As the Pendulı

By
Preston H. Edwards
Book One of the Shattered Genesis Anthology

In Memoriam of John Thurston Edwards III.
Thank you for your love and guidance. Rest in peace.

Copyright © 2023 by Preston H. Edwards

North Carolina
Astra Princeps Publishing

Prologue

"What we do in life, echoes into eternity."
— Meditations, Marcus Aurelius

Beep, beep, beep, beep, beep. Michael turned over and switched off his phone alarm. Rising out of bed, he took a second to stretch out his muscles, still stiff from the night before. He reached over and grabbed his glasses off the nightstand and put them on his face. Michael stood up and walked to the window, peering out at the empty street down below from his hotel room. The streets of D.C. were extremely eerie so early in the morning, devoid of human life. It was as if all of humanity was collectively taking a breath from the chaos.

Michael took a shower, and then put on his clothes. He wore a fitted black suit with an American flag pin on his lapel. His shoes were immaculately shined, a skill honed through years of practice in the military. He walked over to the closet where he had hung his ties and thought for a moment about which one he was going to wear on this particular day. He settled on a solid navy-blue tie, *American colors for an American day,* he thought.

He walked over to the mirror and began reciting his speech for later that day; he was nervous, today would be the start of his career. He walked down to the breakfast area to see what swill the hotel put out for their regularly advertised breakfast. Much to his surprise, Michael entered a large cafeteria area, the walls decorated with blue paint, red and white stars sprinkled sporadically throughout. The aroma was intoxicating, made worse by

2

the distinct rumbling in his stomach. Michael walked over to the buffet line. He placed some eggs and a fluffy biscuit onto his plate and smothered the plate in gravy. He sat down and began to eat, and then a hotel employee began to walk towards him.

"How are you today, sir?" the employee, Karen by her nametag, asked.

"I'm pretty tired this morning, but good. Yourself?" He responded, smiling at the end.

"Good, thanks for asking! Is there anything else I can get for you? Maybe some coffee?" Karen asked.

"I would love a cup of black coffee, thank you very much." Michael had barely finished speaking before Karen whisked away to acquire the coffee.

Michael observed her as she walked away. She had more of a waddle than a walk, she was very short. Something about her eyes had told him that she was completely satisfied with the way her life was, she had grown used to her chains. Michael pulled out his phone and began looking at various news sites. On Wolf News, they were talking about how President Locke was trying to push the country towards socialism. The President had advocated for a harsher tax on people banking outside of the country, and the radical conservative media was having a field day.

Michael then went to ABS's website. They had run a fairer article, in Michael's view, on the nature of these tax hikes for the wealthy, explaining the need for a balanced economy that works for everyone. Ironically, Michael thought this didn't go quite far enough in support. He was getting ready to present a speech in front of the

Lincoln Memorial later that day to end the capitalistic society we lived in and move towards a more equitable society. Many people thought Michael was a socialist, but he didn't see it that way.

A few moments later, Karen returned with the coffee. It is hard to describe that first smell of coffee in the morning, but it made Michael's soul glow every time. It brought him back to the time where he was patrolling in the arid deserts of Afghanistan, and Sergeant First Class Menendez had brought along his French press. The aroma always made him remember how good the world could be. Even in the worst times of his life, the smell of coffee always brought hope to his mind.

Michael finished eating his food, slugged down the rest of his coffee, and gathered his things. He didn't want to be late for this. James, one of his Army buddies and now a political strategist, had been pushing him to get into politics. James had set this whole thing up, giving him a platform to launch his political career from. James told him that this would be fully televised, and that his message would be heard in his home state of Virginia, and hopefully embraced.

A lot of the west coast states had already begun the slow movement towards a wealth-controlled state, passing re-distribution tax codes that proliferated their economies. Those states had massive growth in the first few years of these new codes, and momentum for the movement was starting to pick up rapidly. James hoped that a man with Michael's resume could help the Democrats start to pick up more pace in these traditionally Republican strongholds. Michael was a recipient of the Army cross for his actions in Afghanistan, saving eighteen people's lives in a firefight while serving as a medic. After his time in the military, he went to a prestigious university where he earned a degree in Political Philosophy. Michael, in the view of the Democrat party, was the perfect candidate to influence the momentum.

Michael got into the car that was sent for him and instructed him to go to the Lincoln Memorial. The city was beginning to wake up, like the increasing breaths of the colossus when disturbed from his slumber, the cold air making his ire even worse. Michael saw one old man walking down the road, coat pulled tight against his body. The old man was walking very slowly, aided by a cane, his once proud figure slumped against the weight of prolonged existence. Michael felt a sharp pain in his knee, a distinct reminder of his time in the Army, and knew that was everyone's fate eventually. Some allowed the fear of death to hold them from risk, Michael used the knowledge of death to compel him forward; his need to accomplish something memorable was ingrained deep into his core.

The driver pulled up to the memorial, and a security guard walked up to meet him.

"I.D.?" the guard asked.

"I'm the speaker for today, do you really need my I.D.?" Michael was a little frustrated that the security staff didn't even know who he was. He reached into his pocket to pull his wallet out and then handed it to the guard.

"Sorry sir, just normal security protocols." The guard seemed embarrassed as Michael walked past the security checkpoint. Michael saw James behind the scenes talking to a few younger people in suits, probably some type of senatorial internship program. He seemed particularly delighted with a tall, elegant blonde. That was always James's weakness. Michael walked up to the group, sheepishly trying to edge his way into the circle where everyone was talking.

"Good morning, everyone!" Michael shouted, perhaps a little too loudly. The group turned towards him; James spoke first.

"Are you ready for today, man? This is a big deal." James was smiling. James was a tall man with jet black hair and eyes so dark that they simply looked like pools of blackness. He had a crooked smile that always seemed like he was joking about things, even when he was attempting to be serious.

"Ready as I'll ever be. It's kind of hard to believe that all these people came out to hear my speech about my campaign…" Michael looked out over the crowd, there must be close to 15,000 people in the crowd, waiting to hear him talk.

"Well, the DNC put out a newsletter for volunteers, I guess your star is rising my friend."

Instantly, Michael knew that the DNC had paid people to be here, James was pulling some strings to make this work out. He looked at James knowingly after his comment. He couldn't decide if it was flattering that a friend would be willing to help him so much, or whether he was insulted for having to rely on others for any modicum of success.

A serious looking forty-something guy walked over to where the group was standing. He was wearing a headset and had on khaki pants with a black polo. He looked down at his clipboard, then he looked up at Michael, "It's time to go on, sir."

"Wish me luck everyone." Everyone sung out in a half-hearted chorus of good vibrations. Michael walked up to the stage to loud applause. The crowd was the largest Michael had ever spoken in front of. His campaign was beginning to pick up momentum, and he could feel the energy from the crowd. He lived for these moments.

The sun shone brightly overhead. Its rays pierced through an array of white, fluffy clouds making the atmosphere glow. *If that's not a good sign, I don't know what is.* Michael took to the stage and the crowd went wild. Paid adulation sweeping from the mouths of the capital cronies in such fervor that you might have thought this was a Presidential campaign.

"Good afternoon my fellow Americans!" Michael smiled and waved his hand in the air to the crowd as a cacophony of voices raised into the sky, almost tangible with the taste of zealotry, like when the air is too heavy with a foul scent and the taste sticks on your tongue.

"Today we are here to push forward into a new beginning for America! A new chapter in the grand tradition of democratic ideals and dre—"

The air stood still as the front wave of some explosive burst forth, the podium exploded. Blood and wood erupted into the air like a massive volcano of dust, screams pierced the air as people began to scramble away from the site of the explosion.

Michael, barely able to feel his legs, tried to move his head to get a view of the crowd. He could hear his heartbeat, but he couldn't hear anything else. He reached his hand up to his ears and wiped away blood. He propped himself up and looked down at his legs. His left leg was cut off below the knee, his right leg bleeding with shrapnel lodged inside of it. He pushed his body to look at the crowd. *Thump thump, thump thump,* his heart continued to beat. *Thump, thump, BOOM, thump, BOOM, thump, thump, BOOM.*

Horrified, Michael looked out onto the crowd, explosions were rampant. It was like a warzone, grenade explosions, gunfire was ripping through the crowd of people. Michael fell down onto his back, weeping at the pain of the sight. He looked into the sky and yelled at God. Why would he let this happen? He looked over to his right, James was there, his cold, black eyes smiling back at him. Then, blackness.

Part I: The Election

"The only thing necessary for the triumph of evil is for good men to do nothing" – Edmund Burke

Chapter 1: The Primaries

Luther opened his refrigerator and stared blankly into it momentarily. In a moment he was a weak child, unable to make the simplest of decisions with any sort of conviction. He breathed in the now-cold air from the open refrigerator, and then reached his hand in again towards the back and pulled out a cold beer. Luther walked towards his living room, snatching his remote off of the coffee table in front of his couch. He turned on ABS, they were showing the first of the Republican primary debates.

"Hello, my name is Lisa Young, and in a few moments, we will bring you the first Republican primary debate." She switched to a different camera and then continued, "breaking news across the entire nation as a terrorist attack by the Muslim extremist group Caliphate of Last Dawn, or C.O.L.D., the group is believed to be an extremist group created here in the United States." She seemed rather uncomfortable to continue going forward with the story, something was bothering her.

"A squad consisting of around fifty armed men assaulted a group of 15,000 political activists who had gathered to hear Michael DeLauer, a former Army medic, speak on advancing America towards a wealth-distributive model of American tax policies. DeLauer was running for Congress in the 8th District of Virginia."

"The terrorist group has not come forward to claim any ownership of the action, but simply left a flag with a circle with a trident through it stitched over top an American flag."

She moved back to the center camera and shuffled her paper in front of her. A smile instantly snapped back onto her face, "And now we take you live to the first Republican party primary debate."

Luther took a swig of his beer, put his hand down to the side of the recliner, pulling the lever to lean back. Savannah, his daughter, was sitting on the ground coloring on the coffee table. Aiden, his son, was doing his homework quietly at the kitchen table. He was a shy boy, very unlike his father, but was incredibly dedicated to learning and knowledge. He would often voluntarily do extra studying rather than go to a movie with his father.

Luther looked back to the television; the Republican primaries had started. There were only four candidates this year. The past few times there had been around ten candidates, but the party voted over the past few years to nominate only four to run to have more control over the process. Luther dreamed about running for President someday, it was all he ever wanted, and why he got into politics in the first place. His House race victory in North Carolina had been his crowning achievement in life.

The debate moderator, Aretha Jarvis, asked the first man, Arthur Cross, a question, "Mr. Cross, there has been a violent escalation in the nature of terrorist activities on behalf of Muslims across the world and in this nation, what would you do as President to battle these attacks?"

Cross, the former governor of Florida, leaned back as if shocked by the question, and then rubbed his chin and began to reply, "Well, first I'd like to thank the American people and the Republican Party for the great honor of being here to debate tonight, God Bless America. I think we need tighter border security checks at every access point, including planes and boats."

He slammed his fist on his podium, puffing out his chest slightly, and declared, "We must keep America safe whatever the cost!" The crowd, although instructed otherwise, applauded lightly at the exclamation.

The moderator quieted the crowd, and then turned to the second man, a political newcomer that the party had not wanted to nominate. He was pushed for heavily by the more religious element of the party. Luther had not enjoyed being pushed around at the convention.

"Mr. Drum, same question to you."

Harold Drum, a former Baptist minister from Alabama, was as tall and strikingly handsome as they could come. Golden hair, kept perfectly high and tight, deep blue eyes, bold physique, he was the perfect candidate for the religious right, and he had an air of violent intent about him.

"Well, Ms. Jarvis, thank you for asking me that question, it's an important one. I want to make sure that I give your question the full weight of the consideration it deserves." Harold Drum reached down and grabbed a water bottle, took the top off and took a long drink. He placed the water bottle back down on the podium and walked out from behind it. He walked slowly across the stage for a moment before stopping in the middle.

"What I would do is very different from what we must do. What I would do is what Jesus would do, forgive them and try and convince them to see the light of peace. However, I believe that they will never listen, they will never hear his message, it is too late. What we must do then, in the face of a people who will not accept Jesus Christ as their Lord and Savior, is what God did to Sodom and Gomorrah. We must find these people and eliminate them from our shores, anyone who does not believe in the one true God is no longer allowed in my United States of America." During the last sentence, the words sounded like paint splattered on canvas in a beautiful soliloquy of rage and hatred, of an ideology so ingrained in the very core of someone that the enemy was the antithesis of their soul.

The crowd exploded. The roar was deafening. The first crack in the façade of tolerance spread cleanly across the thin pane of glass separating normalcy from chaos.

Once the crowd settled back down the moderator, asked Mr. Drum a follow up question, "Sir, did you just imply that we should deport non-Christians?"

Harold smiled, he moved his hands to where they were spread out, level with his shoulders. "I am merely speaking a truth which nobody seems to acknowledge. Muslims are destroying this country, they are destroying the moral fabric of America. They are infecting our ideologies with weak liberalism and false promises of collective good-will."

He was walking back and forth across the stage again, like a reverend channeling the passion that God had placed into his soul; proselytizing to his church, and the

12

sheep of the flock were embracing every word as if it was the word of God himself.

"We must reject that which is un-Godly. We must reject the moral codes and well-wishes of a people who only seek to further sequester this great nation from the truth of God's love."

The fourth candidate spoke up at this point. John Grey, a sixty-five-year-old career Senator from the state of Nebraska. He was the odds-on favorite to win the nomination.

"Ms. Jarvis, can you please cease allowing this religious belligerence to continue? We have actual politics to discuss." Senator Grey spoke with a calm significance. He spoke softly, loud enough to where you could hear, but just tacit enough to where you had to focus on his words to hear them. The other two candidates nodded their heads in approval.

Ms. Jarvis addressed Harold, "Mr. Drum, if you would please return to your podium, we have more questions to get to." Harold looked around himself, he looked at the faces of the crowd, their eager eyes locked onto him. These people needed a leader, someone to change the world, and they wanted him to be silent? They asked of him to be sheepish and weak in the face of the enemy? He would not.

"I deny your request, Ms. Jarvis. This world does not need a man to come to power who lives his life in slavish obedience to your decorum! This world needs a man to put the nation back on the path to glory! A path where God is the center of all things, not a path where we bow down to the false prophets of science and weakness!"

Luther audibly scoffed, he grabbed the remote and turned the T.V. off. *The party is going to have to end his candidacy, we can't allow a mad dog like that in the ring,* Luther thought to himself. Harold and Luther had met briefly at the first RNC campaign organization meetings. He had seemed tame, a very well-spoken man, not this rabid animal that he exhibited on that stage.

"This is Trevor Stewart reporting live for Wolf News at the site of the first Democratic Party primary debate. Today the six candidates will debate new tax policies, immigration, and solutions for the rising tide of terrorism in this great nation."

"The current front runner is Dr. Gareth Emory, a former Constitutional Law professor from a prestigious university, and a staunch capitalist. Two candidates that have an outside chance at the nomination are Jacob Young and Emily Benson. We take you now, live, to the beginning of the debate. Our debate moderator, Mr. Yuri Popovich, is standing by."

The scene switched to Mr. Popovich; the camera focused directly on him. "Thank you, Trevor, we will begin with each candidate's opening statements." The candidates each gave their basic boilerplate opening statements, none of the candidates wanted to say anything of substance for fear of losing the nomination before it ever began.

"The first question is for Dr. Emory," Popovich paused for a moment, and looked down at the question card he had been given, "Dr. Emory, what is your plan to equalize the wealth inequality in this nation?"

"Well, Yuri, that's an excellent question. There is only one way to reduce the inequality in this country, and that's to return to an America where people believe that they will have to work for a living. We need to return to an America where nobody has their hand out, but rather has a hand on a tool trying to create something of value."

"Thank you, Dr. Emory," Yuri turned his body slightly, his shoulders had lowered a bit at the response from Dr. Emory, most people were becoming tired of the same old song and dance about capitalism. Yuri spoke again, "Our next question is for Congresswoman Elizabeth Holder, how would you combat the rise of terrorism in this nation?"

Elizabeth Holder was a black Congresswoman from the state of Nebraska. Nobody had expected her to run, and nobody thought that she had a chance, except of course for Elizabeth. She was a tall woman, she had dreads woven into her hair that hung down to her back, and she had piercing hazel eyes that intimidated people.

"I believe that the rise of terrorism is problematic for our society because there's no real way to combat it without destroying the liberties that we believe in. The only way to really stop these attacks is to know when they are about to occur, which would mean that we would have to have unilateral ability to survey individuals. Sometimes, that surveillance would have to take place without a warrant because of time. I believe that is the only solution, but I fear what it will take from Americans in regard to our civil liberties."

The entire auditorium was silent, the truth of the statement astounded people. There were practiced political audience members sitting with their mouths

15

hanging open. The open-faced suggestion that police surveillance of Americans without a warrant was incredibly bold, but that was the type of message Elizabeth Holder was trying to espouse.

"Congresswoman Holder, did you just openly suggest spying on American citizens?"

"Yes, I did." The shock rippled through the crowd once more, open gasps were audible. She stared back at Yuri with an intense, bold glare. Elizabeth had come prepared for a fight.

"The next question is for Mr. Jacob Young. Mr. Young, as a businessman and entrepreneur, what would you do to bolster our economy and fix our rising wealth inequality?"

Mr. Young and Ms. Benson proceeded to answer the same question, but Yuri looked confused the whole time; he had not expected Elizabeth's answer, and it had visibly shaken him. The network had not allowed Yuri to come back to Elizabeth for the entire broadcast, as a traditional Republican network they did not want a person openly suggesting a police state.

"The last question is for Congresswoman Holder—"

"I appreciate the fact that you let me answer a second question tonight, Mr. Popovich." Elizabeth had interrupted him, furious that the network had otherwise silenced her for the entire debate.

"Yes, well, you'll forgive us for our reticence. The question for you is how would you suggest fixing the rise of wealth inequality in this country?" He cringed as he asked the question, he feared the answer.

"I would seek to eradicate capitalism as the basis for our economic policies." Again, the gasps were audible, "I would seek to supplant this capitalist structure for a hardline social economic policy focused on an equitable wealth model. My model would still allow for profit incentives but would place a hard cap on salaries."

"Congresswoman Holder, are you intentionally trying to upset people?" Yuri looked furious.

"No, Mr. Popovich, I am intentionally trying to usher in a new era where people are not afraid to have difficult conversations. It is completely unreasonable to live in the wealthiest nation on Earth and have thirty percent of the population in poverty. It is completely unreasonable to have children who must indebt themselves for the rest of their lives to attend college. It is also completely unreasonable to believe that the laborer is any less entitled to the fruits of their labor than the people that they work for!" Elizabeth delivered this with a cool, calculated demeanor. She had a silent strength that emanated from every word that she said. Her message was the future, and the future was imminent.

Interlude

The world is changing around me. Where I once saw this great unity of purpose and kindness within our society, it has been replaced with fear and hatred. The terrorist attack at the Lincoln Memorial did more damage in one day to this country than 9/11 did in the ten years after. Fifteen-thousand political activists all killed in an instant, it is almost as if you can still hear their screams upon visiting the site.

I fear the repercussions for religious tolerance in this country that this action may have had, if there's even any left. We just keep sinking deeper and deeper into the blackness of fear, rather than standing against the threat, we are eliminating the very people that could stop it. By pushing Muslims away, we are proving these terrorists right. We are fulfilling their prophecies, and the coming wars will make them look as prophets.

It is clear that we must fight this aggression with peace, we must stave this intolerance with tolerance, and that the only path forward is not hate, but love. I only hope that the world agrees.

\-   *A Letter to Trent Kennedy from Luther Washington*

Chapter 2: The First Debate

Luther was sitting in his office at the Capitol building, looking over a budget proposal on an education department funding bill they were voting on tomorrow. Trent Kennedy, the Speaker of the House, walked into Luther's office. Trent was a friend of Luther's; they both went to college in North Carolina and became acquaintances through their alumni network. Trent had a much different path from Luther though, first becoming a prosecutor and then was elected as the District Attorney for Mecklenburg County in North Carolina.

Trent, despite the very famous name, was not related to any of the Kennedys, but nobody would ever make that mistake as Trent was a very large black man. Trent had a completely shaven head, stood 6'6", and was built like an oak tree. He had played offensive line during his time at university. He had a smile that would light up the room, but it was his thick, syrupy voice that would fill every room he ever entered. Trent was from the 3rd District of North Carolina. Luther represented the 12th district.

"My aide told me you were still burnin' the midnight oil up here Lu." Trent was from a backwoods part of North Carolina outside of Jacksonville. He spoke with a degree of familiarity with Luther that he did not with many others. He was a mentor to Luther, and hoped he would carry on the tradition of black men in Congress proudly.

"Yeah, just reading over the budget reports for the education bill we're voting on tomorrow." Luther held up the binder he was poring over.

"Hell man, you actually read that shit? I just have a legislative aide give me some bullet points and call it a day." Trent was chuckling to himself.

"Well, some of us don't have a blank check to hire different people left and right." Luther was chiding Trent at this point.

"Well, some of us didn't have the good looks and charm to get picked as Speaker of the House, did they?" The bluntness with which he spoke always comforted Luther, you always knew when Trent was speaking the truth. You always knew when he was lying, too.

"Good looks? I know you're not trying to say you're prettier than me? After all those beatings you took on the field, I'm surprised your face isn't more disfigured!" Trent and Luther were both laughing now.

"Anywho, was jus' droppin' by to see if you wanted to come over and watch the first debate tonight. This lil' firecracka outta Nebraska is trouble." Trent was referencing Congresswoman Holder who had won the Democratic nomination to run for president; Pastor Drum had won the Republican primary, much to Luther's chagrin.

"I'm considering boycotting the election this year, both candidates are absolutely psychotic." Luther put his hands behind his head and leaned back in his chair.

"Psychotic? I think Pastor Drum has some great things to say. Especially about handling these damned terrorists."

"Trent, you can't be serious! This man is a religious zealot, he's openly advocating for the dissolution of the separation of church and state, how can you support that?"

"Well, you know I'm a Christian, Luther, but you know as well as I do that we'll never have that happen here. It's impossible."

"I don't think you're right on that Trent, but I'm not going to come out and say anything against the candidate. He's at least better than little miss communist."

"Yeah, she's pretty, though. I'd let her take my lawnmower for a ride, heh." Trent was always a little loose with the women.

"Haha, I'm sure Molly would love to hear you say that! Anyways, I gotta get home to the kids, so I can't watch the debate at your place. You're more than welcome to come to mine."

"No worries, man, I'm gonna head home as well, Molly ordered Chinese food for tonight."

After exchanging goodbyes, Trent left the office, and Luther gathered his coat and laptop bag and left as well. He walked to the parking garage and got into his gray sedan. Luther liked to live modestly, unlike his estranged wife, Samantha. Luther had married Samantha shortly after they graduated from college.

Samantha had come from a very wealthy family and was used to a certain type of life. Luther had been dedicated to public service since he left college, unlike many other politicians he had not made much money. Luther started four different non-profits trying to bring food and water to impoverished areas of America. His ventures had led many people to push him to get into politics. Samantha had loved the initial charm and glamour of politics, but when it became clear to her that Luther would rather work for the betterment of others than pay attention to her, the marriage turned south.

Luther was dedicated to his work. He had always felt that the service of others was the most honorable type of work. He had tried to be a good husband and father, but generally failed at both. Luther had lied earlier to Trent, his kids generally stayed with Sam unless she had something better to do. He was just very jealous of Trent's family. They were incredibly supportive of him and his work.

Luther finally arrived home, barely noticing the drive, distracted by his thoughts. He walked into his house and turned on the TV. ABS began to echo throughout the house, starting with its debate coverage.

"Hello, my name is Lisa Young, and we are about to bring you the first presidential debate between Congresswoman Elizabeth Holder and Pastor Harold Drum."

"Congresswoman Holder made waves as a darkhorse candidate in the Democratic primaries. Her hardline stances on security reform being necessary to control domestic terrorism, and creating a system of economic growth outside of traditional capitalism made her very popular with the younger demographic of Democratic voters, who turned out to vote at the highest rate in American history."

"Likewise, Pastor Drum made significant waves with his policies on religious integration into our government. He rallied the traditional conservative religious base with his radical policy agenda, including creating a department that would regulate how media presented religious concepts to the public. This created a lot of backlash in the media, but his message resonated with voters on the backs of the C.O.L.D. terrorist group's horrific attack in D.C. last year."

"We take you now to Walter Brock, and the first presidential debate."

"Thank you, Lisa, and welcome America. Tonight, we will debate a number of topics, based on a format that the candidates have agreed to. Our candidates have agreed to jump straight to questions for time, so we will begin."

"Pastor Drum, what is your first action you will take as President of the United States?"

"Walter, that is an excellent question. The first thing I would do as President of the United States is to put God back in the forefront of our nation's political conversations. There was a time when this nation put its trust in God, and it led to the creation of the most powerful nation on Earth. We have wavered from our true beliefs, and we have been punished by God for our lack of faith."

"Congresswoman Holder, your response?"

"Walter, I cannot believe what I just heard. Did a candidate for President of the United States suggest that we should tear down the walls between church and state? It is incredibly disingenuous to suggest that this country was built by God, this nation was built on the backs of the enslaved and the disenfranchised. The separation of church and state is absolutely necessary to a successful government, and for the perpetuation of a country that believes in religious tolerance."

23

"How *DARE* you! You seek to stomp on the word of God?!" Harold Drum was red-faced and shouting, clearly disturbed by what Elizabeth had said.

"I am not stomping on anything, I am merely not going to allow a candidate for the President of our nation spew religious radicalism on national television."

Harold gripped his podium tightly, and then reached his right hand into his pocket and pulled out his handkerchief and his Bible. He dabbed his forehead with his handkerchief, and then opened his Bible. He seemed to be reading it, and then he abruptly closed it, looked up at the moderator, who was staring at him, then looked over to Elizabeth. He slowly shook his head, and then he began to walk out from behind his podium.

"Pastor Drum, please remain behind the podium." Walter was clearly upset.

"I will not! You cannot bind me, only my God can bind me." Harold pointed at Elizabeth, and then turned towards the camera, "this woman seeks to place this great Christian nation in chains! She seeks to subject us to the will of the Islamists and the atheists! ---"

Elizabeth attempted to interrupt, but Harold just plowed right through, "we stand on the precipice of total annihilation at the hands of the non-believers! I am calling on all God-fearing Americans, if you love Jesus and believe that God is the one true God, absolute in his authority, then you cannot vote for this demon!" Harold was fire, he was channeling thousands of years of religious zealotry and passion. His absolutism was soul crushing.

Elizabeth stood there, mouth hanging open, staring at Harold. Harold finally appeared done with his sermon, and Elizabeth began to speak. "America does not stand for what this man believes in. America stands for tolerance, an open place for all people regardless of religion, race, creed, or gender to live freely without fear of persecution. If you believe in an America that holds that liberty, freedom, and justice for all should be the standard, not an aspiration, vote for me. If you believe that America should become a Baptist church and return back to the dark ages, vote for this zealot."

Walter, clearly at a loss for words, continued the questioning. The two candidates represented a crossroads in America. One, the direction of modernity, a collection of liberal thought created by thousands of years of development of human thought processes. The other relied on the archaic, the known, he channeled an instinctual human fear of the unknown into a ravenous belief in his God and refused to accept compromise.

Elizabeth seemed noble in her answers, but there was something missing. While she expressed these intellectual ideals, she lacked the same outward conviction in her beliefs. Harold was all conviction, fire harnessed by the will of God. It made Elizabeth appear weak, her answers never seemed to resonate because they were so equivocated; well thought out, political equivocations - exactly what America had seen in the past. Exactly what the people weren't looking for.

Harold was new. He didn't allow himself to be told anything by anyone, he was raw emotion. His ideas weren't new, they had been around since the beginning of time. The terrorist attack on the Lincoln Memorial created a fear that America had never experienced before, and that fear cannot be dealt with by politics. Fear can only be dealt with by instinct. This is what Harold knew, he knew instinct; he knew that the world would react violently to violence. He did not hold the liberal beliefs of peace. He knew the truth. He knew peace was a lie, there is only strength; strength as a deterrent for violence was the only possible path to peace. Humans are caged beasts, and the only way to tame a beast is to subjugate.

Interlude

I didn't think it would be so easy for us to fall. We were so close to ushering in a new era for humanity, one of peace and tolerance. We didn't know how fragile our world was, we weren't ready. I believed in an idea of America, an idea of a nation of people that would be the light of the world. A guiding star in the night that allowed the other nations of the world to orient themselves to follow.

Have we fallen so far? Have we allowed ourselves to give in to the base instincts of our primal nature? History will never forgive us for our failures, if there even is a history that includes our brief time in the sun. The chains of tyranny have never left, the tyrants had just been leaving them open until we walked into them willingly.

- *Journal Entry, Nida Mohammed*

Chapter 3: The Fallout

"Hello, my name is Trevor Stewart, reporting for Wolf News. Tonight, we have a set of panelists here to discuss the first debate between Pastor Harold Drum and Congresswoman Elizabeth Holder. Our panelists are former Democratic primary candidate Dr. Gareth Emory, former Navy Admiral Tyler Grant, current Republican Party spokesman Don Hugh, and former Senator for Utah Ezekiel Hartt."

Trevor turned to the panelists, "We'll start first with you, Gareth, what do you think about Congresswoman Holder's economic policies?"

"Well, Trevor, her policies are a disaster. Removing the element of choice for your own profession would be a disaster. Socialism is a flawed system and will never work in America."

"Why do you think that is the case?"

"I know that to be the case because our entire ideology was created based on individualism. Each American is their own American, and they all have their own ambitions and desires. If we switched to socialism, we would remove that element of control over their lives, the government would have to get involved in telling people what to do on a day-to-day basis. That's the definition of oppression."

"I agree with you Gareth, thank you. Now to you, Admiral Grant, what do you think of the two candidates view of the military?"

"Well, Holder's view is a disaster. She wants to reduce the size of the military, and completely strip our nation's ability to defend itself. Pastor Drum wants to make our nation strong and has already announced an expanded budget for the military if he becomes president. We need to keep our nation strong, and Pastor Drum will accomplish that goal."

"I couldn't have said it better myself, Admiral. How else do you think Pastor Drum will help keep our nation strong?"

"I feel like this man has the power and conviction of the Lord on his side. We would be righteous with him as our leader, and that would help our soldiers with morale. President, I mean, Pastor Drum is the future of this nation, and the only candidate that will make us strong."

"Strength is what is necessary to keep us safe, Admiral, thank you for your incredible input."

"I would like to butt in here, Trevor." Gareth spoke up, obviously troubled by the exchange.

"Sorry Gareth, but we have two more panelists to get to, if we have more time we'll come back to you." Trevor knowingly did not want Gareth to speak again, his comments on religion were not the narrative that was being sold tonight.

"Mr. Hugh, what does the RNC think about Pastor Drum's plan to reform our schools?"

"Well Trevor, Pastor Drum wants to put prayer back into schools, and we love that. Freedom of speech is tantamount in this country, and we feel like everyone should be able to express their religion however they see fit, including in our schools."

"Do you think that the election of Pastor Drum would help our schools?"

"Absolutely! I think putting God back into our learning institutions is the solution to a lot of the problems we've been having, including Islamic terrorism."

"I agree with you there, Don, Islamic terrorism is a huge issue, and we need a God-fearing president to combat it."

Trevor switched to a different camera and spoke again, "And now, to our last panelist, former Senator Hartt. Senator, is Pastor Drum the candidate you've been dreaming of?"

"Trevor, Pastor Drum is the next great leader of the United States. He is godly, he is strong, he is passionate, and he will take us to new heights as a nation."

"How high can he take us Senator?"

"How high is God, Trevor?" The senator smiled.

"Hello, my name is Lisa Young, reporting for ABS. Tonight we will be having a panel discussion about the first presidential debate between Pastor Harold Drum and Congresswoman Elizabeth Holder. Our panelists tonight are Rebecca Montagne, a popular women's rights' advocate, Julia Darden, a congressional lobbyist, Anthony Summers, a LGBTQ rights advocate, and La'Tonya Jacobs, a retired circuit court judge."

"La'Tonya, what did you think of Congresswoman Holder's words tonight?"

"Well Lisa, and thanks for having me on, I just think it's great that we live in a time where a woman can be a candidate for the highest office in our nation. I'm not sure I'm convinced that she actually believes in socialism, but I'm so proud that a woman can run for office."

"La'Tonya, you were one of the first female circuit court judges in the United States, isn't that right?"

"Yes, I was a pioneer for women in the judicial branch, just as Congresswoman Holder is going to be for the executive. We have such a great opportunity in front of us to elect the first black woman President of the United States. We need to get out and vote for that opportunity."

"Thank you, La'Tonya; Julia, what are your thoughts on tonight's speech?"

"Well, I think that there's no way that Holder gets elected if she continues down this path of socialism and military reduction. She's going to lose a large portion of voters who believe national defense and individualism are at the forefront of what it means to be an American."

La'Tonya interjected, "Excuse me! If you think that she isn't strong because she's a woman, that makes you a sexist!"

Julia, with a puzzled look on her face responded, "Sexist? I'm a woman, first of all, and second of all I said nothing about her being a woman; I specifically referenced her insistence that we downsize the military in light of the escalation of terrorist attacks on our country."

La'Tonya looked even more upset, "You think she wants to downsize because she is a woman, and that she fears conflict; you being a woman has nothing to do with it, you are chained by the thoughts of those who have brainwashed you."

Anthony Summers spoke at this point, "I agree with La'Tonya, you just think that reducing the military is weak because she is a woman, if a man said the same thing you'd be praising how progressive and peaceful it was. This is just another example of the right in this country trying to marginalize women and minorities."

"What are you people even talking about?" Julia was visibly frustrated, but Lisa did nothing to stop the onslaught of groupthink.

Rebecca, obviously triggered by something Julia had said, "You people? Do you realize that you are just defeating yourself by using language like that? Your microaggressions are crippling the political discourse in this country."

Rebecca continued, "It really makes me sad to see a fellow woman that is so dedicated to the establishment created by these white men that she won't even speak up for her own self-interest. You need to re-evaluate which side you are on."

Julia had enough, "I'm on America's side! It has nothing to do with men versus women, or black versus white. We are all Americans, we need to do what is best for everyone, and stop catering to victimhood mentalities. This is the greatest country on Earth because we can be anything we want to be here. You are screwing it up with your identity and victimhood politics, you are completely destroying rational conversation that deals with the realities of the world we live in. You would rather speak about how offended you are about a particular topic than actually fix anything to do with those problems. YOU ARE THE PROBLEM!"

Lisa Young interrupted at this point, "Okay, we need to go to a commercial, we'll be back."

Off camera at this point, Lisa turns to Julia and says, "This is the last time I have you on my show, we can't have voices like that."

"Voices like what? Voices that tell the truth?"

"No Julia, voices that go against what our viewers believe and want to hear."

"You're supposed to be educating them Lisa! Not pandering to whatever they think is best, do you have no integrity as a journalist?"

"Julia, I'm not a journalist, I'm a talk show anchor, I get paid to get ratings."

Harold was sitting in his chair at the head of the conference table. There were four men in the room, all pastors of one sort or another. There were documents strewn about the table, the men were silent. They had been speaking for hours at this point, their previously perfect hair had begun to lose its form, the jackets had come off. There was a half empty bottle of whiskey in the middle of the table, the room was filled with smoke from the cigars they had been puffing on throughout the day.

Fear and contemplation was set on all the men's faces, the path forward was murky, they didn't know if they had the conviction to execute the plan. They all knew that something had to be done, the world was turning away from God, and that could not be allowed. They had tried peace, love, and tolerance, and that only led to more people not believing. A world where fifty years ago it was just an agreed upon fact, was now a dying breed of people. A people that still restrained themselves because of a book, but the book had to fight back; God must persevere for society to stand strong.

The documents on the table had permits for an event being held at the Lincoln Memorial, they didn't know the name yet, it didn't matter. On another sheet was a shipping manifest. Like in magic, the magicians never reveal how the trick was pulled, as long as nobody notices, it's as if it was real.

Chapter 4: The Second Debate

Harold was sitting at his desk, reading over the potential questions for tonight's debate. Tonight was mainly a foreign policy discussion, but there was a section about which new government agency that each president would push for if elected. Each of Harold's campaign advisors were strewn about the room in different configurations, whether seated directly in front, or laying on top of the filing cabinet rubbing one's eyes, fighting the exhaustion that the campaign was extolling.

"Are we sure this is the best one we've got? I understand what we're trying to do, but it seems a little direct, even for us." Harold was unsure of the naming of the department.

"Sir, with all due respect, I think it will resonate with the voters, we've already got the election pointed towards God, we need to double down, not get cold feet now." Rick Young was one of the men there at the beginning of this journey with Harold and was one of the men Harold truly trusted. He had been right at every turn.

"Alright, we'll go with it. I need some time to relax before the debate, everyone is dismissed until then."

Harold shuffled back slowly to his hotel room and removed his jacket. He went over to his bathroom and turned the faucet on. He delved his hands into the water and splashed the cool liquid over his face. He stood there for a time, staring into his muddled reflection in the pooled water. He had always liked how he looked, but time was not being kind to him; his hair was beginning to gray, and the lines on his face had become much sharper.

Harold closed his eyes, and he heard the screams again. He always heard the screams now, they haunted him always. He shook his head and walked back into the room where he had laid down his jacket. He turned on the TV and began watching mindless cartoons; it was imperative that nobody ever saw him watching cartoons, as he publicly believed them to be a manifestation of the devil, but Harold loved them privately. He took out his cell phone and texted his wife, "Thinking of you." His wife was at home with their three children, she hated the campaign trail. Things had also been strained since the alleged mistress had come forward in the news.

They had been able to discount and deny in the media, and the country seemed to believe, but Cheryl Drum knew the truth. She knew that Harold was a horrible husband, but he couldn't help it, the women just came to him. God put these women in Harold's path for a reason, who was Harold to say no? Harold was honestly surprised that more women had not come forward, although the reputational attack that they had perpetrated on the first accuser probably had something to do with it. *Good*, Harold thought to himself, *a deterrent is a very useful thing.*

There was a light knock on the door, "Sir, it's time for the debate."

Harold sighed heavily, he then stood up and put on his coat. He went to stand in front of the mirror again to make sure everything looked perfect. He thought back to his pastor during college, he always had the finest suits. One suit in particular that Harold could recall was a navy-blue suit with silver pinstripes that ran down the whole suit. He always wore a matching vest and a bright red tie.

The gold cross that he wore as his tie pin shimmered as the diamonds laid into it caught the bright lights of the church. There was one image that always stuck with Harold, one day the congregation was singing hymns. As they were singing, a ray of light showed through the skylight at the top of the church directly on the pastor. The pastor's hands were raised, and the voices of the church resonated within the walls. That was one of the first times Harold had felt God, with a swelling of overwhelming emotion and joy.

Harold walked out of the hotel room to greet his security detail, and they walked to the cars to take them to the venue. This debate was being held at Independence Hall in Philadelphia, a very historic place for the American people. Harold looked out the window as they drove through the dark, musty streets of Philadelphia. He saw a homeless man sitting on the corner with a sign, the sign read, "Iraq War veteran, please help." Harold never knew how to feel about the poor. On one hand, Jesus always told his people to help those in need, but on the other, wouldn't God have given them more if he wanted them to have it? Was he to ignore the will of God in punishing these people?

The cars stopped outside the back entrance to the building, and Harold's door flung open. The security detail had already fully lined the walkway, and Harold was shepherded in quickly. Inside, he saw Congresswoman Holder and her detachment standing backstage, hurriedly reviewing and going through her answers to the questions that were being presented. Harold didn't need to review, the only advice he needed on the topic he got from the big man upstairs, and the pocket bible he always carried with him.

The lights flashed three times backstage, signaling that the broadcast was set to begin. Harold and Elizabeth both walked to their respective podiums and prepared themselves for the spectacle. The moderator was a petite, Korean woman named Peng Xi, she was a professor of Constitutional Law at Penn Valley State.

"Good evening, and welcome to the second debate between the Republican and Democratic nominees for President of the United States of America. Tonight, we will be discussing a multitude of topics pertaining to foreign policy and departmental restructuring of our government. We will begin tonight's debate with opening statements by both parties, Congresswoman Holder, you may begin."

Harold stared straight ahead; he had no interest in what she had to say. He gripped the podium and tried to look completely unfazed and emotionless. "Good evening my fellow Americans, thank you to the affiliated universities for producing the debate. Tonight, we will talk about the image that America portrays to the world, and how we will go about fixing many of the world's issues that are a threat to our way of life. We must balance our thirst for freedom and democracy with the temperance and understanding that the rest of the world may not think like we do; we must be prepared for their plans as well as make our own. Together, we can create a world moving towards peace, free trade, and prosperity." The crowd clapped softly.

"Pastor Drum, you may begin."

"Hello Philadelphia, I hope y'all are having a good evening. Thank you to everyone who was involved with making this debate happen. My opponent here is a very eloquent lady, she speaks proper and believes in an idea of America that many of you believe in as well. It is not the idea of America that I believe in. I believe in an America built on the foundational moral principles of Christianity and God. I believe in an America that acts with conviction that its actions are ordained from the highest possible authority and may act unrestrained with that knowledge. God did not give us this great nation to play political games with other nations, God gave this to us to show them the path, through strength or otherwise. Tonight, I will lay out my plans for moving America towards its rightful place in this world, and moving America towards a moral foundation that will exist for thousands of years." The audience was completely silent, so silent that someone simply uncrossing their legs could be heard by the entire auditorium.

Peng Xi shuffled her papers, and continued, "The first question is for Congresswoman Holder, how would you deal with the rising threat of Islamic-based terrorism in this country and abroad?"

"Well Peng, and this is an important topic so thank you for asking this question, it is important to note that not all Muslims have this tendency towards violence. The vast majority of the Muslim world is peace loving, and not different from our people whatsoever. We created a power vacuum in the middle east during the Russo-Afghan conflict by giving billions of dollars' worth of military equipment to the Mujahadeen. We then abandoned them to their own volition after the USSR pulled out of Afghanistan, and we acted shocked when they became military radicals. We have to understand that our subject here is religious radicalism in general, not just Muslims."

Harold interjected, livid, "Excuse me, did you just suggest that there are Christian radicals that are violent in this country?"

Peng Xi, before Elizabeth could respond, stated, "Excuse me Pastor Drum, but you will have your own time to respond, please do not interrupt the other candidate."

Harold fired back, the blood beginning to rush underneath his skin, "You will not tell me when I am able or unable to speak, I speak when I please. This woman just said that there are Christians that are murdering people by the tens of thousands in this country, and I won't allow it!"

Elizabeth looked confounded, she began to stammer back a response, "I- I-I, guess you've never heard of the Ku Klux Klan? That uses a burning cross as their symbol and lynched and murdered black people in this country in the name of God?"

"Those people don't exist anymore, I'm talking about now, you atheist."

Elizabeth was thrown, she was obviously rattled, "Yes, I am an atheist." The air was immediately sucked out of the room, the world stood still for a moment in time. Harold smiled and stood silently, allowing her to take in the full gravity of what she just admitted. Elizabeth had tried desperately to take the conversation away from religion the entire campaign, and now she had just played directly into Harold's hand.

Peng Xi, unsure of how to continue given the admission, asked a follow up, "Congresswoman Holder, can you elaborate on that last statement?"

Elizabeth was emboldened now, there was no turning back. "Yes, I can. I am an atheist. I do not believe that there is any higher power that controls our everyday lives."

Harold interrupted, "You're aware that the vast majority of the nation and the world all believe in God, right atheist?"

Elizabeth continued, "Yes, I'm aware. I'm also aware that the Greeks and Romans made up their own gods to explain nature. I'm aware that for thousands of years humans thought the Earth was flat. I'm aware that people thought slavery was a moral imperative since the dawn of humanity. I'm aware that if we continue to believe things because society has told us that they are true that we will never reach our potential as a species. I believe that religion, while it has played a positive role in expanding peace and tolerance in the world, is the last great impediment to a world of true equality and peace."

The debate continued. Harold continuously hammered the fact that Elizabeth was an atheist into the minds of the people that were viewing the broadcast. The one great veil that all politicians in this country had to wear, and Elizabeth had removed it. It was a brazen statement made in a moment of weakness and confusion. It was the beginning of the end, there would never be a time where this could be explained away or taken back. Elizabeth had gambled her entire presidency on the hope that most people were just pretending to believe, she hoped that she was not wrong.

Harold returned to his hotel room and opened the bottle of scotch he had laid out for his return. He popped the top, and then his assistant, Diana, walked into the room. She was about 5'7", with deep auburn hair and stark blue eyes. She had run track in university, and still kept the athletic build and shape.

"Sir, the news channels are ripping her apart. We're expecting a massive surge in the polls nationally."

"Nationally? That's incredible!"

"Yes sir, and with the election in a month and a half, there's nothing left for her to make up the gap with. Rick thinks we should avoid doing any appearances and just let the lead fester."

Harold offered Diana a drink, which she took, and then walked over to a chair that had been in the opposite corner and sat down. Rick was probably right, but Harold loved campaigning, the adoration from the people was the one thing that made him feel fulfilled. He would let Rick manage the campaign though, he had been right up until this point. *No reason to change the pitcher throwing a no-hitter in the ninth*, Harold thought.

"Diana, how's the campaign treating you, now that we're nearing the end?"

"Good sir, I'm tired, but I'm excited for the election. I'm excited to call you President."

"I'm excited for that too. It's everything I've been dreaming of since I first thought it might be possible. Everything I've done is for this, and it will all be worth it. I am just so close! I can't fail now!"

Harold was pouring himself another glass. He was getting worked up with the news of his impending victory. He had always been deficient at managing his emotions. While some viewed this as a weakness, Harold viewed it as superior instincts. He knew when to allow his emotions to control him, and when to use the cold rationality that the liberal elite in this country thought was best for a president.

Diana walked over to the chair and began to pour herself another glass of scotch. Harold reached out and grabbed her arm, and she locked eyes with him. In an instant, Harold was up and had pulled up Diana's dress around her waist. He entered her and picked her up, walking her slowly over to the bed. Diana was his favorite girl, and she knew it.

Luther sat in his office watching the debate from the previous evening. The world was still in shock after Holder had admitted on a national broadcast to being an atheist. *The country barely survived a black president, trying to elect a woman and an atheist in one stroke is too progressive*, Luther thought. He was terrified of Drum; this amount of religious rhetoric was dangerous. The separation of church and state was one of the foundational building blocks of the nation. Drum was lighting a fire that could consume the entire country.

Luther stood up and walked over to the door. Upon opening the door, he saw his chief of staff, Eric Jordan, talking to a few staff members. He walked up to them, and the other staff members took Luther's appearance as their cue to leave.

"Eric, did you watch the debate last night?" Luther asked, already knowing the answer.

"Of course, it's my job." Eric was a 29-year-old man from Seattle. He was short, about 5'9"; he had long brown hair that hung down to his shoulders and had thick rimmed glasses. Despite his hipster appearance, the man was a brilliant political strategist; Luther had to steal him from a state politician in Washington.

"What do you think of this religious tension?"

"Well, it's terrifying, but I don't know what other reaction we could expect from the electorate concerning the increasing level of terror attacks. Especially the Lincoln Memorial."

Luther lowered his head. It was always tough to think about that day. So much destruction in such a short time, over 5,000 dead; the authorities never found the perpetrators. The fact that they were never found terrified the populace even more. It was difficult to believe that nobody would come to attack you when they were still at large. Security around the capital had almost doubled since that day. The paranoia was growing collectively. It had always been there, lying just below the collective consciousness of society, a dark shadow that cast itself across the entire species. The shadow was manifesting itself into something darker now, an amalgamation of ingrown fear and radical religious beliefs was growing into something that had no recourse.

"How do we fight this? How do we tell people that their fears are unfounded?" Luther rubbed his temples, trying to figure out a way to lessen the religious fervor that was sweeping the nation.

Eric contemplated his answer momentarily, and then spoke, "Well, all due respect sir, are they?"

The two stared at each other in silence, not knowing how to respond. They both knew the truth, it wasn't unfounded. The vast majority of people in this country believed that they were under attack by the nations of Islam. Although they would never speak such out loud, each of them believed it a little bit, too.

Harold walked up to the podium. His congregation had sat back down after the hymns were finished. They were ready to be infused with the light of God. Harold was their shepherd, and they were his flock.

"Today, we will be learning of the word of God!"

The congregation replied, "Hallelujah!"

"Today, we will be accepting the Lord, Jesus Christ, into our hearts and minds!"

"Hallelujah!"

"Today, we will be learning about the book of Revelations. We will be learning of the great martyr, Antipas! We will be learning of the morning star, and we will be learning of the second coming of Jesus Christ, our Lord and Savior!"

The congregation settled back after another rousing response. There were about 300 people in the church. They were arranged in the traditional pew style seating, with a large balcony set farther back for additional seating. The walls on the left and right were interspersed with stained glass murals of the seven seals of Revelations. There was a large skylight on top of the church to allow for a naturally lit sanctuary. It was a beautiful church, made to mask the words that came from it.

"The Lord tells us of his warnings to Pergamum. He tells us to remember his true martyr, the one named Antipas. King Herod Antipas is known to us as the ruler who plotted to kill Jesus, so why would Jesus believe him to be a true martyr? It is because Jesus planned his death, he planned it so that he could die for our sins, that was his purpose. What this tells us is that sometimes death is necessary for life, to be a true martyr means understanding when one has to kill the few to save the many. We must be like Antipas, willing to make the choices that do not seem good but do the most good."

Harold was beginning to pace back and forth along his parapet now, the podium could not bind him. He was channeling the Lord today and nothing could bind him.

"The Lord also tells of his warnings to Smyrna. He tells us that those who are faithful to the Lord for all eternity will be given the 'crown of life,' and will not be haunted by the second death. Through our faith we are freed from the devil, and through our faith we claim the righteous rewards of God! Faith comes at a price my children, faith requires sacrifice. Sacrifice is what brings us closer to God! We must sacrifice!"

Harold's hands were raised to his sides, palms facing toward the air, the skylight shining down made him look translucent. He was sweating, as all southern Baptist ministers are apt to do. His voice had reached a fever pitch, echoing off the walls of the sanctuary. The reverberation made the hair on the backs of the necks of the congregation stand on edge.

"We must be the children of Pergamum and Smyrna! We must become the true martyrs of Antipas, and we must sacrifice to prove to the Lord we are worthy of the crown of life! We must sacrifice the children of the devil to prove to the Lord once and for all we are faithful and worthy!"

The congregation was on their feet, cheering wildly. They were overcome with a sense of ferocious zealotry that only the truest wordsmiths can produce. Harold was their shepherd and they were his flock.

Chapter 5: The Election

Luther was running. He had his headphones in and was jogging down Monument Avenue. He had on a black hoodie on with black running shorts. He was listening to a podcast on international futures trading, and how the UN was contemplating creating a world currency to allow easier exchanges. He was only half listening. The voices just made it easier not to focus on the knives stabbing his lungs. The cold November air in D.C. was vile.

He kept running. The blood pounding in his ears was so familiar. There was something primal about running, it was like he could see clear back to his ancestors running as a pack to down a wild animal. It brought out a side that wasn't concerned about the frivolous nature of civilization but was merely concerned with survival. Luther dodged around a couple that was awkwardly groping each other on the sidewalk as only teenagers could. It brought him back out of the trance.

He stopped running. He went down to stretch out, his calves were tight. He had been so entranced that he didn't even really know where he was. He looked around, and he saw it at the end of the road. He had avoided it for so long. Luther walked slowly towards it. He began to make out the face in the near distance. Abraham Lincoln was soon gazing down upon him.

This is where it happened, Luther thought. He looked around now, it hardly seemed like anything could have happened here. There was no trace of the attack now, everything had been repaired. It was almost a shame how quickly the area was remedied; no memorials had been constructed.

How did you find the answer? How did you know what was necessary to heal the nation? Why have so few like you come to power? Luther contemplated the gravity of the man upon whom he was gazing. He didn't know what to do, he was supposed to be one of the most powerful people in the world, but he felt powerless. He felt a nation built on tolerance and peace slipping to one of hatred and war. He felt so much fear and pain, he didn't know how to go forward.

Am I even worthy of being a leader? Suddenly, Luther's mind snapped to a calm evening back in college. Luther's frat was throwing a party that evening, various brothers were carrying beer, ice, or party decorations into the house. Luther had an exam on Monday that he was studying for, which his fraternity brothers believed to be less than cool.

Time passed as Luther dedicated himself to defining the area under a curve, he was not succeeding. When he finally realized what time it was, the party was about to begin. The night was calm. The light from the city was low enough to show a few stars, there was a warm breeze. The wind smelled slightly salty, carrying with it the breeze from the Atlantic.

The music started downstairs. Luther decided to turn on his console and play a few games of Donkey Kart. He went to the room next door to his in the frat house and knocked; his friend Jake lived in the room next to his. Jake came to the door, obviously disheveled.

"What's up dude?" Jake seemed nervous, he was looking back and forth.

"Hey man, you wanna play some Donkey Kart?" Jake exhaled and his shoulders visibly dropped. He seemed to calm down.

"Nah, I'm a little busy right now man." Jake closed the door that he had cracked open slightly in order to talk to Luther. Luther heard his footsteps walk back into his room. Luther turned and went down to the party. The party had a ton of people there, in the corner Brian was rallying people for a keg stand. In a different corner, Luther saw two people actively having sex.

Frat parties were always one of the stranger experiences Luther had ever had. Luther was a legacy to the fraternity; his brother was in it when he went to school. He was essentially forced to join, they put a bag over his head on the second night he was in school. Luther shook his head, grabbed a cold beer from the cooler by the stairs, and went back to his room to play Donkey Kart.

Around an hour later, Luther heard a knock on his door. He went to open it. There was a girl standing there once he opened the door. She was around 5'5" and had blonde hair. She had sharp green eyes that were lined by black rims. She was wearing a black and white dress that barely covered her vital organs.

"Hey, I'm looking for my friend Jess, have you seen her?" Her voice was like a perfect chord harmonizing on a piano.

"No, haven't seen anyone but you. You wanna come in?" Luther knew when he was interested.

"No, I really need to find her. She's my little. I'm going to keep looking." The girl turned, drunkenly stumbling down the hall. She turned to Jake's room and knocked on the door.

Jake opened the door and looked at the girl. "Who the fuck are you?" Jake spat.

"My name is Sam. I'm looking for my friend Jess." Jake looked like someone just hit him in the face. His face went pale.

"Uh-uh, I don't k-know who that is." Jake slammed the door in her face. Luther felt that something was off there. He walked out of the doorway where he was watching Sam speak to Jake. He knocked on the door again.

"WHAT THE FUCK DO YOU WANT, BITCH?!" Jake opened the door angrily. When he opened the door, Luther saw what he was trying to hide. There was a naked girl on his bed, she wasn't moving.

"Who is that, Jake?" Luther pushed the door open forcefully.

"It's some girl I met at the party. Not a big deal." Luther walked over to her. She was unconscious. Luther could smell the alcohol on her breath, it was clear that she had passed out from intoxication.

"We need to take her to a hospital. I think she has alcohol poisoning." Luther turned to leave the room, "Hey, somebody call an ambulance!" Luther yelled down the hall, but before he could leave the room Jake stepped into his path.

"I can't let you do that man, she's mine." Jake pressed a hand into Luther's chest. The red began to rush forward in Luther's mind, the animal was right on the edge.

"Dude, she might die, she needs help. I'm going to call the ambulance." Luther started to move towards the door again, and then Jake shoved him backwards. Luther began to walk towards the door again, this time Jake let him pass. When Luther was about to exit the room, he felt a heavy blow to the back of his head.

Luther fell to the ground, dazed from the blow. He tried to reach for the back of his head, but before his hand could get there, he felt Jake jump on top of him. Jake began repeatedly smashing the back of Luther's head with his fists, linking them both together and swinging them like a hammer. Luther felt something snap.

Luther wrenched his torso with all of his might and threw Jake off. There was no sight anymore, there was no sound, there was no thought. All that existed was red. Jake stepped toward the wall where he had a sword mounted on the wall. Luther caught his arm. Then, he snapped Jake's arm down and then shot down on one knee. Simultaneously, Luther launched himself into Jake's midsection, lifting him over his shoulders.

Luther then, with all the strength he possessed, slammed Jake down to the ground. Before Jake could recover from the blow, Luther was on top of him. His fists struck Jake's face like a metronome, thoughtless and uncaring. There was only one outcome from a conflict like this, and Luther knew on which side of the coin he wanted to fall.

He snapped out of it. He looked around and saw the naked girl still lying unconscious on Jake's bed. He looked towards the doorway and Sam was standing there. There were five or six other fraternity brothers at the doorway now. Luther, fists covered with the blood of Jake, stood up and looked at them.

"I- I- I- …." There were no words that could justify or diminish the actions that he had just taken.

The brother in the middle, Jeff, spoke up and said, "We saw the whole thing man, we heard you yelling for an ambulance and came up."

"H-h-h-he attacked me…" Luther didn't know how to process what had happened. He knew that he had been attacked, but the fight was a blur. All he could remember was right before the snap.

Luther snapped back to himself. He was standing again in front of the Lincoln Memorial, headphones still playing his finance podcast. He had formed a cold sweat underneath his shirt, causing the slight breeze to prickle up his skin. Luther hadn't thought about that night in years. That was the night he had met Samantha but was also the night he found something in himself that terrified him.

Luther, finally having shaken off the longing ache of nostalgia, began jogging back to his house. On his run, he got lost in the world again. He ran through the National Mall, and back down to his house. The cool fog clung to his skin like a clammy blanket, it felt like small piercing fleas pecking his cheeks as he ran through. The odd aroma of oil and the woefully preserved vestiges of nature mixed to create an acrid smell unique to metropolises. It was as if nature and humanity were each fighting for survival, and the stench was left over from the fight.

Luther's lawn was in sight. He had been running for ages, and his legs had a dull ache that bid him to stop.

Tonight was important, it was election night. Luther felt this odd clenching in his stomach; the events of the campaign had been highly contentious. The various telecom mouthpieces employed by the parties had been fighting the war on television for almost two years. The war of ideas had dragged on mercilessly, but Congresswoman Holder's admission during a debate of being an atheist seemed to have dire poll consequences. Harold Drum was expected to win the election tonight.

There's something off with him, Luther thought to himself. He couldn't describe it, but every time he saw that man, something inside opened its eyes.

"My name is Trevor Stewart reporting for Wolf News Primetime. We come to you live now with breaking news to report that Harold Drum has won the election for President of the United States by an overwhelming 535-3, Congresswoman Holder winning only her home state of Nebraska. Perhaps even more overwhelming were the popular vote totals, with President-elect Drum winning 74% of the popular vote. This is truly one of the most unprecedented political mandates that a president has received."

He continued, "We now see a president who is untethered by the traditional split of the voters. The country has spoken with one, unmistakable voice. They have said that God is in control, and President Drum is their shepherd."

Part II: The Beginning

"A child who is not embraced by the village will burn it down to feel its warmth." – African proverb

Chapter 6: Harold's Past

Harold sat up from his nap and reached beside him to grab the glass of water he had placed there. He brushed his head with his hand and tossed the blankets to the side. His room was relatively small, only containing his bed and the bed of his roommate, Rick. Rick was studying political science which Harold made fun of him for constantly. *How useless could it be to study politics?* Harold would often think to himself. Harold was an industrial engineering major, but he was still a sophomore.

Rick was still lying down in his bed. He smelled vividly like alcohol from the night before. Harold wasn't much of a partier; his father claimed to be strictly against any sort of alcohol. Although, he suspected his father occasionally snuck a scotch. Rick had jet black hair, and piercing, glowing blue eyes. His face was well-chiseled, he was handsome in a Superman sort of way. Unfortunately, Rick was only 5'8", otherwise people might get the two confused.

Harold walked over to the small black mini-fridge that was halfway between the two beds in the room. He opened the fridge and grabbed a ginger ale. Harold loved that sharp metal clicking sound that always happens when you pop open a soda tab. To Harold, that was really part of the experience of drinking a soda – almost a Pavlovian response.

Walking back to the bed, Harold sat down and pulled the large container of ramen out from under it. He picked up a package and put it in his ramen bowl. His favorite flavor was chicken. Ramen and ginger ale for breakfast was a normal routine for Harold.

After finishing his breakfast, Harold went to get his shower shoes to go clean up before his morning physics class. He began showering, making sure to push the weird suction cup button things on the curtain onto the walls. The water waffled torturously between scalding and freezing; reacting violently to the ill-timed toilet flushing of other residents of the hall.

Harold finally got out of the shower, got dressed, and went to class. The lecture was rather boring, but Harold got to see Cheryl. Cheryl was the most beautiful woman Harold had ever seen. She was a radiant, platinum blonde. She wore sundresses every day to class, just to remind everyone how inadequate they were. Harold was conflicted about his feelings for her. She was very Christian, and Harold didn't think about religion much. It caused Cheryl to tell him that they couldn't go out, though.

After class, Harold was walking back to his dorm when Cheryl called his name out.

"Oh, hey Cher," Harold replied, stopping dead in his tracks to wait for her.

"Hey, I just wanted to let you know that there's an FCA meeting at the fellowship hall if you'd like to go with me." She smiled, and half twisted her body as if to start walking the other way.

"What's FCA, Cher?"

"Fellowship of Christian Athletes. It's a Christian athletic fellowship." Apparently, Harold's ignorance had upset Cheryl.

"Oh yeah? Well, I don't know if I'm really interested in anything like that." Harold wasn't going to let her get any satisfaction from her facetious quip.

"Oh, come on, it'll be fun! We play sports and such, nothing serious, I promise." She smiled again, and grabbed Harold's wrist, pulling him along.

They walked into the fellowship hall. Harold looked around, there were a ton of people there. There was a pounding sound accompanied with squeaking coming from the right. Harold walked over and found a group of guys playing basketball. He stepped inside the gym and sat on the bench next to the court. One of the older men approached him. The man had on faded blue shorts and a white t-shirt that was tucked into his shorts. He wore a bright neon headband and had plain white sneakers on. His hair was slightly receding, revealing a deep widow's peak. It was a light brown color. Everything about this man was plain.

"Hey there bud, do you wanna play some ball with us?" Harold nodded and stood up. The man came over to introduce himself, hand was held out in front from the time Harold had nodded. They shook hands.

"My name is Ken Oaks. Whadda they call ya?" He was incredibly enthusiastic with his introduction. It was like he was eager just for the opportunity to speak.

"My name is Harold Drum."

Later that night, Harold was still at the fellowship hall. He was sitting in a small side room with a small group of young people. Ken was in the room as well, a Bible in his hands, open wide. He was telling them the word of God, and for the first time, Harold listened. Harold listened to the story of Job. A story about how a man had everything stripped away from him, and then was rewarded for faith. They then spoke of the book of Matthew. Ken told them how it was easier for a camel to pass through the eye of a needle, than for a rich man to enter heaven. He spoke of Jesus's deep love for the poor, and how he commanded his flock to give up the lust for worldly wealth and help those in need.

Harold was listening intently, but his thoughts began to wander. *Have I been wrong all my life? Is God real? Is this man lying?* Harold was unsure of what he was hearing. The message sounded righteous, kind, but wrathful. It is a strange dichotomy to be a populace of sinners in the hands of an angry god.

Ken turned to Harold specifically. Harold could tell that the conversation that was about to occur would not end comfortably. Ken closed his Bible and held it out to Harold.

"This Bible is yours, son, if you want it." Harold looked at Ken, locking eyes for a long time. He hesitated. Harold had never read the Bible before, nor had he ever owned one. His parents weren't particularly religious, but he barely knew his mother. She had passed away when Harold was four. He reached out and grabbed the book.

"Th-thank you." Harold was nervous. He felt the hair on the back of his neck stand up. It was a strange feeling of anticipation. This was the first time he had even held the book in his hand, he didn't even believe it was true. And yet, touching the book made a wave of intense heat and emotion wash over him. Harold opened it immediately and began to read. *In the beginning...*

It was like fuel to a flame that Harold didn't even know had existed, and he was unaware that the fuel had been added.

"Harry, are you coming to FCA tonight?" Cheryl had decided to give Harold a nickname, Harold couldn't tell if it was laziness or affection.

"Of course, it was a pretty cool experience." Harold was excited to go. It had been a week since the last one. The meetings occurred every Thursday. They chose Thursday specifically so that they could still attend youth groups on Wednesday at their local churches. Harold didn't think that he wanted THAT much church.

"Well, great! Would you like to walk over with me? I'm going now." It was about half an hour before the meeting was supposed to start. Harold hadn't had time to go to the mess hall to eat dinner yet, he was starving.

"Sure, let's go." They walked off together. Harold's hands were in his pockets. He was wearing a black T-shirt with a large crimson A on it and jeans. Cheryl was wearing a crimson sweater that had a white A scrawled on it, a white headband, and a white skirt that went down to her knees. She was wearing red shoes. In her left arm, she had her schoolbooks and a Bible, she hooked her right arm around Harold's elbow. They walked like this towards the fellowship hall. On the way, they were talking to each other constantly.

"Cher, what do you wanna do?" Harold's light southern accent sounded dignified. His voice was robust, but not intimidating. His demeanor was welcoming, he was always quick to make friends.

"What do you mean? We're going to FCA?" Cheryl looked at him, one eyebrow cocked slightly upward.

"No, I mean in your career, like school n' stuff." Harold spoke while slightly chuckling.

"Oh, well I think I'm gonna be a nurse. I'm in nursing school right now, and I have the grades in science. My daddy thinks it could be a really steady career."

"That's really cool. I'm glad you know what you want to do. I'm still kinda searching for what I want to do." Harold's head was full of ideas, but nothing sounded right to him.

"My dad wants me to be an accountant or something like that. A lawyer maybe. I just don't see myself sitting at a desk all day, ya know? I wanna do something great." Harold talked while looking straight ahead. He didn't really enjoy being this open with people, but with Cheryl it seemed different.

"Well, what do you want to do?" Cheryl stopped, pulling Harold back towards her. Harold turned his body towards hers. She looked him directly in the eyes. Her eyes were blue with little specks of black littered throughout.

"Don't waste my time, Harry. If you just wanna sit around and be a bum with your life, let me know now, I'll go find someone else."

"Hold on, find someone else?" Harry had his palms slightly raised by his sides, a puzzled look on his face.

"Oh, don't act like you don't know what's going on here." She cocked her hip to the side and raised both of her eyebrows.

"No, I don't see it. Why don't you spell it out for me?" Harold had a cocky grin on his face, the type of grin that makes people confused on whether to love him or smack him.

She slapped him in the chest, and then kissed him on the cheek. "That spelled out enough for you?" She turned and walked away. Harold's blood was rushing to his skin, he was brightly blushing. His heart was pounding, he had trouble breathing.

He ran after her and grabbed her wrist. Then, he pulled her back into him. He bent down as if to kiss her. She raised her hand to his lips, putting a single finger in the middle right underneath his nose.

"Uh-uh mister, I'm just shopping right now. I don't know if I've bought it yet, and that's a buying it type of action." Her accent would let little bits of southern slip every now and then. It was like she had to try to keep the country at bay, but sometimes it just came out.

Harold stepped back, equal parts embarrassed, amused, and weirdly, at least Harold thought, more interested in her. She looked at him. She opened her mouth and pulled in air as if to breathe, but then paused. She was searching for the right words to say. Harold's father had always told him that whoever talks first loses, and whatever game was being played, Harold intended to win.

She finally spoke, "I'm pretty sure I'm gonna buy it at some point. Just give me some time, okay?"

Harold smiled, and he walked up to Cheryl. He put his arm around her shoulders. They walked the rest of the way to the fellowship hall. Once they arrived, it was a guys and girls night. That meant that the guys and girls were in large, separate groups. Generally, this was just a lame excuse to let the guys play sports together.

Harold began playing basketball with a few of the guys. His roommate, Rick, was there. Rick was very religious. He grew up in a small southern town in South Carolina called Ninety-Six. He attended a Baptist church there. Ken was there, too. He generally tried to run basketball as much as he could, it was his favorite sport.

They played for about an hour. After the game, a few of the guys were sitting in a small circle. Rick was to Harold's right. There were four other guys in the circle, Jared, Mark, Lucas, and Jacob. Harold didn't really know the others as they were friends of Rick's. Rick had been attending FCA meetings since the beginning of their freshman year but hadn't been able to convince Harold to attend.

Ken walked over to the group. He was wiping his arms off with what looked like a full bath towel. Ken put his arm on Rick's shoulder and leaned down to say something into his ear. Rick then stood up and went to the back of the gym. He grabbed a basketball and ran back to the group. He handed the ball to Ken when he got back. With the basketball in his left hand, Ken turned towards the group.

"When I was a kid, my dad was the one who taught me about basketball. The most important thing about basketball, to my dad, was teamwork. Teamwork requires a lot of common understanding and a lot of working together to make a successful team." Ken was very adamant, almost comically over dramatic as he spoke.

"Oh, teamwork requires lots of teamwork? Thanks, Ken!" Lucas's mouth was hanging open like a hyena, laughing wildly at the completely obvious nature of what Ken had said. None of the other guys laughed.

"My dad also taught me that there is only one real team that matters, and that's God's team." Ken turned around and shot the ball. He missed the shot.

"See guys, at the end of the day, it's not really about winning and losing. What it's really about is your faith in Christ."

Harold, undeterred by Lucas's lack of respect, spoke up. "What does that mean, Ken? People keep talking about it like some hushed whisper, but nobody can ever say what it means." There was a sincerity of curiosity that made Harold's question inoffensive. He wasn't questioning Ken's beliefs, merely inquiring about how to follow them.

"Well, let me tell you." Ken finally sat down next to Harold and began to speak to the group.

Chapter 7: Mission

"I can't believe we're actually doing this!" Cheryl was clearly nervous. She had never been on a plane before. Presumably, Cheryl was about to experience a lot of firsts. Cheryl had never traveled outside of Alabama, except to go visit her grandparents in Pensacola. Harold had been to Canada before to go snowboarding, but that was about it.

"It's what we feel called to do, right?" Ken had encouraged them to go on a mission before their senior year of college. They chose to go to a remote region of Afghanistan. Their church had a partnership with a small church there, and after the effects of 9/11, they thought there was room for Christianity to grow in the region. They were sending the group of missionaries to Islamabad in Pakistan first, and then they would drive into Afghanistan near Dayla. They stepped up to the ticket agent and showed them their boarding pass. Once on the plane, they sat next to each other. It was a very long flight.

The next morning, the group was in the van to go to the remote church. There were four other people in their group. Rick was one, it appeared that Harold and Rick were inseparable. Cheryl's friend, Becca, was another. Ken and his wife, Janet, rounded out the group. They were in a three-row van. The outside of the van was rather dilapidated, the paint had chipped off substantially. What color was left other than rust was a light blue. It sounded like the muffler had abandoned ship years ago.

The van was being driven by a local whom the church had sent. His name was Abbas. He had long hair, down his shoulders. He had hazel eyes, and light brown skin. He wore a navy-blue hoodie with a football team logo on it, and a pair of jeans that had seen better days. There was a Bible in the console of the van.

"How long is the drive, Abbas?" Ken asked politely.

"It is about errr—10 hours mister Ken." Abbas spoke very proper English, but with a sub-continental twinge to it.

Abbas seemed nervous, like he didn't want to be there. He was shifty, looking around nervously. Harold thought that it was most likely because he was scared to be Christian in a Muslim nation. Especially given that he was hauling around missionaries for Christ. Who could blame Abbas for being a little nervous under the circumstances?

Harold looked down at his phone. It didn't have any service. Luckily, Harold had some music pre-downloaded. He put on his headphones; the familiar sounds of the Peak Harmony Church played. Harold laid his head against the opaque window, and he drifted off.

"GET OUT OF THE VAN!" Abbas was shouting at them. They had pulled over to the side of the road. They had barely driven for four hours.

"GET OUT OF THE VAN!" Abbas again repeated. He was shouting louder this time. Harold looked out of the front of the van. He saw Abbas standing with a group of other men. These men were dressed differently. They had on long white linen pants, linen shirts, and leather vests. Each of them had on cloth headdresses, in various styles. Most importantly, they had what looked to be long rifles in their hands. The ammo magazine was curved slightly, and the stock was a glossed burgundy. It was still day out, barely 1 P.M.

"GET OUT OF THE VAN NOW OR YOU ALL DIE!" Abbas sounded desperate, unstably loud.

The group slowly exited the van. The men walked towards the group, holding the guns up the entire way over. When they finally got to the group, they began to grab onto them. The men threw Rick to the ground and tied his hands behind his back. They put a dark sack over his head. They did the same with the rest.

They were put back in the van. This time, however, the van veered off the road. The ground made the trip much more difficult. The trip to their destination took another hour. When they finally arrived, the men walked up to the van. They opened the doors and grabbed the members of the group one by one, ushering them into a small metal shack outside of the small mosque they had arrived at.

After being violently handled out of the van, the group walked across the hard desert sand. They entered a building, and the abductors took the sacks off everyone's heads. A man walked in. He was round in the midsection. He was older, mid-fifties probably. His hair was peppered with gray, and he had a large beard that was similarly colored. He wore a round white hat, and a gray robe.

"Hello, I am Iskandar. I am the Imam here."

Ken spoke up at this point, "What is going on? What do you mean Imam? We're going to a Christian church!" He was holding back tears, obviously terrified. His emotions were confused between the need to protect the group and his desire to run away and hide.

"Are you the leader here?" Iskandar looked at Ken. He had a kind look in his eyes. Almost like a father.

"Yes, I am the leader." Iskandar walked slowly over to where Ken was knelt down on the ground. He put his hand on Ken's shoulder.

"Kill him."

Without hesitation, the guard at the door, who was one of the men who had seized them on the road, leveled his rifle at Ken. Ken tried to stand. *POP POP POP.* Ken's body fell lifeless to the floor. Harold stared at Ken's warm corpse with a feeling of horror. His gut twisted as his body rejected the image of his dead mentor on the ground. Everything in his soul screamed at the agony he felt. A new sensation began to take hold in his heart. Fear.

"Would anyone else like to ask questions?" The group was silent. The Imam smiled and began to walk around the room, he looked at each one of the group members intently. He walked over to Cheryl. He grabbed her jaw with his palm facing upward. He made her eyes come into contact with his.

"This one is pretty. Are you married, little one?"

Cheryl looked over at Harold with desperation in her eyes.

Harold spoke up, "Yes, she's my wife." The Imam snapped his eyes towards Harold. He walked over to him and slapped him in the face with the back of his hand. When Harold brought his face around, he slapped him in the face again. Harold fell to the ground. His mouth was beginning to fill with blood.

"The first was for speaking without being addressed. The second was for being married to such a

68

beautiful woman but being so unworthy." The Imam spit on Harold. The fear in Harold's heart kept him cowed. He didn't respond, he didn't move. Iskandar walked back over to Cheryl and caressed her check. He then walked over to Janet, Ken's widow. Looking down at Ken on the ground beside her, Janet was as pale as a ghost.

"I assume that was your husband?" Iskandar put his hooked finger under her chin and made her look up at him. Janet's eyes were bloodshot, tears streamed down her face. She was broken. Iskandar knelt down and kissed her on the check. Janet looked horrified.

"My dear, you are in need of a husband." Iskandar motioned to one of the guards. There were eight guards in the room. The guard put the bag back over Janet's head and picked her up. Janet began to scream and kick, to little avail. They carried her out of the shack. Iskandar motioned to another guard, who looked at Harold. The guard walked over to Harold and placed a bag over his head.

The guard stood Harold up. Harold could feel the cold steel of the guard's gun press against his back. He walked where directed, the fear making him complicit. After about five minutes of walking, Harold heard a door open. The guard sat him down in what felt like a small metal chair. He used a plastic wire tie to lash Harold's hands to the chair. He did the same with Harold's ankles and took the bag off.

There was a dim overhead light. There was music playing lowly, strange music with weird sounds. It smelled like warm sand baked in the sweltering heat of the desert sun. The wind was blowing strongly against the building that Harold was in, creating a howling echo that resonated throughout the small metal shack. He looked around, but it was dark by this point. It was difficult to make anything out with how dim the light was. Harold checked the upper part of the wall to see if there were any windows, but he couldn't find any.

Harold's mind was racing. *Where am I? What happened? Why is God doing this to me? Where's Cheryl?* His thoughts were uncontrollable. They were a chaotic tempest raging inside an emotional cataclysm of fear, anger, hatred, confusion, and pain. Harold didn't sleep. He stared at the corners of the room, paralyzed with fear.

Morning broke, there were small gaps in between the top of the walls and the ceiling which allowed a small amount of sunlight to peek through. Harold finally got a full glimpse of the room. He wished he hadn't. It revealed a small, barren room. The only fixture in the room was the chair on which he sat. He returned to his catatonic state.

After a while, Harold heard footsteps outside the door. The sand must have been almost brick from the heat. The door opened, and Iskandar walked in. He was wearing the same robe from the day before. A guard was behind him, carrying a chair. The guard placed the chair down, and Iskandar sat in it. He was about three feet in front of Harold. He crossed his legs and pulled out a long pipe. After stuffing it with what appeared to be hashish, he lit the pipe and puffed it.

"What is your name?" Iskandar spoke like an American. It was strange to hear such a clear accent come from someone in Afghanistan.

"My name?" Harold paused for a minute. He was unsure of whether to give him an honest answer or not.

"Harry." Iskandar puffed his pipe again. He blew the smoke directly into Harold's face.

"That's your first lie. I would suggest it be your last, Harold."

Harold was even more scared than he was before. The paralyzing cognitive storm pulsed vividly in the back of his subconscious again, looking for an excuse to come out of its temporary box. *How did he know my name? Has he talked to someone else?*

"Your wife told me all about you." Iskandar puffed his pipe, chuckling softly to himself. "She didn't tell me you were a liar, though. She seems to have left that part out."

He seemed sincerely perturbed, as if she had owed him that insight. "I will not lay with your wife, she is yours. I wanted you to know that." Harold pulled his head back, looking him directly in the eyes.

"What are we doing here?" The question left Harold's mouth before he had time to consider its effect. Ken had been killed for far less. Harold didn't want to die.

"What do you mean? You came here voluntarily. We just didn't think you would actually come. We killed your Christian friends a long time ago." Tears began to well up in Harold's eyes again. Dead. The entire village, over a hundred Christians, all dead. Fear began to evolve into something much darker.

"We are the Last Dawn. You are our guests. For now." Iskandar puffed his pipe and then walked out of the room. The guard quickly grabbed his chair and then walked out behind him. Closing the door on Harold once again. The storm rushed quickly back over Harold's mind.

"YYYYYYYYYAAAAAAAAAAAAAAAAAHH HHHHHHHHHHHHHH!!!!!!!!!!!!!" Harold let out a primal scream. He wept.

Harold was awoken by the door opening. It was early, barely daybreak. Two guards walked in. Iskandar wasn't with them. One of them had what looked to be a long metal rod in his hand. The other had a book, Harold couldn't tell what book it was. He could only make out the symbol of a trident and a circle. They began chanting in some language that Harold couldn't understand.

The guard with the rod walked up to Harold. He stuck the rod to Harold's side. Harold screamed at the sensation. It was like an electric shock. He felt it in his entire body and only one spot all at the same time. His skin felt like icy fire. The guard struck him again. And again. And again. Harold blacked out.

Harold was hit with a bucket of water. He woke up, feeling disoriented. He was dizzy, and the room was spinning rapidly. He looked at what he thought was up and saw Iskandar. The Imam was standing there smiling down at Harold.

"This is just the first day of many down your path to enlightenment. His will be praised." Iskandar patted Harold on the head, and then he walked out of the room. Leaving Harold there alone. The storm returned, and Harold lost sense of time. Time was a meaningless thing to Harold. It was strange to him how time could feel small and infinite. He was experiencing time constantly, but he had no way to perceive it. Days became amorphous, it didn't matter what was going on. This room was reality.

An amount of time passed, and the door opened again. This time Iskandar walked in first. Two of the other guards were behind him. One of the guards carried an empty metal oil drum. The other carried a large basin that was filled with water. The guard placed the drum behind Harold's chair. The second guard began filling a few pitchers that he pulled from inside the drum with the water from the basin. Iskandar stood in the corner.

The guard who had placed the drum took a black sack from his back pocket and placed it over Harold's face. Darkness. The guard then pulled Harold's head back. Harold felt water hit the sack. He tried to breathe in, but he couldn't. The water stopped momentarily, as soon as Harold tried to breathe but the water hit the sack again and Harold was forced to inhale a gulp of water. It made him cough uncontrollably. The water got into his nose as a result. The pain in his lungs became severe. The water stopped again, when Harold tried to gasp for air the pain in his nose was excruciating.

Harold's mind began to panic. Survival responses from deep in his animal psyche began to kick in. His body began to thrash wildly, his muscles violently contracted. Anything to fight against this, anything to struggle. Harold began to figure out how long it took for the pitcher to empty. He timed his breathing better. The pain became tolerable. Harold intended to win whatever game they were playing.

Eventually, they had to pour the water from the drum back into the basin to begin the process again. They took the sack off of Harold's head. Harold hadn't let out any noise after his initial coughing fit. Harold's fear had hardened into rage. His fury was compelling him to resist.

He looked directly into Iskandar's eyes, and his jaw was set.

"You are a fighter. We will see how much fight you have." The men placed the sack back over Harold's head and resumed. After another four full rounds, they took the sack off of Harold's head again. He was barely conscious, he looked like a boxer who was outclassed but refused to get knocked out. His mouth hung open loosely, his muscles sore from resisting the water pushing furiously to get into his lungs. His hair hung down in tattered strands.

Iskandar came over to him and put his hand on his shoulder. He nodded to the guards. They began to collect their heinous tool kit and then walked out of the room. Iskandar paced back and forth in front of Harold. He was stroking his beard, and it looked like he was thinking intently. He had a very pointed nose and pronounced wrinkles around his mouth. When he smiled it looked like a Cheshire cat.

"You have been lied to, my friend." Iskandar continued pacing back and forth. "You have been told that your God is the one true God."

He stopped in front of Harold. He put his face directly in front of Harold's. His face appeared angry, a pronounced frown decorated his mouth, and his eyes were slightly tensed. "Your Catholic Church lied to the world. They said that Jesus was the Messiah. That he died for your sins."

"Jesus is the Messiah, he is the King of Ki—" Iskandar smacked Harold with the back of his hand before he could finish. Harold continued, screaming with recalcitrant rage, "Our father, who art in heav—" Iskandar smacked him again, this time with significantly more force. Blood spewed across the sun-hardened sand bricks on the ground. "Hallowed be thy—" This time Iskandar used his fist. Once. Twice. Three times. Darkness.

Harold heard loud popping sounds off in the distance. He could also hear the familiar sound of engines. They sounded louder than car engines though, more like loud diesel trucks. There was shuffling outside, the men of the mosque were running around. Harold heard popping much closer to him. With the pops being so close, Harold was able to discern it was gunfire. It began to escalate, gunfire sounding out like a grim symphony of human advancement.

The fear in Harold began to surface again. Something – or someone – was coming to take out their captors. Harold didn't know how long they had been here. Days had blurred together. A week? A month? Harold couldn't tell. Reality outside of these four walls felt like a dream, so real yet unattainable. The sound of the steel tempest raging outside snapped him back to the present. Harold heard a new noise in the distance. It was a warping of the air, almost like a giant was running. The warps were consistent, but they grew faster.

Helicopters, Harold recognized the sounds, *Americans!* The cold grip of fear turned into the warm light of hope in Harold's heart. The arsenal of democracy had come to save him. What Harold heard next was indescribable. It was as if the entirety of the morning's gunfight was compressed into ten seconds. He couldn't see what was going on outside, but if the sight matched his hearing it was a hellacious display of overwhelming force. The yells from the men outside slowed.

Harold heard English being yelled outside. He began to scream. "Help me!" He yelled over and over again. Reckless hope compelled him to keep yelling. "PLLEEAAASSEE!!" Eventually, Harold heard footsteps outside. There was a lot of shuffling and whispering. Suddenly, an explosion blew the door of its hinges and sent a cloud of sand and dust scattered throughout the room. Harold began coughing and wheezing due to the shock and awe.

"Clear!" Someone shouted.

"Clear!" Another shouted.

"All clear, Sergeant!"

"Hostage secure."

"Call it in to LT."

"Hua."

Harold still couldn't see through all of the dust that had gotten in his eyes. The water from his eyes was continuing to run down his cheeks. The coughing was beginning to hurt his lungs, and he eventually began dry heaving. Someone walked over and took the sack off of his head. The men were wearing black uniforms. They had a black and gray scale American flag on the shoulder. They were bearded, which Harold thought was strange.

"Cut him loose, grab him and let's go, we can't stay here for very long."

"Hua."

Harold was forced to stand for the first time in as long as he could remember. He had been lashed to that chair since the first day that they arrived, however long ago that was. The soldiers took him outside the shack. The light of the sun was blinding. The warmth felt like nails being driven into his skin. The storm clouds in his mind had triumphant beams of light shining through.

The helicopter had landed right outside of the mosque on a large, flat clearing. The layout of the complex was rather simple, there was a series of shacks outside of the mosque, the whole complex was surrounded by a wire fence. The mosque was rather large and had two halls attached to it. Harold looked around, but he didn't see his friends anywhere. *Were they already dead?* Harold wondered.

One of the soldiers looked at Harold, "Were you alone, son?"

Harold shook his head. He couldn't find the strength to speak. The soldier then ran over to another soldier who looked different than the others. He had the calm aura of someone who had seen too much death. On his chest were two vertical, silver bars. He didn't wear a beard, but he had on dark black sunglasses and had a large radio receiver in his hand. He stood next to a Humvee that had a large gun manned by another soldier on it.

Harold couldn't make out what he was saying because of the helicopter. The soldier who was carrying Harold put him on the floor of the helicopter's cabin. Harold tried to stand, but quickly passed out.

Harold awoke to sterile, fluorescent lights. There was a steady, rhythmic beeping. Harold looked to the side and saw a heart monitor. He looked down at his body and realized he was in a hospital bed, attached to that heart monitor. *How long have I been here? Where am I? Where is Cheryl?* Harold began to feel panicked. The walls began to close in as the panic from the room returned to his mind.

A nurse who had observed the panic attack, rushed over to restrain Harold. "Calm down, sweetie. Everything is okay." Her voice was soothing. Harold had panicked breathing, his skin looked clammy from the cold sweat of anxious fear. Her name tag said Ayala. *Last name? Military hospital?* The helicopter rescue popped back into Harold's mind. He began to remember what happened.

He turned to Ayala, "What happened to me? Where are my friends?" The nurse turned towards him. She looked forlorn. She obviously wanted to answer but restrained herself and walked away. Harold was confused. *Why won't she give me answers?* He began to feel anger well in his chest. Childish. Unrestrained. Unstable.

"Answer me!" Harold screamed after the nurse who had already left his room.

Harold noticed there was a clock on the wall, and he began to stare at it. He felt every waking tick as if it were a personal attack on himself. It was as if time was taunting him, making him feel the inadequacy of his fleeting nature.

After one hour, twelve minutes, and thirty-six seconds, a man walked into the room. He was a slight man, barely 5'5". He was bald, and his face was clean shaven. He wore a white lab coat and his name tag said Tyler. He had the two vertical bars on his chest, too.

"Hello, I'm Dr. Ron Tyler. I've been treating you." He had an out of place voice for someone his size. It sounded warm and deep, like a ten-year smoker who was talking even deeper to tell a story. Harold's theory was backed up by the pack of cigarettes in the front pocket of his lab coat.

"What happened, doctor? Where are my friends? Are they okay?" The doctor shuffled into the room and closed the door.

"I've been authorized to share these details with you because you were a victim but understand that you cannot spread this information." The doctor sat down on the bedside and gave Harold a look that implied he needed to respond in order to hear the information.

"I understand."

"One of your group was apparently killed on your arrival to the camp. Another, we believe his wife, was also dead when we arrived. Three others were recovered but they remain unconscious. They are here at the hospital. The others were discovered in rooms similar to yours." Dr. Tyler paused, unsure of how to proceed.

"How did you find us?"

"Your church reported that you had never checked in with them upon arrival, and then the authorities contacted the Army after a few days. We've been searching for your group for over a month."

A month. Harold felt that it was an eternity, a ceaseless abyss of suffering, but it was only a month. The feeling of helplessness when the water hit his face roared back to the front of his mind. He began to panic again. His breathing became shallow, and the blood rushed to his skin to create a burning sensation. Harold began to reach out towards the doctor for something real to grab onto.

"I got you." Dr. Tyler grabbed both of Harold's arms and held them down to his sides, and then wrapped him in a hug. "You've been through a lot, okay? Take some time, we'll get you some help." Dr. Tyler stood up, handed Harold a juice box from the food that had been left on the side table, and walked out of the room. He was clearly uncomfortable dealing with the type of emotional trauma Harold was exhibiting.

Harold pulled his knees into his chest and put his head down. He began to rock back and forth rapidly. Whispering to himself just to fill the room with some sort of noise. *I will never go back into a box. I will never go back into a box. I will never go back into a box.*

Chapter 8: Farmboy

Cock-a-doodle-doo! Cock-a doodle-doo! The sun hadn't even risen, and the roosters were already carrying on like one of their hens told them a joke. Luther threw the blankets off and got up. He looked at the digital clock beside his bed. It was 4:30 AM. He loved coming back from school to stay with his grandparents, but the roosters were always an unfortunate condition of doing so. He began the process of getting ready to go downstairs. To no surprise, his grandparents were both already up and out of bed. Luther could smell coffee wafting up the steps to the small, slanted loft where he slept.

His grandparents had offered him the much larger guest room, but Luther had been staying in that loft since he was a boy. He had no intention of changing that particular tradition. He put on a pair of jeans and his boots and walked down the steps. He had a black shirt on with a gothic, blue D on it.

"Boy, didn't I tell you that devil shirt can't be worn in my house?" Luther's grandfather was standing at the base of the stairs waiting for Luther. Marcus, Luther's grandfather, was a tall man, standing around 6'2". He was slender, and his skin was aged like roughly hewn hide. With an aged Carolina blue ballcap on his head, he wore a red plaid shirt with the sleeves rolled up to the elbows. In the pocket of his plaid shirt was a pouch of tobacco and a pipe; these ever present companions of Marcus Washington. His pants were blue jeans that looked as if they had been through a war zone. The kind that people would pay top designer price for.

"Sorry gramps, I'm only interested in top schools." Luther clapped Marcus playfully on the shoulder. Marcus wrapped Luther's head with his arm and gave him a noogie. Luther was getting ready to start applying for colleges. He was really only interested in one school.

Luther walked into the kitchen. His grandmother was pouring a cup of coffee. She made the coffee in a percolator to get the maximum amount of caffeine. Outside, looking through the window above the sink, Luther looked over the whole farm. It was around twelve-hundred acres of beautiful eastern North Carolina farmland. Used to grow the one thing that it grew better than any other state in the entire world: tobacco. Rows and rows of long green leaves, tobacco had sustained the Washington family for generations even though Marcus was the first landowner in the family. Before that, the Washington's spent decades as tenant farmers.

Marcus walked into the room, "Joanne, I'm fixin' ta let the cows into the back pasture."

Joanne, Luther's grandmother, walked over to Marcus and kissed him on the cheek. "Good morning handsome." Marcus cracked a smile, "Mornin'." He stooped down to kiss her on the lips. Luther audibly groaned.

Marcus started to walk out of the room, Luther pulled the coffee up to his lips while staring blankly out the window. Suddenly, Luther felt something grab his ear and jerk him backwards.

"Come on, boy, we got work to do." Marcus dragged Luther out of the house and finally let his ear go.

They walked to the barn to gather their equipment for the day. They arrived at the equipment barn, and Luther went over to the racks that were placed up on the wall to the right of the front door. Luther pulled on some thick, oiled leather gloves. There was a strange feeling of history in these gloves, they were made from the hide of one of the cows that had died when Luther was a boy. Marcus was adamant that every piece of every animal must be used; to do otherwise was to diminish that animal's sacrifice.

The life of a farmer is a strange one. Their solemn task is to kill that which they raised and created. A good farmer loves his animals and tends his crops, primarily for the sole purpose of harvest. This weighed heavily on those stewards of the land, Marcus was no exception. Marcus was not an educated man, he dropped out of school in the eighth grade to work on his family's farm. His family was extremely poor when he was a child. At fifteen, Marcus got a small bank loan to buy a tractor to reap the hay in neighboring fields for a small fee for other farmers.

From this small tractor, Marcus bought his first farm. From his first farm, he bought the farm that they now live on. He pulled himself up from nothing to owning a twelve-hundred-acre farm and supported his family the entire time. This is not a land of opulence. This is a land of toil and sweat. Marcus couldn't tell the difference, this was his kingdom, and it was the joy of his life to be its king.

They walked out to the cow pasture. Marcus was slightly ahead of Luther, a subtle indication of who was in charge. They opened an intervening gate between two pastures. Following the two men the entire time was a squad of three border collies, Yip, Deek, and Xena. At the

83

snap of Marcus's fingers, the once still and silly dogs were suddenly filled with purpose. They bolted into the field and began to nip and bark at the back line of the cows. The bovine armada began to shuffle obediently into another pasture.

Now Luther's real task began: shoveling the manure into bags to sell at the market. *Everything has a use*, Marcus's words echoed in Luther's head as he bowed his head and went about his duty. Luther took a large plastic utility bag and placed it inside of a 55-gallon drum. He put this drum on a cart next to three other identical drums. He placed bags in the other drums and wheeled the cart out onto the pasture.

Scoop. Pour. Scoop. Pour. Scoop. Pour. Luther began to lose track of reality. Minutes stretching tortuously into hours. The punishing rays of the North Carolina sun beat down on his neck. The sweat rolled down from his hair which both cooled him and irritated him as it rubbed raw against his collar. His hands began to ache, but he could barely sense it. The monotony of the task blinded Luther from the pain. Scoop. Pour. Scoop. Pour. Scoop. Pour. Luther felt the echo of thousands of years of his ancestors in the depths of his mind, the shared generational experience filling his mind with a determination of singular purpose.

Across the field, Marcus watched Luther. Marcus watched the single-minded nature of Luther's labor. He watched as he would break momentarily to wipe the sweat from his neck but would return immediately to the task. Marcus puffed on his pipe and walked towards the shop. There were a few things to tend to before the day was over.

Time snapped back into relevance, and Luther looked up to find the sun setting on his herculean penance. He wheeled the much heavier cart back to the barn and sealed the utility bags with zip ties. Luther stumbled back into the house, worn ragged from the day's labor.

After Luther grabbed what was left of dinner from the stove where Gramma Jo had left it out for him, he went up to his room to strip off the manure-caked clothes he was wearing. Walking down to the bathroom to take a shower, Luther began to think about what he was going to say to his father when he got back home.

Luther felt the sharp inhale caused by the not-yet hot water from the shower. The hair on his skin stood straight up from the shock. As the water continued to pour over him, sheets of mud and dirt flowed onto the floor. There was a unique feeling of accomplishment when you could see the geological representation of labor being rinsed from the skin. It was as if you felt that you deserved to be cleaned as a reward for your work.

Walking back to his room with a towel wrapped around his waist, Luther put on a soft t-shirt and some athletic shorts. He went downstairs to the back porch where his grandfather was smoking his pipe and took the rocking chair next to him. The porch was painted white, but the color had begun to fade. The wood looked like it hadn't been treated in a good ten years, and the beams had begun to warp upwards at the ends. The porch wrapped around the entire base floor of the house, but the back portion was screened in to keep mosquitoes out. Not that it was entirely necessary as the tobacco smoke generally kept them at bay.

There were two rocking chairs off to the left, Marcus sat in one of them, and now Luther sat in the other. The other end of the porch had a swing chair. The chains were rusted, and it looked like a sketchy proposition at best to sit down in it. Luther stared out over the rolling hills of the farm. The cows gnawed slowly at their just rewards. Marcus said nothing but continued to puff his pipe.

Marcus patted Luther on the shoulder and walked inside momentarily. He came back out with a bottle of brown liquid and two glasses. The bottle was unlabeled, probably some bootleg moonshine he had gotten from another farmer in the area. He poured the liquid into the glasses and handed one to Luther. Luther had never drank alcohol before, he was a rule follower. Luther put the glass up to his nose and took a whiff, the smell caused him to cough weakly.

"Drink it, boy. It'll put hair on your chest." Marcus was smiling at Luther. Luther put the glass up to his lips and opened his mouth as if to take a drink of water. He drew in a gulp and swallowed it down. Luther began to cough uncontrollably, the burn in his throat was overwhelming. He felt a little dizzy, his young liver processing the alcohol almost instantly. Marcus laughed wildly and a hint of true joy flashed in his eyes.

"That's your reward for the hard work you did today." Marcus patted Luther on his shoulder. Luther, after recovering from his rookie mistake, looked over at his grandfather and managed to crack a smile.

"Thanks, grandpa." Luther looked back down at the glass, and this time took a small sip as he observed Marcus doing.

"Look boy, I ain't got a whole lotta time left in this world." He took another sip and looked solemnly over his kingdom. "And you are the only thing that will ever survive me. I know I ain't educated, but I don't know if all the education is good or not."

His eyes were glassy, he was holding back a river of emotions that had been suppressed for a long time. "I wanted you to know that I love you, boy. You make me proud. You always have. I see a lot of myself in you, and I just wanted you to know that."

Luther just stared at him, not saying a single word. He had never heard those words leave his grandfather's mouth before. He didn't know how to react. He felt a pulse in the world as if time had stopped for this brief moment.

"Now, I know you don't wanna be a farmer, and I get that. It's a dying breed it seems, more run by these fancy machines than by the sweat off a farmer's brow. I just want you to remember one thing from me." Marcus turned towards Luther and put his hand on his shoulder, "Don't you ever forget where you come from. Don't you ever forget the shoulders that you are standing on to reach for your stars. This land made you who you are, and it can just as easily unmake you if you don't respect it. The people who create are the folk that the rest of the world depends on. Don't forget that."

Tears welled up in his eyes. Despite all of his shortcomings in education and the lack of intellectual desires, Marcus was a brilliant businessman and a brilliant farmer. He knew that his way of life was no longer a viable way to make a living for young people, and he hated it. He hated the world that the intellectuals had created, he hated that his simple agrarian life was being demolished. Most importantly, he hated that he couldn't share this with his family.

Luther, who hadn't spoken in a long time, turned to his grandfather. He opened his mouth to speak, but words seemed like a shallow response to such a statement. Not knowing how to respond, Luther took another sip of the liquor. The two men sat there in silence as brothers. Luther couldn't know it, but that was the last time he would ever speak to his grandfather.

Chapter 9: Last Dawn

Harold looked down at his hands, they were shaking. He was panting heavily and rocking slightly. He was glistening, his skin was clammy. His hair was caked to his face in soaked strands, visibly stunned.

Harold put his head down on the table he was sitting at. He was in his kitchen. In the middle of the table was a bottle of whiskey, half empty. There was no glass at the table. The shock and grief from the mission trip had still not subsided. At this point, he doubted it ever would. Cheryl had left him, unable to deal with his constant outbursts and newly formed habits. Friendless, alone, broken, Harold resigned himself to his anguish. He drank to dull the pain of his forced continued existence, too cowardly to take his own life, at least in his mind.

He fell asleep on the table. Hours passed. Harold continued to slumber in the blacked-out abyss for a long time. When he awoke, time was irrelevant. The only thing he could perceive was his own fear. Panic swelling in his chest, he reached for the whiskey. To his surprise, a hand grabbed his arm. Harold looked up to his right, looking up, Harold saw that it was Rick Young.

"Stop it, Harold. I'm tired of seeing you like this." Rick spoke with no emotion. It was like he was catatonic but had learned the things to say at different times. Like a different species trying to act naturally, it was as if he was mimicking a caring person actively. Rick walked over to the kitchen and filled up a glass with water. He brought it over to Harold and put it down in front of him.

"Drink it. There's someone you must speak to."

Harold looked into Rick's eyes; something had changed. "Okay man, who am I meeting? Why are you even here?"

"No questions. Either drink this or we leave now, either way we're going." Harold was shocked by the forward nature of what Rick just said. It wasn't like Rick, who had always been so submissive.

"Alright, let me drink this and shower."

"No, no shower. We don't have time. We have to go, now."

Rick grabbed Harold by the arm and dragged him outside. There were three men in a van waiting for them. The men grabbed Harold and threw him into the back of the van. They put a bag over his head and tied his hands behind his back with wire zip ties. Harold started to scream, shriek, terrified. *I WILL NOT GO BACK IN THE BOX*. He continued screaming inside of his head, they had put a rag in his mouth after the initial yelling.

They eventually came to a stop, and the doors opened. Harold still had the bag over his head, unable to see anything. He heard a door being opened ahead of them. He was being dragged over some sort of asphalt surface by someone. When Harold felt the breeze of air conditioning, he reasoned they must have entered into some sort of building. They took a left down a hallway, the floor felt like cheap carpet underneath his feet. Another door opened ahead, and the man leading Harold turned into where the sound had originated. The guard sat Harold down in a chair and removed the bag.

Sitting in front of Harold in a black suit with a gold tie and a white linen turban was Iskandar. Heart thumping wildly in Harold's chest, he felt like the room was going to collapse. Iskandar smiled in his Cheshire cat way.

"Hello, Harold." He spoke very clear, proper English.

While Harold certainly would have loved to yell or respond in some manner, the cloth was still shoved into his mouth. Trying his best to put up some sort of resistance, Harold stopped struggling against his restraints and leveled the meanest glare he could muster towards Iskandar. This made Iskandar laugh audibly. He had a hyena-like chuckle; it was horrifying to listen to. It almost sounded like a suffocating bird.

After a minute, Harold finally managed to stop glaring at Iskandar long enough to survey the room. To his utter shock, Rick was standing behind Iskandar. *Fucking traitor.* Harold was furious.

"Harold, you need to listen to what he has to say."

Iskandar interjected, "Let me talk." It was a command, harshly issued, and Rick looked completely obedient to it. Iskandar got up from his chair and walked over to a table to the left of where he was. He poured himself a glass of wine, a pinot noir.

"What I am going to tell you will be hard to accept. It will be a long story, and I will present my best evidence to convince you of its truth. I only ask that at the end, if you believe me, that you will join us. You must promise nothing right now, nobody who has ever believed has said no." Iskandar swirled the wine in his glass and took a sip.

"Are you familiar with the legends of the Knights Templar, Harold?" Iskandar had cocked an eyebrow towards Harold. Harold nodded slightly, he knew of them, but not much else.

"Good. The Knights Templar, as you must know, were a holy order of knights that were charged with defending the Catholic Church under the direct command of the Pope himself. They were the Sword of God, or so they thought. At dawn on Friday the 13th of 1307, the Templar Grand Master and his closest commanders were arrested by King Philip the IV at the command of Pope Clement V." It sounded like a lecture, but it was masterful. It was a story that had been rehearsed and performed hundreds, if not thousands of times. Almost as if watching a hypnotist charm you into submission, the lecture made the images almost appear real in Harold's mind.

"They died because they discovered the truth. The truth that caused the Great Schism, the truth that scared Atilla the Hun away, and a truth that still haunts the world to this day. Before I tell you this truth, I must tell you why we hurt you in the desert." Memories flashed in Harold's mind, driving him crazy.

"We needed Americans. We needed strong Americans. The villagers in that town had left long ago, we did not kill them. We found your letter to them and replied to you as them. The plan only works with a white man." Harold was confused, *what plan?*

"Just know that your indomitable spirit has made you the choice to lead this. We had to know how strong your will was. Your friend Rick here was strong, but he broke after about a week. The same story was told to him after he broke, and he joined. Do not hate him, he has seen the light."

"This truth was that the one known as Saint Peter, the founder of the Catholic Church, was none other than Lucifer himself. The truth is that Lucifer was struck down and stripped of his powers by God, and he was banished to Earth. It was intended that he suffer the remorse and consequences of his failure for eternity. Lucifer was not so easily deterred, he would corrupt God's creation."

"When God sent his son down to the Earth, he ceded his control over the planet. He sent his son down to rule the planet, the Prince of Peace to unite all and rule forever. It was not Judas who betrayed Jesus, but Lucifer masquerading as Peter. When you write the book, you can make the villain whoever you choose. He then founded the Catholic Church and ruled over the souls of Christendom, forever corrupting God's creation."

Iskandar had sat down now, visibly tired from telling the story. In this light, Iskandar looked less intimidating, he looked old and worn. Like he was struggling to continue moving. Nevertheless, he continued.

"There has been evidence of this truth throughout history. The Great Schism actually was provoked when a cardinal found out this truth, and engineered a scenario where he could split the church to attempt to save Christianity from Satan. Atilla the Hun, once stood triumphantly outside the gates of Rome. The Pope walked calmly to his tent and spoke with him. Atilla, with the superior army and almost assured of a victory, walked away. The Pope told Atilla the truth, that the

Catholic Church was the will of Lucifer, and that he would be eternally damned if he attacked it."

Puffing his pipe slowly, he exhaled. "We are the Last Dawn, and we seek to destroy the Catholic Church and the word of Islam. If you will join us, we will succeed."

Iskandar continued to present his evidence for the next three hours. He told the story of the Battle of the Ethereal Plains, a thousand epoch long conflict between God and Lucifer. Eventually, the forces of Heaven were victorious, and God cast Lucifer down to Earth as punishment. He stripped him of his power and divinity but left his immortality. It was intended as an eternal punishment. However, God could not strip Lucifer of his hatred and his malice. When Lucifer heard that God had sent his son down, he knew that this was the conduit of God's power on Earth.

He continued, telling of how God had created many worlds with many different humanities on them. Each different humanity had a different defining characteristic. Earth, however, was a special experiment in the heart of God. It was the only planet on which he put all of the different races he had created into one place. Each of the beloved families he had created, living in harmony under his only son. God, while powerful and mighty, could not pay attention to all of his creations at once. So, he sent down governors to each one, to exact his will.

Jesus, like Earth and its population, was special to God. He was an amalgamation of God's will, created for the specific purpose of ruling over the harmonious nations of man. Lucifer knew this. In his malice, he sought Jesus out, and began to corrupt him.

Iskandar stood up and stamped out the contents of his pipe into the ashtray. Sitting back down, he looked down at his clasped hands. It was a brief moment before he continued. Harold wasn't sure how long he'd been listening to this story; could have been minutes, could have been days. He still felt the sharp edge of the wire ties pressing into the skin around his wrists. Iskandar's story was still echoing in his mind. Harold wasn't sure if he believed it or not, but he knew the consequences of saying no in this situation. He *would not* go back into the box.

"I believe you." Harold spoke quietly, almost reverently. He was doing his best to sound sincere.

"Good. I am going to have to teach you how to believe in yourself, though." Iskandar stood up while waving at the other men in the room. "Come now, gentlemen. Our newest member's training starts in the morning."

They all left without question. They left Harold sitting in the chair, tied up and restrained. Iskandar was the last one out, and he turned all of the lights off except for one. Harold wept.

Chapter 10: Anvil

Harold laid on the concrete floor with only a blanket underneath, he had no idea where he was. They had gone underground at some point, but Harold's eyes were covered by a black t-shirt. His hands were tied behind his back, tightly grinding every little fiber into his wrists. The stiffness in his shoulders from being locked behind him was excruciating. He had been stuck like this for hours now.

He tried to wriggle forward, but he touched the wall. He hit something behind him, and he heard something stir from what he felt should be the corner. A hand touched the back of his head. The fingers grabbed his hair through the sack and gripped tightly. Whoever had Harold's skull dragged him across the floor. Harold's foot hit a wooden wall, *Doorway*, Harold thought, *he's taking me somewhere*. Gritting his teeth, Harold went as limp as possible; he would not assist his captors in any regard. *I thought I was joining them. I don't understand why they are doing this. Did I do something wrong?* Harold's panicked mind was a cloud of fear and confusion.

"Please stop!" Harold screamed out, unable to take the pain anymore. "PLEASE!" The person let him down, Harold's head cracked against the floor.

"FUCK!" Harold yelled out. The pain was too much to bear.

Suddenly, light filled Harold's eyes, his pupils restricted rapidly. The pain of the adjustment made Harold recoil and close his eyes, falling back down onto his hands with his knees on the ground. A heavy kick landed on his side, Harold yelled out and rolled to the side. He tried clutching his side, but before he could someone grabbed the rope attached to his hands and held it. Kicks continuously landed on Harold's side.

"Stop." Iskandar's unmistakable voice rang out. The men immediately stopped. Harold opened his eyes. His vision was blurry, and he could barely see Iskandar. Blinking rapidly, he began to come into focus, he stared up at him. Iskandar was dressed differently than before. Rather than the black suit and gold tie he was wearing before, he wore robes of deep blue, with gold trimmed down the front creating a trident shape. There was a gold circle embroidered halfway on the spear.

Iskandar stooped down, and he grabbed Harold's chin. Staring right into his eyes, Iskandar smiled while staring daggers into Harold's soul. The smile was eerie, unsettling, like a puppeteer gleefully observing a new toy.

"He's got fight in him. See that does not remain the case by the time that I return from Rome." *Rome?* Harold thought to himself, *I thought he was trying to destroy the Catholic Church?* Confused, in pain, barely able to think, Harold yelled out.

"LET ME OUT OF HERE!" The kicks began to land again, heavy enough to cause pain but not heavy enough to do any real damage. Purposefully restrained to prolong the suffering, it was like craftsmen practicing a trade – emotionless, dispassionate, skilled.

After a time, the kicks stopped. Harold laid on the floor, crying. It was difficult to tell what was reality and what was pain. Weeping quietly, tears no longer came; Harold had none left to give. Numbness set in. *Steel, I must become like steel. They cannot break me.*

Someone picked Harold up, blessedly this person chose to grab him by the waist. Thrown over this large man's shoulder, Harold felt like a sack of flour. A commodity. Harold let the sweet abyss of sleep take him.

Harold awoke on a small cot in a single room. His hands were no longer tied, nor were his feet. He looked at his sides, deep purple bruises ran up his entire torso. It hurt to move, it hurt to breathe. *I have to get out of here, I'm going to die either way I think,* Harold thought. He moved toward the door. Feeling up and down, Harold realized that it was locked from the outside. *More prison than bedroom, figures,* Harold started looking around the room to take full stock of his surroundings.

There was a small wooden bucket with banded iron around the outside. Harold assumed that was for using the bathroom, but it seemed a little out of place with modern plumbing. Walking over to the bucket, Harold pulled down his pants and relieved himself.

As he was pulling his pants up, the latch on the door sounded like it was moving. Harold crouched down instinctively into the corner. He didn't know how he was going to react when they came into the room. To Harold's great surprise, the person who entered the room was a very tall, older man. He had stark white hair that was pulled back into a bun with a thin, white beard on his face. His eyes were a piercing blue that seemed to glow. Harold looked at him and cocked his head slightly.

"Sorry about what they did to you." The old man seemed sincere, but Harold hadn't let his guard down quite yet. The old man found this humorous and chuckled softly to himself.

"Son, I couldn't hurt you if I wanted to, I promise. I'm here to tend to your wounds."

Harold relaxed a bit, and then went to sit on the bed. The old man came over to him, and then he started to pull Harold's shirt up. Harold tried to lift his arms above his head, but he couldn't manage with the pain in his shoulders and sides. He grunted loudly, wincing at the pain. The old man pulled a pair of scissors out of his medical bag and began to cut Harold's shirt off.

"Don't worry, we will get you some new clothes." The old man began to poke Harold's bruises, especially around the rib area. While it was painful, Harold figured he was looking for broken ribs, so he let the old man continue. The old man shuffled over to the bucket and looked inside.

"Why did you pee in the bucket? There's a toilet right over there." The old man pointed to the opposite corner of the room across from the door. Harold's gaze turned to where the old man pointed and there was a small frame in the wall. The old man was having trouble containing his laughter.

"Young man, didn't your mother ever teach you anything?" He rapped Harold's knuckles lightly with a stick. *Where did he get that stick?* Harold flipped his hand wildly to try and relieve some of the pain from the stick hit. The old man took some pills out of his bag and handed them to Harold.

"These are for the pain, nothing narcotic."

Harold reached out and took the pills, "What's your name, old man?"

The old man turned around and looked at him. He smiled a warm smile, it was inviting. It felt like you were being pulled into sitting by a warm fire and reading a book. His bright blue eyes drew Harold in even further.

"My name is not important, just call me Brother, for now." The old man walked over to the door and walked out. The latch was locked back into place. Harold was alone again. Sitting back on the cot, Harold tried to relax again.

There was a clanging from down the hall. It seemed like the entire place had concrete floors, so sounds echoed loudly enough for Harold to hear inside his cell. The latch on the door moved again. This time, four men walked into the room. Harold didn't recognize any of them.

None of the men moved, they just stared at Harold. Seemingly out of nowhere, a small woman walked through the men. Barely five feet by Harold's eye. She had black hair that went down to her jaw, parted directly in the middle. She had wire rimmed glasses over her eyes, and she wore a dark black dress that went down to the floor. It was a mix of elegance and terror, and Harold was intrigued.

"It is time to go, Acolyte." They motioned towards the door. Not wanting to endure any more punishment, Harold went willingly. They led him to a room that had a small altar and a knee pad. The woman motioned for Harold to sit down on the pillow. He complied, kneeling down.

"You must pray." The woman patted Harold's shoulder as he knelt.

"For how long?" Harold asked.

"That is completely up to you." The woman patted his shoulder again, and then turned and left. The door closed behind them, and Harold heard a latch clang down. *Who am I even praying to?* Harold stared at the trident and circle on the altar. He bowed his head and clasped his hands in front of him. *Okay, I'll play your game.* Harold prayed.

For several days, Harold repeated this ritual. He would be awoken before dawn and taken to the strange altar to pray until he either passed out from boredom or the sun set. There seemed to be no end to this cycle. Time passed like water through a canyon, the flow was uncontrollable and its passing imperceptible. All around Harold the chaotic tempest of reality marched on towards our shared calamity, but Harold sat and prayed.

Finally, after time unknowable, Harold's day took a different turn. Instead of going into the altar room which had become his second home, the priestess took him down the hall. At the end of the hall was a large, steel door with a symbol on it. Harold recognized the symbol as the same that was on Iskandar's shawl, a circle with a trident piercing through it in the upper right side and coming out on the bottom left. The priestess knocked on the door that they arrived at, and the door opened without further action.

Behind the door appeared a small but ornate office. Harold stepped inside and was taken aback by what he saw. Books of all sorts from different ages. On his right he saw leather bound tomes that looked like they would be in a medieval history museum, not a small office library. Before Harold could look too closely at what was around him, a man appeared at the desk. It was the kind old man that Harold met earlier, Brother.

"Sit my boy, sit." Brother waved his hand to the chair in front of the large oak desk. The desk was obviously handmade, you could see the chips from where the wood was worked with a hand chisel. It was thick and smelled of deep wood lacquer that filled the room. The scent of that combined with the old books gave the room a truly ancient feeling.

"You have prayed for twenty straight days. Do you know what you were praying for?"

Harold shook his head. *I don't know why I'm here,* Harold thought. Brother chuckled.

"Ah, none of us know why we're here, my boy. It is irrelevant." Brother stood up and walked over to Harold. Brother was wearing a white linen button down and a pair of dark blue jeans. He appeared lithe and spry which belied his apparent age.

Placing a hand on Harold's shoulder which immediately made Harold feel a sense of peace, Brother produced a book from behind his back and handed it to Harold. The book was leather bound with a thick binding. On the front was the now familiar symbol of the trident circle, and above the circle was written *Veritas.* Harold looked at Brother very confused.

"What you have been told your whole life is a lie, my boy."

"Iskandar told me a story about that, I didn't believe it." Harold whispered a reply, he hadn't talked in days.

"Iskandar is a very useful tool, but he has never seen this book. There are only two living humans that have laid eyes on that tome. Me and you." Harold's eyes snapped up to Brother, looking for something, anything to explain what was happening.

"You see, humanity's story spans a much longer time than this neophyte civilization is ready to hear. This book is my personal journal through the storm that is my cruelly prolonged existence. It depicts the rise and fall of the Atlantean Empire on my world, and the subsequent near destruction of our species."

Harold audibly scoffed. "Oh, you don't believe me, do you?"

"You're talking about other planets with humans on them. I know that's crap. There are no aliens." At this, Brother began to laugh. He reached out his hand and touched Harold's forehead.

"Let me show you." Harold began to see. When the vision subsided, Harold looked up at Brother.

"Tell me what I must do." Brother smiled.

Chapter 11: Encounter

The sky was dark, there were no stars. There was a large Ferris wheel lighting the sky, sending beams of light into the night sky. The sound of carnival music disrupted the silence like an old friend. A sweet smell of burnt cake permeated the pier causing mouths to slightly water while the nose turned up slightly. It was a bustling cacophony of human abundance.

Samantha was walking down the pier with a huge blue cotton candy ball, comically larger than her face. She was wearing a red sundress that flowed down to her knees. Her blond hair was pulled behind her head in a ponytail, and her smile competed with the Ferris wheel for how much it lit up the world. Luther followed behind her like an obedient puppy.

"Luther, why don't we go somewhere else?" She curled into his arms and nuzzled her nose into Luther's neck.

"Yeah sure, let's go." Luther's opinion didn't matter anyway, he was going wherever she was.

"Where can we go? A bar?" Looking at him expectantly, she flashed that smile again.

"I mean, can we get into a bar? I don't have a fake." Luther was trapped between his desire to please this creature and his desire to not go to jail. It was a compelling tension.

They walked back down the pier towards the car. Her hands felt warm in his, a slight sweaty film formed between their hands. Neither cared. When Luther looked down at this perfect little angel, nothing mattered. The world paused each time until he no longer looked. He pulled her into him, and their lips met. Luther's heart was beating nearly out of his chest. He couldn't contain whatever animal was inside of him. He grabbed her ass and pulled her body into his. He wanted to feel every little inch of her.

Laughing and kissing in rapid succession, they slowly meandered their way back to Luther's car. Luther had built his car from scratch, and he loved it. It was an old-school Pontiac GTO. It was dark blue with bright red racing stripes in the middle of the car. The interior was ragged, but Luther didn't care. Samantha didn't seem to, either. As the keys went into the ignition, Samantha asked where they were going. Luther looked at her, but he did not answer. He cranked the engine and listened to the roar. There was something primal in that roar that struck into the core of who Luther was.

Rapidly accelerating backwards, Luther didn't realize there was somebody behind him until it was too late. He bumped into someone. Freaking out, Luther got out of the car and went to see what happened. There was a couple behind the car, and the guy looked furious.

"You almost killed us man! What were you thinking?" The guy was tall, blue eyed, and wore a white t-shirt with that obnoxious "A" in the middle.

"Sorry man, I didn't see anyone behind me." Luther walked forward with his hand out, "I'm really sorry about this. Are ya okay?"

The guy didn't offer his hand back, and then reached down to his knee. He pressed against it and started flexing it back and forth to see if it still worked right. The girl stood there, completely silent. She was seemingly horrified, or maybe she was just dull? Luther couldn't tell, but he didn't really care either. He was just worried about getting sued.

"Like, do you need my insurance or something? Or are you okay?" The guy looked back at Luther. He had bright blue eyes that were very intense, and Luther got the impression that the guy was trying to look intimidating. He hadn't quite mastered the skill yet though, and Luther wasn't easily intimidated.

"I could really put your feet to the fire here, ya know?" The guy looked at Luther with a sinister type of smile, "I could call the cops and tell them you hit me. Put you through the ringer. Tell me why I shouldn't."

Luther was shocked. He was trying to be kind to this guy and was clearly apologetic and sorrowful. This dude was going to try and manipulate a situation? Luther stepped back slightly and scratched his head; he was trying to figure out his next move. He walked over to the car to get a paper and pen. He wrote his number and insurance card info on the piece of paper and handed it to the guy.

"Here, this is what I got. I don't wanna play any games with ya man." The guy didn't put out his hand, keeping them pushed violently into his pockets. His shoulders were slightly hunched up, like a predator ready to strike.

"Games? I wasn't playing a game. I am in control here, you just hit me with a car. You will sit here while I call the cops." The guy pulled out his cell phone and started to dial. Luther stepped over and smacked the phone out of his hands.

"No cops." Luther said. The phone cracked on the pavement and broke into a few pieces.

The guy looked shocked. His mouth was hanging down to the floor. He bent down to pick up the pieces of the phone. Luther bent down to help him pick them up and started to reach for his wallet. He held $20 out to the guy.

"Here's money for your shitty phone." The guy finally reached out his hand and pushed the money back towards Luther. He was clearly still shocked at Luther smacking the phone out of his hand.

"Why did you do that?" The guy's voice was shaking, he was clearly upset.

"You were gonna call the cops on me." Luther said it with complete seriousness. *He probably could have figured that one out himself*, Luther thought.

"Because you hit me with a car?!" The guy flung his hands out to his sides like a preacher.

"Sorry man, I offered to give you my insurance to call, and my number if you needed anything. I can't afford a police report about me hitting a dude with a car though, it's a bad look." Luther shrugged as he said this.

"It was my right! I could have been hurt!" The guy's voice was cracking.

Luther sort of half-chuckled, "Lot of good your rights do without anyone around to make them real." Luther started to turn away, but the guy reached out and grabbed his shoulder.

"What do you mean by that?" The guy looked sincerely interested in the answer. *This is an odd fellow I hit*, Luther thought.

"I mean that laws only matter when there's a cop around to make it matter. Laws come from the people, and if there's nobody around that the people use to enforce the law, they are essentially meaningless. Don't you know anything?"

The guy reeled backwards. He clearly had a large emotional range. He was red in the face, "Laws come from God you jerk, you're gonna be judged in heaven for not following them." He had a noticeable southern drawl, he wasn't from North Carolina or the Outer Banks, Luther figured.

"You keep right on thinking that, dude. I ain't got time for all this." Luther started to walk away. The guy was still standing there, mouth agape.

"Hey, don't just walk away from me! At least give me your information." Luther smiled, *Got him*. He turned around and handed the guy the piece of paper.

"Luther, eh? Cool name. My name's Harold." He reached out his hand and Luther shook it.

"Well, I look forward to never talking to you again." Luther laughed and got into his car where Samantha was still waiting.

"Is he okay?" She asked.

"He's an idiot, we're fine."

Interlude: Induction

The cold air bit Jimmy's hands. The cold was out of character for Dothan. He was standing in the middle of a grove of trees, wildflowers were blooming on the edge of the grove. A few other guys were there, but he didn't know who they were. He was sent here by Pastor Drum. The Pastor hadn't told him anyone else was going to be there.

Jimmy walked further into the grove. Reaching the group of the others, he let out a warm greeting.

"Hello, Pastor Drum told me to come here for some community service work. Do you know what we're supposed to be doing?" Jimmy was there to pick up some trash, as the church had a certain section of the highway they were supposed to clean. He had even worn a reflective vest, just to be safe.

The men stared at him but did not speak. They stood completely still and stared uncaringly back at Jimmy. From the highway, Pastor Drum got out of his car and walked through the small tree bank separating the road from the grove. He was wearing a long robe, sort of like what a Methodist preacher would wear, but it wasn't quite the same. There was a shawl around his neck, it was a deep purple with gold trim. Jimmy noticed that there weren't crosses on the ends of the shawl, however. Instead, there was a circle with a trident piercing through. The trident was angled with the points downward to the left. Jimmy found that very out of place for the Pastor.

Perhaps it's a costume to brighten the trash pick-up, Jimmy thought to himself. The Pastor walked over to

Jimmy and placed his hand on his shoulder. Upon doing this, he also reached up to Jimmy's forehead and drew a pattern. The longer this exchange went on, the stranger Jimmy felt.

"Son, it's time." The Pastor walked into the middle of the grove, as he did so, he motioned for the other men to follow him. Each of the men walked towards where the Pastor was walking. A large man grabbed Jimmy's arm and pulled him to the middle of the grove. His heart began to beat out of his chest, the nervous energy that was boiling just beneath the surface had exploded into his mind. He was terrified, but he couldn't put his finger on why.

"P-p-pastor Drum, what's going on? I thought we were picking up trash?" Jimmy's voice cracked wildly as he was dragged forcefully towards the center of the grove.

There was no answer. None of the men spoke either. Once they reached the middle of the grove, the Pastor stomped on the ground three times. It made a hollow thud each time as if there was something underneath. To Jimmy's surprise, a hatch creaked open from under the ground. Each of the men in front of him climbed down into the hole that was under the hatch.

The man behind Jimmy pushed him to the edge of the hole and waved his hand down towards the hole. He started climbing down the ladder that was inside of the hole. The ladder wasn't rusted at all, almost as if it was maintained regularly. There was no musty smell like Jimmy expected, like he had smelled in all of the caves he had been to during his Boy Scout trips. The tunnel continued down for almost twenty feet. As he was clearing the bottom of the ladder, someone grabbed his legs and helped him down.

When he got to his feet, he looked around to see a narrow hall with a large metal door at the far end. The door had the same symbol that the Pastor had on his shawl. The line of men walked up to the door with the Pastor at the front of the column. As he approached the door, it opened. The men filed through the door, and Jimmy's companion pushed him through dutifully.

The next room took the breath out of Jimmy's lungs. It was a large sanctuary. The walls had massive stone columns running up the sides. The columns were a rose-colored stone, and each one was adorned by an intricate golden trident running from the bottom of the column until about halfway up the columns. There were pews arrayed at even intervals at a slight decline down to the parapet.

A large podium was on the dais, the symbol of the circle with the trident through it was prominently displayed on this. There were two large banners hanging down to the left and the right with the same symbol displayed. Between the two banners stood a massive statue. The statue was a man holding what appeared to be a globe upwards with his arm extended. In the other hand, a large golden trident. The man appeared to be about to thrust the trident into the globe. The party continued down to the parapet, and the Pastor walked up to the podium.

"Let us begin." The Pastor waved to the others.

The man behind Jimmy pushed him forward. When they got to the front of the dais, the man kicked the back of his knees so that he collapsed harshly to the floor. His knees cracked heavily against the cement.

"Who gives this child?" The Pastor had his hands extended out to his sides.

Jimmy's parents walked out from behind the statue from a door that he had not seen. They were smiling, warmly. Jimmy immediately relaxed, the tension that had been rippling through his body dissipated instantly.

"We do, Praetor." They both spoke in unison.

The Pastor walked down from the podium and put his hands on Jimmy's shoulders. He began speaking in a strange language that Jimmy didn't understand. It was rhythmic, it sounded like a prayer. Once the Pastor finally stopped his chant, he motioned to one of the other men. They handed him a golden trident. He held the trident with both hands placed a foot apart on the haft and closed his eyes.

"The Last Dawn arises." The Pastor had returned to speaking English and spoke this phrase with a solemn tone.

"The sun of God will shine once again." All of the other people spoke this in unison.

"The blood of God was spilled." Jimmy was reminded of church when they would speak the Apostle's Creed. Pastor Drum was leading them, and they were responding, but Jimmy had never heard this before.

"The debt must be repaid." The people responded again.

"Who shall bear this burden?" As the Pastor spoke these words, he thrust the trident out in front of his body with his arms extended. He pointed the trident at Jimmy and slowly lowered it down until it touched the top of his head.

The flock replied, "The Army of God."

Part III: Manifesto

"If you must break the law, do it to seize power: in all other cases, observe it." – Julius Caesar

Chapter 12: Passion

Luther walked slowly down the marble-floored hallway that led to his office. He was reading a short briefing on social issues that persisted in the Middle East due to various conflicts in that area. Chief among these were asylum seekers who were being rounded into large camps to await a hearing. The new President, Harold Drum, had begun to restrict the amount of allowable asylum seekers.

President Drum had only been in office for about three months, but the changes were sweeping. The previous President, a democrat named Edward Locke, was generally considered powerless. Markedly, he had achieved almost no singular success that made his presidency meaningful. However, he had done nothing wrong either; he was a mouthpiece for the powerful people who elected him. Drum seemed different.

Luther sat down at his desk, briefly waving at Eric to come into his office. Eric came in, looking sweaty and disheveled. He was carrying a stack of papers all tucked underneath his arm, and a tablet computer in his hands. Eric sat down and crossed his legs.

"Polls are good today, boss. Up 12 points over any current challenger for next term. President Drum is polling well at 65% approval but is getting shelled over the recent asylum policies in the liberal news."

Luther had just been through a general election in the last cycle, but Eric insisted on continuing to watch poll numbers to ensure future electability. To his credit, they had been able to secure a number of donors based on their longevity in office. *Who knew that people would give you more money if they knew they could extort you longer?* Luther thought.

"What did he actually do with this?" Luther got the general concept, but Eric would always explain the more technical aspects of the operation. Eric had attended law school at a prestigious university, and he was always a bit of a Poindexter. Could not manage to pass the bar, though.

"Well, technically, he upgraded the background check requirement legal threshold to be 'clear and convincing' that the asylum seeker has no connections with terrorism. This essentially almost fully stops anyone seeking asylum though because we don't have the resources to do that sort of check on anyone." Eric pushed his large-rimmed glasses up his nose. He had a toothy smile, but it always seemed like it was forced as a way to hide the crippling despair that lingered right beneath the surface.

Luther stood up and walked over to the coffee pot that his secretary had put out for him. He promised himself that he would remember her name, but he couldn't. His last secretary, Janet, had passed away last year. It was tough not having her around, she had been like a surrogate mother to Luther after his real mother passed away.

After looking over a series of documents, it was time for a vote. Luther wasn't sure what was being voted on today, but he would go talk to the whip, Tuck Hampton, to figure out what he was supposed to do. The bill had something to do with military equipment funding. Often, low level Congressmen like Luther didn't have the opportunity to read bills until after they were passed. They restricted the making of the sausage to the butchers who didn't mind all the blood on their hands.

Having walked across from the office buildings to the Capitol, Luther walked into the open doors of the House floor. Luther had dreamed of coming here as a boy. His father had taken him to the White House when he was a kid, but they weren't able to take the tour. Luther's father had put all sorts of ideas into his head about what it meant to be a good person, but never was able to live up to his own standards. After Luther's mother died, his father became deeply depressed and all but gave up on life. He had decided a long time ago that he would be all of the things his father aspired to be to honor his mother and give a measure of redemption to his father. Luther didn't know whether his father was alive or not, but he had not spoken with him in several years.

The gavel rapped the podium and the mindless herd of leaders shuffled into their respective seats. The room quieted, and Speaker of the House Trent Kennedy began to speak.

"Hear ye, hear ye, we call this session of the 125th United States' House of Representatives to order. Our first order of business is discussion of a House Bill 1701. The Honorable Congressman from Texas has the floor."

116

A decrepit figure stood up from the front row and walked to the podium at the front of the chamber. His name was Terry Orr, he was a senior representative from Texas, and he was one of the most aggressive war hawks in modern history.

"This bill represents a renewed dedication to the United States military and its fast strike capabilities." That sentence alone took an entire minute. The man carried on for another twenty-five long minutes about the need for increased military spending. When Trent called out for any dissent from the vote, none of the opposition party moved to speak. It was not very politically expedient to deny the military money, even for the peaceful.

The bill passed without any significant debate. There were always a few of the more extreme Democrats who would disapprove of military expansion, but the economic military machine swallowed up most of both sides. Every good congressman and senator knew that a war production facility in their district meant jobs. And votes.

Luther was scrolling on his cell phone when Trent walked up to him. It was always a startling experience when he walked up due to his size. He placed his hand on Luther's shoulder and then walked on without saying anything. Many of the other senior Republicans disliked Luther because of his relationship to Trent. Trent was a Republican political star, and he had helped win a large amount of the black vote for President Drum in the most recent election. Although, it's not clear how much help he needed after Elizabeth Holder admitted she was an atheist. Holder was incredibly powerful in her home district, though. The candidate, a lady named Emily Childress, who won that Congressional seat while Holder ran for President vacated her seat so that Holder could be reappointed. Clinging to power with a manifestation of pure political will, it was clear that Elizabeth Holder's opposition to President Drum was not over.

Walking out of the chamber onto the beautiful, marbled floor, Luther was looking at his calendar to see what was planned for the afternoon. After a quick donor lunch at the Capitol Cafe, he had to start making phone calls begging for more money. It was frustrating to Luther to have to essentially become an influence peddler. He had to sell himself to win re-election, and he was never able to help the people who elected him as a result. There was a deep conflict created by this. *Never forget where you came from*, his grandfather's words echoed in his head. *Never forget who you are.* Luther never knew what to say to that voice. Not now? If not now, when? Every response seemed hollow. Every response felt like a wedge was being driven further and further into who Luther was and who Luther wanted to be.

Upon going back to his office, Luther checked in with Eric. Eric was asleep on his desk, snoring softly. He had obviously fallen asleep typing, as his hands were still on the keyboard. Luther never asked Eric to work this hard, but the kid felt like he was saving the world in his role; he was unable to turn off generally as a result.

The phone in Luther's office rang. A voice rang out on the other side of the phone that was tinged with a slight Arabic accent. The man was noticeably angry by the inflection in his voice.

"How could you vote for a bill that gives more arms to harm people in the United States?" It was hard to

118

make out what he was saying, but the man was obviously a constituent.

"How'd you get this number, sir?" Luther replied, shocked at how someone who wasn't a donor was able to reach his personal office phone.

"You have caused the death of hundreds of immigrants and Muslims, do you know what these weapons will be used for?"

Luther was annoyed now. He was a peace advocate, but he knew that it was a thin veneer. The only reason that there was peace now, or ever, is that there is a dominant military power in the world. Very rarely in the course of human existence has the world order been stable without an alpha, and for all the good intentions that the peace-loving members of the nation had, Luther was unwilling to test fate and remove that status.

"I voted to increase the security of every American citizen. Even you."

The man wasn't even listening, and based on his tone it didn't seem likely that he would. He continued to shout in broken English about how much fear his Muslim community felt with this new President. Many of them were looking at going to neighboring Canada to escape what they thought was going to happen. Luther wasn't tone deaf, and he knew that a lot of President Drum's rhetoric was based on religious differences. *That's what happens when you elect a preacher, I suppose*, Luther thought to himself.

Luther, used to ending unwanted conversations efficiently, promptly hung up the phone. Leaning back in his chair, he turned on the TV that sat in the upper corner above the door. Unfortunately, the only channels that he was able to get in his office were the news. Luther began watching Wolf News. It came back from commercial break to a re-run of an interview between Trevor Stewart and President Drum.

"Mr. President, many people in this country fear that your administration is bordering on religious discrimination with your recent restrictions on asylum for Islamic countries. How do you respond to this criticism?"

The President leaned back in his chair, crossing his left leg over his right. He scratched the side of his head. Wearing a navy suit, the aura of power was palpable. "Well, Trevor, I would say that some discrimination is justified. We're not discriminating against any American born Muslims. Honestly, we're just trying to do what we feel is best to keep America safe." His slight southern drawl made him seem almost innocent, as if he was too gentle to really have any real intent to harm anyone.

This appearance seemingly disarmed Trevor. "I think a lot of us understand that what you're doing is necessary and just, but how do you respond to those families that have been separated by these policies? Are their family members not trustworthy?" Luther audibly scoffed to himself, which apparently woke Eric up in the other room. *He doesn't know the first thing about justice.*

Luther turned the TV off and walked into Eric's office. "Eric, I think its time to make some noise."

Looking up from the small puddle of drool that had formed on his desk, Eric had an eyebrow slightly cocked. Thus far in his career, Luther had been a conformist. He did what the party asked him to do, when the party asked him to do it. His father-in-law was a big

Republican donor, and that got him all of the opportunities he had in life. Then, when he ran, Samantha's parents donated heavily to him in addition to all of the doors they had opened for Luther. However, after three terms of playing the obedient lapdog, Luther felt that the debt had been paid.

"I can't stand this religious divide in the country right now. I think it's time to speak up about the necessary separation we need to get back to with this type of stuff." Luther was pacing, he very rarely felt anything, but speaking this out loud made him feel alive. He felt his skin tingling, on the edge of euphoria, he felt purpose.

"What do you mean? That's not going to be a very popular poll position, we just had an election almost exclusively revolving around religion. Do you think that's just gonna go away? People don't have long memories, but I don't think they're *that* short." Eric was typing something mindlessly while talking, most likely notes of their conversations. He had gotten in the habit because Luther would often forget some of the things he had promised to do for donors, it was a workable system.

"I'm tired of pandering for re-election. I want to lead. I want to do what I came here to do." Eric smiled.

"Well, what do you want to say?" Luther began to speak. Eric began to type.

Chapter 13: Poisonous Roots

Harold walked through the Rose Garden in the White House. Rick was walking behind him to his right, as he always was. As they walked into the Oval Office, Harold took his seat behind the desk and kicked his feet up onto the table. James was standing behind the desk, watching protectively. James was the President's personal Secret Service attaché, a post that Harold had personally appointed him to.

"We need to move forward with our plans, Rick." Harold was half eating a sandwich while talking.

"I just don't think it's the right time, Harold. We just got into office. We should wait for something new to happen." Rick was scared, he had always been scared.

"Don't lose your nerve now my friend, there are many things yet to come." Harold got up from his desk, he had finished his sandwich and handed it to one of the many interns.

He was walking down the hallway towards the back entrance where the cars would be waiting to pick them up. Harold's personal driver was a black man named Eugene. Eugene was a fifty-three-year-old Army veteran, and he was one of the few that Harold had not replaced when he got into the White House. Harold liked his company.

They were driving over to the Executive Office Building to see the Director of Homeland Security. The director was a man named Luke Farnsworth; he was a nobody who Harold had appointed. Fortunately, the Republicans controlled the Senate, so every single person who Harold nominated was appointed. To Harold, loyalty was the only character trait that meant anything.

"Eugene, what do you think about all these Muslims?" Harold liked to talk to him whenever they drove anywhere. It had only been four months since he had taken office, but Harold knew what he was elected for.

"Iunno, sir. Feels like they are tryin' to come here and take our country from us." Eugene was a veteran of Operation Iraqi Freedom, so his opinion meant a lot to Harold. Harold tried to keep his finger on the pulse of how the base of his voters felt. He did this, in some measure, by talking to Eugene.

About four minutes later, they arrived at the offices. Rick got out of the car that was behind them. Harold had been keeping Rick at arms-length as of late, they had been more divided since they took control of the Caliphate.

Harold walked into Director Farnsworth's office. The man was a short little gremlin, he was completely bald and his face looked like it had been stung by bees one too many times. His ears had scar tissue that made them look like an old school boxer. Glasses adorned the end of his nose and gave him the appearance of an old librarian. When he looked up, his voice croaked out like a five-pack-a-day smoker.

"Good morning, Mr. President. To what do I owe the honor?" There was no fear in his voice, but there was the unmistakable accent of a New Yorker.

"I want to move forward with the plans that I told you about when I nominated you." Harold sat down in his chair. He had no time for small talk, and he wouldn't waste time with it now.

"Mr. President, I think it's best if we wait for a more politically opportune time. It will be seen as rather drastic at the moment, especially since there hasn't been an attack since the—" Harold raised his hand to stop him before he could finish the sentence.

"The Last Dawn arises, this is my command." Harold stood as he said this.

Understanding the weight of the command given, Director Farnsworth nodded. "It shall be done, Praetor."

Rick interjected, "This is too extreme a move. We have to play the game correctly or everything we have done will be for nothing!"

Harold walked over to him and placed his hand on his shoulder. He stared into Rick's eyes for a brief moment. The fear behind those brown eyes was palpable, the man feared death more than he feared Harold. That was a problem.

Luther was sitting at his desk. The news was playing in the background, it was on ABS today. Eric was reading the newspaper in the corner, always watching the polls. Luther saw that President Drum was giving an address in the Rose Garden and reached over to turn up the volume.

"My fellow Americans, I come before you today to announce a new policy to keep America safe from domestic terrorism. My administration feels that we were elected for a specific purpose, and in keeping with that purpose we are announcing this policy. The Department of Homeland Security will be collecting threat level data on persons who may be prone to radicalization and terrorism. These people will be moved to holding areas to undergo restricted observation for their violent propensities. As such, for these individuals, Habeas Corpus will be suspended. We will release any persons deemed to not have sufficient violent tendencies. Thank you and God Bless America."

Luther's mouth was on the floor. *Did he just try and suspend Habeas Corpus?* There were no words for this, the President was vastly overreaching his authority. Luther's phone began to ring wildly, no doubt constituents' response to the recent announcement. There was no doubt in Luther's mind about which individuals would be targeted by this proclamation, President Drum had campaigned wholly against the Islamic faith. He was making good on those promises in quick fashion.

"Eric, I think we found our cause." Luther got up from his desk and looked out the window of his office towards the direction of the White House. He had a glass of scotch in his hand, and a cigar in the other. *Never forget whose shoulders you stand on*, his grandfather's words echoed in his head.

"What are you thinking, Lu?" Very few people called Luther that, but Eric had started recently. Still felt odd to hear it from a subordinate. *Is it that difficult to say an extra syllable?* Luther thought to himself.

"This is obviously an anti-Muslim move that they're pulling. We need to come down hard on the line between church and state. He's trying to use the government to enforce his theocracy, and we need to

125

change the conversation." Harold's heart began to beat rapidly. He felt alive like he hadn't in years.

"You want to fight the President on religion after he won this past election on it? That's a terrible political move. The party will be furious with you, you might even get kicked out." Eric looked skeptical. Luther could never tell whether Eric was loyal to him or the Republicans, but he would figure it out soon enough.

"Honestly, I am fearful of what this religious division will do to the country. People can justify all sorts of terrible things in the name of God. I think we can carve out just as big of an electorate in our district by coming out with a message of tolerance and inclusion."

Eric scoffed at this and went back to reading his paper. Luther kept staring out the window, he had never turned to look at Eric. Luther looked out over the National Mall, staring at the Lincoln Memorial as he often did. Standing in the center of the window, Luther looked like a painting. This painting drew feelings of confusion, remorse, and trepidation. A man, single in the world, alone with his thoughts. This was a terrible thing.

"Nida, where are you my love?" Abdul had made a cup of tea for his wife. He walked into their prayer room to find her saying her prayers. She was always much more devout than he was, insisting that she pray all five times. Abdul had lost faith a few times over the years, but she kept bringing him back.

Nida looked up at him and smiled, she took the cup of tea from his hands and put it up to her lips. She coughed a little bit, the heat always made it difficult to swallow the first time. The cup was still steaming. Nida stood up, her hair was so beautiful. It was strange to think about her hair, as he was one of the few people that had ever seen it. Abdul had been raised in America, so the Sharia practice of forcing women to cover themselves seemed strange to him. Nida, however, had been raised in Saudi Arabia and only came over here to marry Abdul. It was an arranged marriage through his family. It seemed that not even the liberal Americas could cure his family entirely of their deeply rooted traditions.

She was absolutely beautiful. She was tall and slender with jet black hair that hung down to her waist. Her eyes were a glowing hazel, which belied her half-Egyptian heritage. Her skin was light brown, almost white. Nida's family was a low-level royalty in Saudi Arabia. Abdul's family owned a series of jewelry stores in America and had become very wealthy as a result. Thus, their marriage made perfect sense for both families. Nobody expected them to love each other, but they fell in love anyways.

Their child, Tahir, was laying peacefully in his crib beside her. His beautiful little black ringlets hung down slightly over his closed cherubic eyes. He was dreaming, and his little fists were flailing slightly because of his dream. Abdul felt so fulfilled, he never knew life could be so perfect.

There was a knock at the front door. Abdul went to answer it, "I'll be back in a second. Going to see who is at the door."

As Abdul opened the door, he saw something he did not expect. There were about fifty men outside the door in black suits. The man at the door tackled Abdul and pinned his arms behind his back.

"DON'T FUCKING MOVE, OR WE'LL KILL YOU." The man on top of Abdul had a gun to his head and another one handcuffed his arms and legs. More men stormed into the house. He heard Nida screaming in the other room. Tahir began to cry.

Abdul heard one of the men talk into a radio, "Got three more incoming, sir." Abdul tried to struggle against the restraints. The man on top of him raised his arm with the pistol in it and swung it down violently against the back of his head.

Chapter 14: Battle Lines

On one side of the table sat the Republican Congressional leadership. The other side of the table had the Democratic Congressional leadership. At the head of the table sat President Drum. The Democratic Senate minority leader was a woman named Alice Pullman. She was from New York and had been an outspoken opponent of the President after his recent anti-terrorism crackdown. The Republican Senate majority leader was essentially a walking corpse of a human being, Sturm Thurgood. He was from South Carolina, and he had already had a reputation for being a sycophant for the President.

Trent Kennedy was there as well. Across the table from him was the Democratic House minority leader, John Aberle. Aberle was a dyed in the wool public defender who had been a vocal supporter of Elizabeth Holder. There were cameras in the room to mark the historic occasion of the meeting. Not that it was particularly momentous, but that this President agreed to meet with his opposition was noteworthy. He had refused to meet with any Democrats for the first six months of his time in office. Often accusing them of being atheists, he said that their voice was no longer relevant in the government.

The President was not a shrewd political animal. His anti-terror crackdown had largely targeted Muslims, and there were now large internment camps forming at various places across the United States to contain them. The images of these camps drove the less religious elements of society into a blood frenzy. The President's approval ratings had gone from a sky high 74% after his asylum restrictions to 45% as a result.

Rick was right, I should have waited, Harold thought to himself. Still smiling vividly into the camera while the media gave the mice their cheese. *I can't back down now, though.* After the media left the room, nobody spoke. They just sat there until finally Speaker Kennedy opened his mouth to speak, he was preempted by Senator Pullman.

"We need to end this, now. This is sick and cruel, and I cannot believe any American leader would sign off on such a heinous plan." Her words spat out of her mouth like bullets, each intended to be insulting.

Senator Thurgood spoke, the dust seemingly dislodging from his throat as he choked through his words, "Women never seem to understand what is necessary. We must do this."

At this point Congressman Aberle started yelling, "Are you serious? Women never understand? How about you explain that to the wives and mothers you threw in a prison because of their skin color, can you explain that?"

His face was instantly red. He sounded like a bulldog that had just gotten to the end of his chain and started barking ferociously. The reinforced hatred of injustice made his delivery passionate and a bit extreme.

Well, clearly nothing will be accomplished today, Harold thought to himself. He looked over at Rick who was standing in the corner. Rick tapped his wrist, as if to indicate that this was a waste of time. Harold nodded, and Rick walked out of the room.

"Gentlemen and lady, it is clear to me that nothing will be accomplished here today. I have no interest in changing the policy, I am simply doing what I was elected to do. Which, in my view, is to keep America safe by eliminating potential threats." Harold had started to learn how to politic his way through things. The religious rhetoric worked wonderfully for the campaign trail, but these people in Washington were a different breed. A word out of place would dominate a news cycle for weeks, Harold had to be careful not to associate his words with religion as much.

Aberle and Pullman got up and stormed out of the room. Trent and Sturm stayed behind to speak with Harold. Trent's head was in his hands, he was clearly a little upset. The entire meeting was his idea, and he had spent a tremendous amount of political capital to make it happen.

"Sturm, I thought I told you to keep your mouth shut." Trent was towering over the old man at this point. Real frustration tinged Trent's words.

"Look here boy, I will speak whenever I damn well please." The old man hadn't quite lost his edge after all, it seemed.

"Gentlemen, calm down." Harold interjected to avoid further confrontation, "we knew it was unlikely for anything to change anyway."

Trent scoffed, "Mr. President, I know you're new to this, but we had to at least make a real effort for optics sake. They are going to smear us relentlessly with this. They came all this way to sit down and the President threw them out on the street with nothing. Your poll numbers will take a huge hit."

Harold sat back in his seat. This Trent Kennedy had no fear in his voice when he spoke to him, which was a rare trait. He was one of the men who had helped set the Caliphate's plan in motion all those years ago. The shared experience gave them a level of comfortability that Harold only shared with Rick. All the rest of the people in the world who considered Harold a friend were dead, or his wife. The latter of whom did not talk to Harold much anymore.

"Mr. Kennedy, please leave us." Trent looked stunned at the dismissal. He had stuck his neck out for the President, and this was the return he received. Trent would not make the same mistake twice, however. Trent walked out of the room leaving only Harold, Sturm, and James.

Harold turned towards Sturm, "Should we be afraid of him?"

Sturm chuckled softly, "I don't think so, he's fallen in line every time before."

"What's the move here, Sturm? I'm out of my element with these people."

Sturm uncrossed his legs and leaned forward onto the table. "There's only one solution when you're forced into a corner. Attack."

"How do we fight? Everything I say gets turned into a circus."

Sturm laughed at this, "Did I say speak? That's not your way, Harold. It has never been."

Harold turned and looked at the old man. *How long had they known each other?* Harold honestly couldn't remember. Sturm was one of the first people he had met in this journey, and one of the very first of his supporters for President.

Attack, Harold thought to himself. Such a simple suggestion, but it felt right. *How do we attack?* Harold began to form a plan. He looked at James and smiled.

"Sturm, we have work to do. Come with me." Harold began to walk out of the room.

"Yes, Praetor." Sturm followed obediently.

"My name is Lisa Young and we're live, reporting for ABS News Network. Today our main story is the President's refusal to come to the negotiating table over his anti-Islamic policies. Today, leaders from both parties sat down to talk about a solution to end the large-scale internment camps installed to detain potential terrorist threats within the United States. Although the President initially stated that no particular class of people would be targeted by these policies, it is unquestionable that it has specifically targeted members of the Muslim communities.

At this point, it is unclear whether the President will ever negotiate over these policies. Currently, there are over 75,000 Muslim-Americans being held in these camps, including women and small children connected to their allegedly radical husbands or extended family members. These policies have been widely regarded as extremely xenophobic, and many political figures on both sides of the aisle have called for their immediate end."

"Joining us tonight to talk about these policies is Congressman Luther Washington. Good evening, Congressman Washington." The camera panned out to

133

end the soliloquy, revealing Luther sitting next to her at the news desk.

"Good evening, Lisa. Although, I cannot say it is actually good."

"Well, Congressman, let's talk about this. How can these policies be constitutional?"

Luther clasped his hands in front of him on the desk, "Quite simply, Lisa, they aren't. Any distinction based on religion is strictly forbidden based on the First Amendment of the Constitution, and every distinction based on race is forbidden by the Thirteenth and Fourteenth. The President is attempting to subvert the very structure of our Republic, and we are in dangerous waters. No President since Lincoln during the bloodiest conflict in our history has seen fit to do something as drastic as suspend Habeas Corpus."

"Congressman, you've been very vocal about your disapproval of these policies. Do you not see any validity in controlling the threat of domestic terrorism in the wake of the Lincoln Memorial?"

Luther paused for a moment. *Shouldn't have mentioned Lincoln*, he thought to himself. He shifted slightly in his chair and put his hand to his chin.

"I think that there is a difference between taking active security measures and tyrannical trampling on the rights of minority members of our nation out of racial fear. The President is clearly playing off of the racial biases of his electoral base to accomplish his religious goals. He spoke very clearly on the campaign trail that he was going to put God back in the White House, and I think he's being consistent with those ideas. We should have seen this coming and we didn't. Those biases have no national security justification."

Lisa smiled. It was an honest answer. Something she had so rarely seen on television, and something even more seldom that she appreciated. It was the exact sound byte she wanted to smear this President with for the next few weeks. Sometimes in life the most important interactions appear innocuous on their face. It is the small handshake at a restaurant that echo through time to bring down empires. It is the shared bottle of wine that creates them.

"Mr. Washington, these stances have no doubt had political ramifications for you, how is your standing within the Republican party?"

Luther sat up straight and looked deadpan into the camera, "At this point Lisa, the Republican party has chosen to support a President who has no concept of democracy. I can no longer be a member of a party who chooses love of their party and hatred of minorities over the love of their country. I am proud to announce I will be personally spear-heading a new political party, the Constitutionalist Party."

Lisa blinked wildly. She had no idea that this was coming. She had wanted to watch the Congressman squirm around his own hypocrisy but found none of that here.

"W-w-what will your platform be?" Lisa's shock had not worn off, but the show must go on.

"We will announce the more specific details later this month, but the motto of the party, in keeping with the idea of its founding, is 'Country over Party.' That should tell you everything you need to know." Luther smiled. His heart was pounding wildly. He had just dug his own political grave, his entire existence from now on was trying not to be buried in it.

"Thank you, Congressman, for joining us tonight. We'll be right back."

"THREE MINUTE COMMERCIAL BREAK!" An aide yelled from off stage. Luther got up to walk away, but Lisa called out to him.

"Hey! That was a hell of a thing to throw out on my show, a heads up would have been nice." She was livid, but still political.

"Sorry, the party probably would have shut it down if I'd told you. You would have told your producers." Luther spoke so unapologetically. He had thought this through.

Lisa's lips pressed together sideways. She was both annoyed and impressed. She held out her hand to shake Luther's. Luther took her hand and pulled her closer to him and whispered in her ear.

"We can take him down together." Luther stood back and let go of her hand. He began to walk away, but he turned back and winked at her.

Lisa was standing at the mirror attached to her bathroom sink. She smiled and tried to make sure her grin was symmetrical. While everyone always told her she was beautiful, she always felt like she needed to improve. After a while in the news industry, it was obvious that the women who lost their luster lost their spot. She watched her image carefully, determined to stay at the top.

She walked back into her bedroom. On her bed was a tall drink of water, but she wouldn't be caught dead in public with him. A tall, blond-haired, blue-eyed newscaster who everyone in the world would assume she hated, Trevor Stewart, turned to look at her. His eyes took in her naked body and he smiled.

"Come back over here. I've got an hour before I have to leave." Trevor held out his hand and his smile turned into a suggestive grin.

"Oh, that's so romantic." Lisa rolled her eyes and smacked his hand away. She pushed him back into the sheets and straddled him with her legs. She took both of his wrists in her hands and pushed them up above his head.

Leaning down into his ear, she whispered, "You and I both know this won't take an hour."

Trevor burst into a laughing fit. Thrusting his hips upward, he threw her back down onto the bed. He put his body directly onto hers and swooped in for a kiss.

"Maybe that's why I'm always early to work when we're together." He kissed her again, and they continued their previous activity.

Chapter 15: Momentum

Luther was standing at a podium in front of a series of cameras and news microphones. There was a blue backdrop behind him with U.S. House of Representatives logos patterned throughout the backdrop. The lights were bright, Luther had to shield the lights to see the faces of the people behind them. The heat made Luther's skin glisten slightly.

"Yesterday I announced that I am leaving the Republican party and creating a new party, The Constitutionalist Party. This party will be founded on the principles of absolute individual autonomy. This party will believe that all people have a fundamental right to self-determination, to prosper, and to be treated fairly and justly. Most importantly, we will not impose our beliefs on others, but rather make a system where all beliefs are free to exist in harmony."

Luther paused, the questions from the reporters started almost immediately. "Does this mean you're running for President against President Drum in 2032?" Luther scoffed a little.

"No comment." The press audibly gasped, expecting a flat denial.

"Has anyone else stepped forward to join your party?"

"No, I am currently the only member, but I am sure that as the President's true beliefs and policies begin to reveal themselves more and more Republicans will find that they can't support the President."

"What do you have to say to the President?"

"I say to President Harold Drum, end these atrocious religious crackdowns, free these citizens who have been imprisoned without due process, and resign from office." Luther was doubling down, there was no backing out when the media was giving you this sort of attention. This was Luther's moment in the sun, and he intended to bask in the glow for as long as possible.

Nida was laying down on the cot next to her baby son, Tahir. They had just eaten their food allotment for the evening, and they were waiting for Abdul to return. The men were required to perform public labor during their time in the internment camps to offset the government costs. They were baling hay for local farmers often to generate revenue for the state. None of the men were being paid for their work, though. Many of them were extremely disgruntled at the level of extortion going on and were beginning to make noise.

Nida had begged Abdul to stay out of the troublemaker's camp. She just wanted to live through what she believed to be a temporary moment in the history of the country. After moving to America, Nida had read a lot about American history, including the horrifying details about the Japanese internment. She figured, while the Japanese were devastated from a commercial and cultural standpoint as a result, at least the American government at the time had not engaged in genocide. They may be exploited, but as long as their family stayed together, everything would be fine. Nida thought.

Nida was playing with Tahir's ringlets when one of the guards walked into the barracks. There weren't many people currently in the barracks. The other two were an older lady and an older man. They didn't speak much, and generally stayed in a far corner of the barracks by themselves. Whatever had happened to them during their abduction had clearly troubled them, and they were having trouble communicating as a result. Nida also found that when they did speak, it was Ordu which Nida did not understand. Nida only spoke English and Arabic.

The guard had his guard stick in his hand and walked up and down the barracks. He stopped at Nida's bunk where she was laying with Tahir. Grabbing her ankle, the guard shook her leg. "WAKE UP!" the guard yelled. Nida kicked his hand off of her ankle. She reared back and protectively pulled Tahir against her.

"Get away from me, we're not doing anything wrong!" Nida howled. The guard was furious and redfaced. Nida's kick had pulled the guard forward and his head hit the metal bar on the bunk. He dashed under the bunk at her and ripped Tahir from her arms. He threw Tahir onto an adjacent bunk, luckily Tahir seemed uninjured. Turning back towards Nida, he dashed at her again. She clawed at his face with her nails and poked his eyes. He was relentless, eventually he reared back and hit Nida square in the nose. Nida heard her nose break, and the pain immobilized her momentarily. The guard started to pull up Nida's dress and unzipped his pants.

Nida was dazed, she could barely see the outline of the guard. She lifted her hand to try and strike the guard but he held her hand down. The guard looked down, and from the corner of her eye Nida saw a shape. She heard an audible crack, and the guard fell to the side limp. Nida's head was still swimming. She passed out.

The television in the Oval Office had the news on all morning. Harold was sitting behind his desk, looking at the screens blankly while avoiding the dull minutiae of governance. He wasn't very fond of that part of the job, admittedly. Much to Harold's surprise, almost every news station cut to a clip of Congressman Luther Washington giving a press conference earlier today. *Why are there so many cameras there?* Harold was furious this peon was being given such a huge platform. *Where do I know him from?* The familiarity screamed in Harold's brain whenever he saw the man, but he didn't know where from.

Harold watched the interview mouth wide open. *Resign?* Harold was on the brink of an exhausted rage. He had barely slept in months because of the constant national security issues, and now when he finally got to turn his attention back to his actual plans this putz tells him to resign? Harold couldn't take it. He stormed into Rick's office, right beside his own as the Chief of Staff, and slammed the door.

"So, you saw the interview, huh?" Rick had a dour look on his face and leaned back into his chair.

"How long has this been out there? You knew about this and didn't tell me?" Harold couldn't contain his anger any longer, it had to go out on someone.

"I saw it when you saw it, I don't know when it was. How did he get so many cameras there?" Rick seemed honestly perplexed.

"I don't know, that's exactly what I thought. Who is paying attention to this guy?"

"Our enemies?" Rick asked, very quietly.

Harold thought to himself for a second. They had eliminated the *Illuminati* centuries ago. Supposedly, the Last Dawn had free reign over the world and was actively continuing to exert their chokehold on world power. There hadn't been a known enemy in a very long time, and Harold wasn't informed of any prior to his seizure of power from Iskandar. Unfortunately, a lot of the older members of the Caliphate had chosen Iskandar's side in the conflict, so even if there were one there would be nobody who knew of it.

"I don't think so, who would it be? He's probably just acting on his own. Perhaps we overestimated the religious zeal of the country?" Harold looked at Rick.

Rick seemed perturbed, "You mean, *you* overestimated the religious zeal of the country. I told you to wait!"

"You don't need to parse words with me Rick, I know it was my decision. That's not what I meant." Rick seemed to calm down. They were both so stressed and fatigued from the burden of leadership. It had been a long road to get here.

"Remember Nur-Sultan?" Harold said to Rick, reminiscing.

"Yeah, take me back, man." They both sat down and Rick poured a glass of whiskey for the two of them. Rick merely topped off the one he was already working on when Harold had walked in. Post lunch drinks were the modus operandi of this particular White House.

After a while of just sitting and sipping, Harold set his glass down. He stood up again and started to spin the globe that Rick had set up behind his desk. The globe spun easily, it was slightly discolored and made of marble. It was antique and had slight relief edges to notate mountainous regions. When Rick had it brought here, he explained he bought it from a merchant in Marrakesh. The deep beauty of it reminded Harold of something truly ancient, though. The edges of the continents and the portrayal of the national boundaries made Harold believe it was much older. At the same time, there was something mercurial about the globe, every time Harold spun it the lines seemed to change and ebb. It was like the globe was trying to keep time with the world but was trapped in the same state it started. Forever shackled by its creator's flawed understanding.

"What should we do about Washington?" Harold asked Rick after what had seemed like hours.

"I'm not sure. It's a tough call, if we go after him it only draws more attention to his cause. If we ignore him, he might have time to gain real momentum. He only needs to turn one of the high-profile people that aren't in the know. There are enough of them to hinder our goals if we let this get out of hand." Rick scratched his head. His black beady eyes seemed to be patiently waiting for Harold to make the call. Rick was great at analysis, but when it came to pulling the trigger, he always hesitated too much.

"Leave him be for now, I think. This media attention will die down soon enough. Ironic that his last name is Washington." Rick nodded and poured another whiskey. Harold went back into his office and began to type an e-mail. Furiously pounding on the keys.

Harold started the e-mail, *"Brother…"*

James walked into the Oval Office and saw Harold sitting behind his desk. His hair was disheveled, his tie was slightly undone, and the clerical sheen that normally accompanied him was nowhere to be found. This was the Harold that James had become used to, the quiet face he hid from the world. It was always astounding how once the cameras were off, Harold went from the fire and brimstone preacher to the quiet and reserved drunk. His contempt for the man grew daily, but James had no choice but to follow.

Thus far, James had been simply an advisor to the President, but that meant simply being a part of his entourage. Harold had never asked for advice a single time in the few months that he had been in office. He waved James in and he walked in and grabbed a seat on one of the chairs that had been arranged in front of the desk.

"Jimmy, my boy, it's good to see you!" Harold's words were intelligible but slurred.

"Mr. President, we've discussed this, I go by James now." James was one of the few who felt he could speak plainly with Harold. After all, he was the first soldier Harold had ever personally recruited.

"Ah, right. Well, Jim, look, I've got an assignment for you. Something, I think, worthy of your talents." He took out another glass and then lifted a bottle from a drawer in the desk and poured himself and James a glass of whiskey.

James took the glass and took a sip. *At least it's good whiskey,* James thought. "Well, sir, I'm all ears, what can I help you with?"

"Jim, you gotta understand. This assignment must have the utmost discretion attached to it. Nobody can know. Got me?" Harold broke through the buzzed haze and became incredibly serious. James nodded.

"I've orchestrated approval from Congress to have you appointed as the Director of the Secret Service. I've done this for one reason and that's to ensure the loyalty of the people who protect me. We have a lot of enemies, as you're aware." Harold put the glass up to his lips again and took a sip.

James, honored and humbled to receive such an appointment gleefully spoke up, "Absolutely sir, anything that you ask." At this, Harold smiled.

"I knew I could count on you, my boy. And look, while you're the director, try to get as many of our men into the service as possible. Make it difficult for those who aren't our people to continue in the service and get as many of them out as you can." He paused for a moment, "We got a deal?" Harold stuck out his hand to James and James shook it.

"It will be done, Praetor." With that, James wheeled around to get to work preparing for his confirmation hearing.

Chapter 16: The Storm Wall

Trent was napping on his sofa with peaceful ocean sounds playing from his central room console. There was a soft pulsing sound from the console that interrupted the music. Trent's secretary Stephanie called to him over his intercom.

"Sir, Congressman Washington is here to see you."

Trent sat up and wiped his face. He walked over to his stocked mini-fridge and grabbed a soda. Sitting back down in his office chair, he turned on his computer and opened up the bottle. He poured the bottle into a glass and then reached under his desk. There was a cooler Trent always kept stocked with ice under the desk. Stephanie didn't bring the ice fast enough, so he stocked it himself. He began reading an e-mail that had come from one of his donors. He opened it immediately and began to read it. One of his major donors, Pelaris Pharmaceuticals, had sent him an e-mail complaining heavily over the President's new anti-terrorism policies. Seventeen of their top development engineers had been targeted by the policy, and it had brought major research projects to an absolute standstill.

After about ten minutes of waking up, Trent finally buzzed Luther in. When Luther walked in, he had a huge smile on his face. He walked right up to Trent and shook his hand.

"Long time, no see, my friend." Luther spoke kindly as he approached Trent.

"Yeah man, been a while. How're the kids?" Trent sat back down after shaking Luther's hand.

"They're good. They mainly stay with their mother while we're in session though. They still go to school in North Carolina." Trent nodded along patiently. Not the short and sweet southern answer he was looking for, but Luther wasn't quite the southerner he always claimed.

"Well, that's fine, I guess. Glad they're okay. Sorry to keep you waiting, I was on an important call." Trent adjusted his tie at the end of the lie.

"No worries. Have you heard about my recent decisions?" Luther asked, one eyebrow cocked and a smile cracked across his face.

"A little. The hell are you thinking, man? This is the end of your political career." Trent was so disappointed. Luther had been a growing star in the party, it was only a matter of time before he earned a leadership position.

"I don't think so, Trent. My donors are still with me, they don't like this guy. If I can turn a few key allies, we can establish a new Republican party divorced from these zealots. I can't take it anymore, Trent. I just can't." Luther had clearly crossed a mental Rubicon and there was no return.

Trent sat back in his chair and looked at his computer screen again. He pondered how to move forward. *I have to know how this ends,* Trent thought to himself.

"I may know a few people that would be willing to listen to your ideas." Trent stated softly.

Luther perked up. This is what he had come here for. He had always thought that Trent and he were great friends. Trent had been somewhat of a mentor for Luther in the early days of his Congressional career. One day early on, Luther had reached an impasse with one of his donors. They wanted Luther to agree to pressure a local municipality into granting this water consortium rights over the water in the district. The issue was that one of Luther's close friends currently ran the water utility that oversaw that city's water. Trent coached Luther into handling the friend's distress. They gave the friend a lobbying job at a large firm in Raleigh, NC. He was happy to cede his rights after that. This was Luther's first real lesson in soft power. It was also his first lesson in employer-employee loyalty. Of course, it was all above board.

"Dick DeAngelis is an atheist in the Republican party. I'm sure he'd be looking for any chance to jump ship. He isn't long for this one anyways, I can tell you that much."

"Anyone else?" Trent looked a little disappointed in the ask. *Should never give them cookies…* Trent thought to himself.

"Kelli Jacobs. She's Jewish. I don't think she likes the President too much for all this religious rhetoric. That's all I got for you. Good luck."

Luther smiled and got out of his chair. He shook Trent's hand and went towards the door. He turned back towards Trent with the doorknob in one hand.

"Thank you. Your friendship means a lot to me." Luther turned and walked out the door.

Trent sat down at his desk and began typing an e-mail to Kelli Jacobs and Dick DeAngelis. He had to get the message just right so that they would understand what was required of them.

"Kelli and Dick,

Luther Washington has become an obstacle in the path of Dawn. I have informed him that the two of you are likely to be willing to defect from the Party. Obviously, I have no doubts about your loyalty. You are to support, encourage, and flush out whatever Washington has in mind. When the time comes, he must be beyond evidence for his fate.

Order By,
T. Kennedy
Centurion, COLD"

Luther walked back into his office at the Congressional Office Building. He sat back down into his chair and turned on his computer. There were two e-mails from Kelli and Dick already in his inbox. Eric walked into Luther's office before he could think too deeply on the topic. He had his tablet in his hand and was looking at some sort of graphical data.

"Our polling numbers are up slightly since we announced. Have you been able to work anything out about who to start to convince?" Eric was talking very fast;

he was nervous he'd be out of a job soon. This was a huge risk for both of their careers.

"I went and talked to Trent –" Eric interrupted. "YOU, WHAT?!" Obviously furious, he had slammed down his tablet and was now leaning over Luther's desk towards him.

"How could you be so short sighted? He's the freaking Speaker of the House, Lu." Luther leaned back in his chair, shocked by Eric's outrage.

"I had no other options, I don't have a lot of friends in the Republican party. I had my own donors through Sam's family, so I wasn't very well connected in the party to begin with." Luther looked down at the floor, clearly ashamed of what he just inadvertently admitted about his political career. He had only achieved anything in life because Sam's family was absurdly wealthy. He wasn't really looking for a rich girl when they met, but she had him wrapped around her finger before he could think twice.

"Well, what did he say?" Eric whispered.

"He said Dick DeAngelis was an atheist and would be willing to help us and that Kelli Jacobs was disgruntled." Luther smiled, clearly pleased with himself.

"Sir, with all due respect to Speaker Kennedy, Dick DeAngelis is a devout Baptist. He attends church every week with Speaker Kennedy, in fact."

Quickly, Luther realized what had happened. *Trent wanted to keep tabs on me. He didn't want to help me.* The shattered trust left Luther embittered. A viscous reaction from his stomach burned the bottom of his throat. The anguish at the betrayal of someone he considered a friend boiled Luther's soul.

"I know what I have to do now. If I can't convince the power, I must convince the people." *Never forget who you are.* Marcus's admonition flashed into Luther's mind. He hadn't thought about that day in a long time. It always brought a smile to his face to see the weathered face of his grandfather again. That warm, loving smile accompanied with that harsh, disciplined temperament always made Luther feel calm. *It's time.*

Chapter 17: The Constitutionalist Manifesto

*"I, Luther Washington, as the declared leader of the
Constitutionalist Party declare that the ideals and governing
principles laid out in this document will govern all future decisions
and actions of the Constitutionalist Party.*

*First, We believe in absolute individual autonomy. A person is free
to act in whatever manner they so choose until it effects the life,
liberty, or property of another. All moralistic prohibitions on that
autonomy will be dismantled.*

*Second, We believe in absolute diplomatic hegemony. The force of
our arms must never be diminished. There is a world peace slowly
falling over the human race. Our military dominance must continue
until that continued peace is beyond doubt.*

*Third, We reject the ideology of racial codification. There is only one
intelligent race on this planet, human beings. There are no races,
there is only One Humanity.*

*Fourth, We believe that the Separation of Church and State must
be absolute. The Divine Right of leadership was extinguished when
the Declaration of Independence granted the right of leadership to
the People of the United States. In order to ensure that the
democratic will of the people is properly carried out, that separation
must continue eternally.*

*Fifth, We believe in the absolute right to the privacy of one's
internal livelihood. All collected information on any U.S. Citizen
is property of the same.*

Finally, We believe in the Eternal Republic. We believe in the permanent continued existence of the greatest nation to ever exist on this planet. The United States of America must continue forever in order to pass the blessings of life, liberty, property, equality, and justice to our posterity. Any threats to the institutions of democracy which so enshrine the will of the People must be cast aside."

-    Luther Washington

"Read it to me again." Eric said.

"You sure? I've read it three times." Luther was starting to doubt whether it was any good. He tried really hard to be eloquent with this stuff, but it was difficult. He started to read again.

"I, Luther Washington - " The phone began to ring when he started speaking. He picked up the phone.

"Is this Luther Washington?" The voice sounded angry and aggressive.

"Congressman Luther Washington, but yes. Who is this?" Luther only made people use the title when they were rude.

"This is Congressman John Aberle of the Democratic Party."

"Oh, uhh. Hello, Congressman. What can I do for you?" His voice barely covered for his genuine shock at the phone call he had received.

"On behalf of the Democratic Party, we would like to heavily discourage you from your current intended path of starting a new political party."

Luther audibly scoffed into the phone, "Why, you think I'll steal too many votes?"

"No, we would like to offer you a position in the Democratic Party."

Luther hesitated. *A Democrat?* It just felt wrong to Luther. He was a Republican. There was no way in hell he would ever call himself a Democrat in public.

"I appreciate your offer sir, but I can't help you. I have no interest in joining your party." Luther tried to sound legitimately professional. It wasn't really Luther's voice. It was like he was pretending to be somebody who sounded like that. That was Luther's real talent, he could be whoever he needed to be at the drop of a hat.

Luther hung up the phone after Aberle had given his diatribe and goodbyes. There wasn't any convincing Luther, though. He had made up his mind and for once in his life he felt free. He opened up his e-mail on his phone. He had fifteen e-mails from Sam alone. *Oh, so now you want to talk to me?* Luther asked his phone politely to call his estranged wife.

"Luther, why haven't you returned my phone calls or talked to me?!" She poured into the phone as soon as Luther had slightly breathed.

"We haven't talked in months, Sam. You don't just get to turn this back on when you want to." Luther was honestly still deeply hurt. Sam had left right after the last election. She said she couldn't take the constant campaigning, and she hated D.C. Luther definitely agreed with her on that last part, D.C. was the worst.

"How dare you! I am your wife! Do you know how mad daddy is that you spoke out against the

President?! He's not going to donate to your next campaign. We're getting a divorce." Sam's voice was shrill, her throat sounded hoarse.

Luther paused momentarily. He had just lost a consistent donor, but he didn't care. He was finally free to be his own person. He was finally free to lead and there were just a few more steps to take. First, he had to find some friends.

Phillip Hammond was a nobody Congressman from the middle of nowhere West Virginia. He was one of the few people who had spoken out against President Drum's immigration policies. Most of his town had been destroyed when the coal industry left, and he had negotiated with a Muslim religious organization to have their mosque and people move into their town. There had been a lot of work getting all of the necessary paperwork complete, and they were set to come under the new asylum program that the former President Locke had instituted during his second term in office.

When Drum took office, he almost immediately reversed the asylum grants that had allowed these people to come to the United States. Hammond had to sit there and watch as his entire town was forced into the internment camps. He had been furious at the time but had fallen back in line afterwards.

Luther approached where he was sitting at the coffee shop near the Capitol building. Hammond was reading some sort of newspaper, but the title was obscured. However, Luther could clearly make out "Sports" on the top of the page.

He looked up. He had short brown hair that was pulled to the side with copious hair products. His hair formed a weird, comical loop. The navy jacket he had on went well with his khaki pants. For a man from the middle of nowhere, he was remarkably well dressed.

"Hello, Phil. Can I sit down?" Luther gestured towards the open chair on the other side of the coffee shop table.

"Sure, but I ain't gonna buy what you're sellin', brother. Promise you that." Phil laughed a belly laugh as Luther sat down.

The coffee shop was a small corner of an office building. The entire front side of the coffee shops were windows looking out onto the National Mall. The floors looked like they were solid wood but were clearly some sort of processed material. The table Luther was sitting at was round and had only room for two chairs. It was pressed up against the wall, and there was a power outlet right above the coffee table. *Going to have to come back here with my laptop sometime,* Luther thought to himself.

"Phil, look. We have to do something. This is only going to get worse." Luther tried to flag down the waitress. She clearly had other priorities at the moment than serving customers.

"I agree, man. What're we gonna do, we're only two guys. I don't have the war chest you do, either." Luther cringed. He had nothing.

"We have to be ready to lose an election. We have to work with the Democrats to impeach this guy. It's the only way. The Senate is deadlocked, and they're furious that the President flipped the national emergency switch for his internment camps. I think there's real momentum here." Luther had switched into full sales mode.

"How many do we need to make an impact?" Phil seemed intrigued.

"Four. Two more including you and I." Luther smiled.

"How so? I count an eight-seat deficit in the house for impeachment." Hammond was counting on his fingers.

"It's not about quantity my friend, it's about quality. We just need two more in the judiciary committee to start the process." Phil's mouth pressed into an O.

"Who else do you think you can turn?" Phil said.

"Kelli Jacobs and Dick DeAngelis. I have reason to believe they have serious doubts about this clown in the office."

"Man, really? I just talked to Dick the other day and he was talkin' about how they had just given him a shot at the Senate. I doubt he's willing to walk away from that." Phil had this strange mix of southern drawl with New York speed. It was honestly difficult to understand when he was running at full speed.

"I have it on good authority that they'll work with us." Luther didn't want to reveal his sources, especially because Luther was highly doubtful either of them would actually join. He had to start somewhere, though.

"Well, I ain't in if that bitch is in, either. She trashed me on Wolf the other day for my no on her appropriations bill. Not working with her."

Well, shit. Luther thought for a moment about paths forward. Pacing back and forth, Luther certainly seemed the most confident person in the world. He rubbed his thumb and forefinger on the tip of his chin. Turning back to Phil, he sipped his coffee.

"Do you have any friends?" Luther smiled.

"We could try a couple that I know have some Muslim majorities in their districts. They probably would be willin' to help us the most." Phil got up and put his newspaper in the trash.

"So, you're in?" Luther's voice sounded like a little kid asking if he can go to his friend's house.

"Not publicly, yet. We get a few more on board and I'm in."

Luther was smiling from ear to ear. He had not expected to get this on the first try. Ecstatic from his stunning personal victory, it was hard to contain the excitement in his voice.

"We're going to take him down. I promise you." Luther had a strong tone of determination and confidence in his voice.

"Oh, and Luther. One more thing. I have a high-level position in the party if this actually does work out. Something like Secretary of the Treasury." Phil then laid the newspaper down, put on his aviator sunglasses, stood up and walked towards the door. Luther saw him turn the corner away from Capitol Hill when he left the coffee shop. *I guess that's one cabinet position filled.* Luther's dreams were as farfetched as they were absurd, but he still dreamed them.

Chapter 18: The Harbinger

Abdul was sitting beside Nida on the bed. Lying unconscious, Nida hadn't woken up since the attack. It had been about two hours since Abdul returned to the barracks, and nobody would tell him how long ago she was attacked. The man who saved her, Captain Billy Winters, was standing in the barracks speaking to a few of the witnesses. One of the camp guards had been sneaking into different barracks facilities and sexually assaulting the women while the men were away. Captain Winters had personally witnessed him enter this time and couldn't let that continue.

The guard, Staff Sergeant Jerry Harrington, had been sent to a holding cell to await a court martial. Captain Winters had informed everyone in the barracks that there would be entirely new management coming to operate the facilities. They had an inherent trust in him after he saved Nida and her son Tahir. There was something strange about trusting your captors to act honorably, but these were strange times.

Nida began to rise, and Abdul immediately put his hand on her shoulder to lie down. She had cracked her head against the wall in addition to being punched in the nose. Her nose was broken and in a white, molded cast.

"W-what happened?" Nida was struggling to speak. The blood from the nose break had caked into the back of her throat. Her voice was hoarse and scratchy, barely audible. She began to cough, and when she did, blood spewed out of her mouth onto the blanket she was still covered in. Abdul reached for her with a towel. The towel was soaked in blood, Nida had been bleeding for a while. Everyone kept pleading with the guards to allow her to go to the infirmary, but there had apparently been an outbreak of some sort in the hospital. The guards said it was safer here.

Nida passed back out. Captain Winters was still standing at the end of the bunk, and he watched her. He was a tall, white southerner. He had a high-top fade; the guards all had the same haircut. He was slender, almost 6'5", had brown hair and brown eyes. His eyes were sunken and he looked drained. His face was drawn against his skin and his cheeks were hollow. His demeanor echoed a haunting viciousness, but the heroism of his actions belied his appearance.

Abdul got up and shook Captain Winters hand. After he had saved Nida, Abdul had been effusive with praise and thanks for him. When Abdul stood up, there was a knock on the door of the barracks. Abdul stepped out into the passageway between the rows of cots. He looked down the passageway. There were bunks spaced evenly starting at the far end of the wall. They were double stacked cots with stacked footlockers at the end. There was about six feet of space between the row on the opposite side that could be walked through. This was where Abdul stood now, and he looked at the door at the far end of the passageway and walked towards it.

When Abdul opened the door, there was a doctor with a bag of blood and what appeared to be a medical kit. The doctor was a black man and was almost comically short. However, the man looked like he could lift a brick house up, his legs exceeded the size of most people's torso. Abdul had to restrain himself from laughing at the man, he found the combination amusing.

"We heard there was someone who needed a blood transfusion in here?" The doctor walked into the barracks without asking. He had a military uniform on, so he was not a civilian doctor like many in the camp were. *He probably was deployed here after whatever outbreak happened in the hospital*, Abdul thought.

The doctor knelt down beside Nida and began to feel for a vein. He took a while to find one. He sterilized the area he identified, and then slid the needle almost parallel to the arm under her skin. He hooked the bag to the top of the bunk and then plugged the bag of blood into the injection needle. Such a simple use of gravity, giving life to someone who has lost too much.

Color returned to Nida's face. Her breathing relaxed. Clearly, the blood was having the intended effect. *Such simple creatures we are, in the end*, Abdul thought to himself. Sitting down next to Nida, Abdul put his hand on her forehead to test her temperature. She was cool to the touch.

"Is it normal for her to be cool like this?" Abdul asked the doctor. He turned around and looked at Abdul with a puzzled look on his face. He rushed over to Nida's side and put a thermometer in her mouth while listening to her heart with his stethoscope.

"She's in shock. Someone get your body heat next to her. The less clothing the better. We have to keep her internal temperature up." The doctor looked expectantly at Abdul, who stripped down to his underwear. He got next to Nida and put his arms around her. It was a true test of love because the blankets had not yet been exchanged for new ones. The doctor pulled out a radio.

"Hotel Bravo, this is Delta Romeo 23." The doctor spoke into the radio.

"Delta Romeo 23, this is Hotel Bravo, go ahead." The radio spat back a harsh male voice.

"Do we have any shock blankets near the barracks area? Over." The doctor had his hand on his hip while he talked.

"Negative, you'll have to go to the depot for a shock blanket, sir. Over." The radio spat back.

"Hooah, over and out." The doctor put the radio back into its holder on his belt, "alright everyone, keep her warm and make sure that blood keeps getting into her body. If we can get liquids into her system, do so. I'm going to the depot to get a shock blanket. I will return shortly." Without waiting for anyone's response or acknowledgement, the doctor turned and walked out.

Abdul began to cry. He had a nice life. His father was a jewelry merchant who immigrated to America. Attending private school had allowed him to attend a prestigious university in New York City. He majored in business and then joined his father's company. He got to marry his princess and they had a son. *What more can they take from me?* Abdul's chest ached from the sorrow he was feeling. Tears streamed from his face uncontrollably. He was not losing Nida. *Where is Tahir?* Abdul thought.

He frantically began to look around, and shouted out, "Where is Tahir?!" his voice was panicked.

"I have him." Abdul heard from the corner. The old married couple were playing with Tahir in the corner.

Abdul breathed a sigh of relief. *Thank Allah.* "Thank you. Do you, uhh, mind watching him for a while

162

longer?" Abdul sort of motioned with his head towards Nida while he talked and raised his eyebrows.

"Of course, dear, we'll watch him as long as necessary," she turned to her husband and smiled, "you just take care of her." Her smile was so warm. Abdul let his guard down, and out of exhaustion, fell asleep.

Nida awoke. She was covered in a strange, metallic blanket. There was a needle in her arm attached to a bag of blood. The bag seemed fresh and was still flowing. Abdul was talking to a short black man at the end of the bunk.

"Aby?" Nida spoke so quietly. Abdul and the doctor rushed over to her.

"Put your head down, my love." Abdul pushed her gently back towards the bed. Nida let herself be pushed, not having the energy to fight back. There was a throbbing pain emanating from the back of her head and her nose. She could barely focus on staying awake, she could ---

---

Abdul sat next to the bed holding Nida's hand. He was too terrified of losing her to sleep. The structure of his life was crumbling. The things that had defined him for so long had been taken away by these people. *For what? For what did they do this? We are Americans!* Abdul was so angry he couldn't stand it. The resentment churning inside him cried out for one thing, justice.

Nida awoke. The spell over Abdul broke instantly. He stood over her, waiting for her to fully open her eyes. He could barely contain his excitement, the joy

163

in his soul was immeasurable. The sun had risen again in his spirit.

"My love, my love, my love, my love..." Abdul was stroking the top of Nida's head gently, panicked and delicate.

"Aby, what happened?" Nida was awake now. It seemed she had finally recovered. She had been out for three days straight.

"You were attacked by a guard. He broke your nose and smashed your head into the wall." Abdul hesitated.

"Go on." Nida was remembering, slowly.

"He was trying to rape you. Captain Winters hit him in the head with his pistol to knock him unconscious. We didn't realize how much blood you had lost, but a doctor came and patched you up." Abdul attempted to grace over the first part of the sentence as best he could. He felt he had to tell her what had happened, but he didn't want to dwell on the fact that he wasn't there to protect his wife in her hour of need. Nida's hair was caked with sweat, her shock had broken it appeared.

"I thought I lost you. I was so scared." Abdul was crying again. The mixture of terror and relief was impossible to control.

Nida put her arm around Abdul and they fell back asleep. Tahir was asleep in his crib next to the couple, he was sleeping. For a while, they rested together.

Captain Winters was sitting at a table in the mess hall. He was sipping on a glass of the standard issue tea. Eyes aware, the Captain surveyed the mess hall. Always on the prowl for non-conforming soldiers, the Captain ensured the discipline of his men this way. Garrison military often saw the discipline of the soldiers' decay, and it had been years since any major conflict.

This post was not an ideal one for Captain Winters, who was on track to become a Major any day now. Generally, you want an infantry command for your first one if you plan to make general, and Captain Winters didn't get that. He had started in the military a little later in life, around thirty. So, it had taken him a while to climb the ladder and he was much older than his peers. The eight years he had already been in the Army had aged him considerably.

He was part of the last wave that crushed the uprising in Iraq after it was officially re-organized as a state. Many people blamed the heavy-handed treatment of the population during that uprising as a catalyst for the Lincoln Memorial attacks. When the officers who were responsible for the heavy-handed treatment came up for advancement, they were routinely delayed for promotion. To say he was displeased that this was his post would be an understatement.

He eventually snapped out of his stream of intense subordinate observation and walked out of the mess hall. He walked towards the Depot. There was a small convenience store at the Depot that the Army stocked to provide their soldiers with small amenities. The Depot also housed some of the supplies for the camp. It was supplied by a much larger supply depot about forty-five minutes away from the camp. *Can't have too much food lying around for the prisoners to steal,* Winters thought to himself.

There was a food freezer that meats and other perishables were stored in, and a full bunker in case of attack. The contractor that had built them had mastered the technique with an advanced molding facility capable of molding and binding carbon fiber strands. The buildings were constructed in almost a day, and they were all of similar design and capabilities. They were one of the modern marvels of the military.

He walked into the store. He grabbed a green energy drink from the cooler and picked up a candy bar. After paying for the snacks, he walked out of the Depot and back towards the barracks area. As he approached, he witnessed a contingent of soldiers walking towards him. At their helm was an older gentleman who walked with an air of newly found authority. They were currently near the main control tower, where Captain Winters' office was located. There were two buildings located on either side where the soldiers generally slept. In two parallel lines, there were concrete, single-story containment barracks for the involuntarily detained civilians. The guard units referred to them as IDCs.

The guards finally made their way down the middle pathway between the parallel IDC barracks towards where Captain Winters was standing. The Depot was at the far end of the lane. It was a standard building set-up for the instant fortification camps that the Army had been developing since the Iranian conflict. The entire encampment was surrounded by a chain link fence with barbed wire at the top. There were guard towers at each corner and one halfway on the long ends of the encampment fence. They were simple towers, fit to hold one soldier. Not very comfortably, just how the Army preferred it.

"Captain Winters, sir!" Lieutenant Alvarez ran up to him first, while saluting. Captain Winters touched his hand briefly to the tip of his cap to return the salute.

"What seems to be the problem, LT?" As he said that another man approached. This man had a black oak leaf in the center of his chest. Captain Winter's demeanor immediately changed, and his spine straightened.

"Colonel, sir!" Winters snapped to attention and saluted. The Lieutenant Colonel returned his salute. This was a physically imposing human being. His large, brutish shoulders hinted at the raw physical strength this man possessed. His eyes were piercing blue, and his hair was blonde cut into a high-top fade. The amount of product required to keep this man's hair in place was enough to make him smell like the chemicals. He stood around 6' tall.

"Captain, I am here to relieve you of command." There was no hesitation, and the Lieutenant Colonel expected to be followed.

"Sir? This is a company-level command, why would a field grade officer be given this command?" Captain Winters was shocked and confused. Winters knew that he was being relieved, but he still thought he would have a great deal of authority within the camp. Now that a Lieutenant Colonel was here, he would be completely irrelevant.

"The explanation is above your pay grade, Captain. I'm Lieutenant Colonel Arthur McAdams, and you are now under my command. I don't expect any issues. Dismissed." Colonel McAdams handed Captain

Winters an envelope and walked away. Captain Winters opened the envelope. It contained his new orders from the Pentagon. *You are hereby relieved of command...*

Chapter 19: No Greater Friend, No Worse Enemy

Trent was sitting in the oval office. There were two couches parallel to each other placed in the middle of the room. There was a fine oak coffee table in between the two couches. Harold was sitting across from him, drinking his bourbon. It was four o'clock in the afternoon.

"Well, what did you come here to talk about, Trent? You called this meeting, didn't you?" Harold was already very impatient.

"Sir, yes I did. I jus' wanted to express my apologies for the mix up the other day. These Democrats play a different type-uh game. Ya gotta be real careful about optics, Mr. Pres-ee-dent." Trent was trying to be diplomatic and educational, but his tone was sarcastic and chiding.

"Did you really come all the way down here to tell me how to play politics, son?" The inherent disdain was apparent in Harold's tone. What thinly veiled respect he pretended to give to Trent disappeared almost instantaneously.

"Get out of my office. Not only did you disrespect me in public, you came and disrespected me to my face by way of apology. Why do we even keep you around? You can't do anything right. You even failed to get your little lap dog to recruit our members. Give me one god damn reason I shouldn't get rid of you!" Harold, already drunk for the day, was sloshing his words and was clearly agitated.

"I helped you get here Harold, you need me. Nothing you do is sustainable unless I'm on board and you

169

know it. Spare me the theatrics you drunken fool." Trent turned off the kind southerner routine and went into a completely different persona. The persona that won him political victories and acclaim. The real Trent, not the politician. The highly educated Speaker of the House was no pushover, he just pretended to be. Harold was made suddenly aware of with whom he was dealing.

Harold smiled and put the glass down. "Ah, that's your one reason. I need you." Harold stood up, slightly off balance. He walked over to his desk and pulled out a piece of paper. Taking a pen out of his coat, he began to write on the paper. Trent sat patiently on the couch. He was unsure of what to do.

When Harold was done writing, he pulled out a candle from his desk drawer. He lit the candle with a light that he had also pulled out of the door. He let the hot wax drip onto the paper. Taking his right hand, he placed a ring on his ring finger into the wax on the paper. He blew on the wax.

Harold walked over and handed the piece of paper to Trent. Trent took it and began to read:

T. Kennedy, Centurion,

You are discharged from the Last Dawn effectively immediately.

Submitted,
H. Drum, Praetor

"You can't take my position away, you don't have that power." Trent stood up and threw the paper in Harold's face.

"I can do whatever I want, I am in charge around here." Harold was leaning on the desk, arms crossed facing Trent.

"If that's what you think, then I'm not really sure how you made it this far. You are not in charge of a damn thing without the money behind the party. I control the money, not you!" Trent spit the last part of his sentence.

"For now, there's an election in a year, Trent. Would be a shame to have a special vote during the primary season to elect a new finance chair. Wouldn't it?" Trent shuffled back. *He's in control of the party, he could vote me out...* Trent turned and began to walk out of the office, unsure of what else to do.

"Oh, and Trent," Trent stopped, but didn't turn around, "turn around when I speak to you." Trent turned around this time, deeply humiliated.

"Make sure everything goes smoothly with the motion for my State of the Union address this afternoon." Harold then waved his hand twice towards Trent, like shooing a pest.

Trent sat back in his office chair. He was stunned at what had just happened. Power was seemingly snatched away from him at the drop of a hat. For years he had waited patiently, working his way up the political ladder. He had only even involved himself in the Caliphate after they had taken over the party. It wasn't a willful move, it was adapt or die for the most part.

Adapt or die. Trent thought to himself. It was his internal motto. He had a ton of them. It was how his father had taught him to stay committed and how to react to any situation. *How can I adapt? He has the whole party under his thumb.* Trent leaned forward in his chair and began to look through polls that he could find. The President's approval ratings had plummeted. It seemed that the national consensus was that the Muslim camps were radical and illegal. His approval was virtually non-existent outside of his super religious voter base who were keeping him in office. Still, it was the lowest it had ever been.

Trent pondered how to use this as an opportunity. *Could I reveal this whole religious cult?* Instantly, Trent recognized that would probably lead to his swift demise. Trent saw an article on his news feed about Luther Washington and clicked it. The article was titled "True Republican" by Lisa Young.

"The Republican Party has a new challenger to the conservative voter base: The Constitutionalist Party. Started by Luther Washington in response to President Drum's unconstitutional Muslim internment camps, the Constitutionalist Party has the potential to bring back what many believe to be the true Republican Party.

Luther Washington has stated that his new party will be the party of Lincoln and Jefferson. A party that will reduce the size of the government, cut national spending, break up unions, and continue the traditions of the free exercise of American speech and religious rights. Instead of entangling itself with religious extremist organizations, the Constitutionalist Party will strictly adhere to policies of church and state separation.

In an earlier interview with Washington, he revealed that the internment of Muslims had no legitimate national security justification. This type of rational and fair thinking makes a person almost hopeful about the potential for a three-party system to take root in American politics. Bravo Mr. Washington, a true Constitutionalist."

Trent read the article three times. He couldn't believe what he was reading. This was supposed to be a joke, but there were thirty million views on the article. Clearly, this man had caught something that captivated the nation. Trent leaned back in his chair. He smiled. *Opportunity.*

Luther was making his morning coffee. He was at his apartment in D.C., it was about six in the morning. The sun hadn't risen yet, the early winter mornings were the worst. He poured milk into his coffee from a silver pitcher he kept it in during the mornings. He put one sugar in and stirred. Sipping his coffee slowly, he breathed in. The aroma alone was enough to wake him up.

Shuffling back to the table, he picked up his phone. Scrolling through his text messages, he noticed a text from Sam. *Lu, daddy's backing your Republican challenger. Thought you should know.* Luther scoffed. *Moved on rather quickly,* Luther thought to himself. Luther began to get dressed. His phone began to ring.

Luther looked at the screen. "Trent" showed up on the screen. Luther answered the phone. He put it on speaker and placed it on the table.

"Mr. Speaker, what can I help you with today?" Luther was trying to suck up, he needed Trent's aid now more than ever.

"Luther, I want you to know that a lot of us at the party support your cause. We want to split off with you." Luther choked on his coffee, spitting it back up.

"What? You said you couldn't help me the other day." There was a cold sweat forming on Luther's brow. He never expected this.

"Let's just say that the President hasn't made a lot of friends recently." Luther grunted slightly with approval.

"How many people do you have? We're gonna need a lot." Luther's initial shock had worn off, he trusted Trent and figured that Trent was simply returning that trust.

"We have about forty total. Enough to swing the vote in favor of impeachment, at the least. We are working on getting the Democrats on board. Can we work with you?"

"I have two, myself and Phil Hammond. Let's do this." Trent paused. He had expected a lot more people to already be a part of Luther's movement. Given the media attention that it had gotten, he figured that there were a lot more people in the shadows pushing the narrative. Apparently, Trent was speaking to an accomplished propagandist.

"Meet me in my office at 8." Trent said, hoping that Luther would pay him the deference.

"Why don't we do my office?" Luther said.

There were four people in Luther's office. Luther sat behind his desk, and the other three were strewn about the room. Luther was a junior Congressional member, so his office wasn't exactly one of the largest. Nonetheless, he had insisted on conducting the meeting here. He had told the others that it was the safest because nobody comes to this part of the office building due to its remote location. The others had agreed that was a reasonable assumption.

"I don't get it, why now? This has been going on for over a year, Trent. We've been asking for a vote for over a year." Elizabeth Holder was standing while leaning on a wall. She was her same powerful, Atheist self. She had changed her hair. It was now short and straight down to her shoulders. Her hazel eyes were still entrancing, intelligent and knowing. Hers was the look of a woman who had been raised free of patriarchal mental restraints. A woman who had been baptized in the world of feminism and had embraced its core teachings of individual self-worth. A true believer in American equality.

"Look, I'm going to have to leave the Republican party if I do this. The majority will still follow him. I've got 42 people, including myself, Luther and Phil. I need you all to name me Speaker again so we can retain control. We only have the majority if we work together, and y'all need me to get what you want done. There's a Senate deadlock, so you never know what might happen there." Trent was selling.

Holder and Aberle, the other man in the room, were listening intently. They both looked at each other for a moment and stared blankly. This was clearly beyond anything they had expected to occur at this meeting. They hadn't been informed of its purpose prior to its occurrence.

Luther chimed in, "We have to get rid of this guy. This is the only way. I won't support anyone besides

Trent, and if we don't choose the person the other members of our coalition might balk. It has to be Trent, and you have to accept. There's no choice in this." He had clearly bought in to his own new found idealism.

"How do you propose we impeach him? His base seems onboard with the internment of the Muslims." Aberle was unconvinced that the coalition would even work.

Trent sighed. *The conspiracy is already in motion, there's no walking this back.* Standing up, Trent handed everyone a piece of paper. The paper contained an Army grid map, depicting central Washington D.C. Along the edges of some of the grid patterns were markings, and there was a key that denoted what the markings meant. Some of the key indicated "Alpha Team" and some indicated "Rendezvous points." The other people in the room looked up at Trent with extremely puzzled looks on their faces.

"What am I reading here, Trent?" Holder was not amused by the theatrics, but it was only because she didn't understand what it was she was holding.

"What you have in your hands are the battle plans for a group called the Caliphate of Last Dawn that perpetrated the attack on the Lincoln Memorial two years ago." The air was immediately still. The group tension escalated, it felt like a warm blanket that immobilized the tongues and minds of all in the room.

"First, how in the hell did you get these? Second, why does this matter for the President?"

Trent leaned back in his chair, coffee cup in one hand. He began to tell a story.

"There's no easy way to relay this, so I'm going to start at the beginning. I was a young man when I was first contacted by the group. They refer to themselves simply as the Caliphate. As a young Congressman, nobody listened to anything that I said. The Caliphate offered power, and the only thing that they asked was loyalty."

Interrupting the flow of consciousness, Holder interjected, "Get to the point, Trent. I have better things to do today." Elizabeth and Trent had many public battles over all sorts of legislation, their personal disdain for each other was public record.

"I promise you, Elizabeth, you do not." Trent put his coffee down and stood up. He began pacing back and forth while continuing to recount his story.

"I never questioned much about the loyalty part, I just assumed these were some of those 'secret groups' you hear about in history. They never seemed too hostile to me, but they did have a religious fervor to them that was unsettling. In public, they act like normal everyday Christians, but in private, they conduct themselves according to a rigid hierarchical system. At the top of this system, that is, at the top of the Caliphate is a man known as the Praetor," Trent paused for a moment before continuing.

"When I joined, the Praetor was a man named Iskandar. He was a Palestinian born Christian. He was a vicious man and worked only from the shadows. After a few years, though, things began to descend into a level of strange I was unaware existed. Eventually, a man named Harold Drum killed Iskandar and seized control of the Caliphate." At this point, Trent looked up at the faces of the three political animals.

A politician's poker face is the most important aspect of their existence. The ability to wheel and deal in the currency of words is central to the puppeteering that is required of politicians. The best politicians would never blink an eye if you told them that their father or mother was sick. These three were among the absolute best politicians in Washington. All three of their mouths were hanging wide open, and a look of utter shock and disgust colored their faces.

It was ten minutes of silence before anyone spoke. Elizabeth was the first to break her silence. She stood up and grabbed the paper copies of the map again. She began to read the inscriptions and the legend more carefully.

"Oh, God… it wasn't a terrorist attack at all was it? It was a military operation!" She fell to her knees. She began to fully comprehend the animal she was fighting against. Her entire world view shattered, she stood up once more. The calm demeanor of steel that had been so practiced eroded into something more venomous. This was no longer a game of politics. This was war.

"Not exactly. The Caliphate has been kidnapping and indoctrinating young men and women for years at multiple training bases around the country. They have an army of zealots that number in the thousands, all fully combat trained and prepared to kill for their leader at any moment. Those are the people they had perpetrate the attacks."

"How many members of Congress are members?" Luther had recovered enough at this point to begin asking questions. So many conversations made sense to him now. So many overtures concerning loyalty and "playing ball," suddenly rushed back into the forefront of his mind. *How many times did they try to recruit me?* Luther wondered.

"The majority of the Republican party are members of the Caliphate. The Senate Majority leader, and every other major Republican leader. The only major member of the party they have yet to convince is the Chairman of the National Security Commission, Rhett Yarborough." All three of the others in the room looked at Trent with a horrified expression.

"T-t-the majority?" Aberle had not recovered from the shock. The mind is a fickle thing, often vastly difficult concepts are easy for some to understand. However, when you place a fact in front of someone's face that is simple, it is often harder to grasp if they do not want to believe its contents.

"Enough that if we walk out of this room without a decision being made, they will figure it out and kill all of us before we can say another word." Trent's blood was boiling. He had pulled the trigger on a life. He was just unsure whose it was.

Elizabeth walked over to where Trent had finished pacing. She stood there for a moment and looked into Trent's eyes. Without saying a word, she reached out her hand. Trent took it.

"Liberty or death." Elizabeth said.

The coffee had finished brewing, and Lisa poured some of it into her mug. She generally just used one of her single pods for making coffee, but Trevor had stayed over from the previous evening so she brewed a full pot. She poured coffee into another mug for him and walked back to the bedroom.

Trevor was sitting up reading his tablet and looked at Lisa when she walked in. He didn't look especially pleased. Eventually, he put the tablet down and took the coffee. Lisa couldn't bear the silence anymore and so she broke it.

"Good Mo-"

Trevor interjected before she could speak, "True Republican? Are you serious? How could you write this?"

Oh, Lisa thought. They generally never talked about work given how far apart their respective viewpoints were. This was a physical relationship, but both of them knew that if it weren't for their careers they would be much more. Trevor seemed honestly upset by the article.

"It's just an article Trev, nothing more. You write stuff like this all of the time. What's the difference?" She was shocked, this was the first time that he had ever told her that he had even read anything that she'd written.

"The difference is I don't accuse your side of being tangled up with extremists. We're not just a bunch of religious nut jobs, ya know?" He was pouring his heart out.

"I don't think that of you, I don't, but you know Drum is dangerous. You know he is. Look at the type of following he has, that's not normal." If he wanted to fight, she certainly was going to fight.

"Dangerous? All I see is a person willing to do what it takes to make this country great. Is he a little religious? Yea, totally, but he's not trying to impose some

180

sort of theocracy. The Republicans wouldn't go for that."
Lisa hesitated. She hadn't said anything about a theocracy,
she didn't go that far.

"What do you know that you aren't telling me,
Trev?" She sat down on the bed beside him and put her
hand on his shoulder.

"Nothing, Lisa. It's nothing." He slicked back his
golden hair and stared blankly at the article on the tablet.

Chapter 20: The Night of the Long Knives

Harold stood by the window looking out over the lawn of the White House. There were people gathered in the Oval Office discussing something Harold didn't know. Harold didn't care. Picking up the bottle of scotch he had been working on since earlier this morning, he poured himself another drink.

He walked over to where the men were discussing this bit of governance and sat down. Pretending to look interested in what the men had to say, Harold leaned in and formed his face into a quizzical look. From the corner of his eye, Harold saw James. James was special to Harold as he was the first of his army, and the most loyal of all of them.

James gave a hand signal to Harold. The hand signal was part of a code that his operatives had developed over the years spent together. The signal indicated that James needed to speak privately at the next opportunity. James placed his hand out and his opposite index finger in it and wrapped his hand around the index finger.

"Well, gentlemen. That'sh abouth all the shtime we haff today." Harold hiccupped and stared blankly at the men.

"Mr. President, are you... are you drunk?" The younger of the two men asked. Apparently, he had not been taught manners in school.

"Get the hell out of my office and don't come back with your stupid projects!" Harold was screaming now, the drunken stupor fueling his outrage.

"Sir, this is a national defense grid that you asked for, we take this very seriously." The older man stood up in defense of the younger one.

Just as Harold was about to unleash every bit of angst, anger and hate he had accumulated over the past five minutes onto these two misbegotten souls, James ushered the two men out of the room. Rick walked in after the men had left and stared coldly at Harold.

"What – *hic* – seemshto be the problem, Jimmy?" James hesitated to answer.

"Sir, don't call me Jimmy. We've been over this. Also, we've been getting some odd reports about Speaker Kennedy meeting with high level Democrats and Congressman Washington behind closed doors." Harold laughed. He was too drunk to understand the implication. He was too drunk to remember the argument with Trent.

"Hesh prolly just lettin' them haff the busin—" As Harold trailed off, he passed out and landed face first on the floor.

Rick didn't move to help. Instead, he just turned and walked out of the office. His disappointment was immeasurable. *After all of the careful scheming, maneuvering, and politics that the two of them had perpetrated to get here, Harold was going to drink it all away.* Rick thought to himself. He was trapped because the Caliphate saw Rick as a necessary holdover from the previous regime. Rick wasn't part of their revolution, but he was the inside man who opened the door. That's who he had always been, and nothing Rick did now would change that. Rick sat down in his office chair and stared blankly at the ceiling.

Luther was standing backstage. Lisa Young was giving her introductory "rundown" of all the hot news topics that nobody cared about. Lisa had pushed arduously to make the network give her equal time for human interest stories. To publish news that was worthy of being news, not just network manufactured jargon to give people their regularly scheduled dopamine hits. Lisa's show was close to shutting down until Luther had announced his new party on it. Now, her show had basically been co-opted by a political movement that the network forced her to cover. She was the mouthpiece of the movement Luther had started, and it wasn't even much of a movement yet.

"My next guest needs no introduction on this show, please welcome Luther Washington."

As Luther walked on stage, a manufactured applause rang out. Luther gave a wave to the audience that didn't exist and sat down at the interview desk across from Lisa.

"Congressman, welcome back to 'Talking Points,' thank you for coming on today." Lisa smiled that showbiz smile the entire way through the sentence.

"Thank you for having me again. Feels good to be back." Luther replied.

"Let me start today by asking the big question: what is happening with your new party?" Lisa leaned in. Her producer believed that Luther was a hack and was doing all of this for some ill-begotten shot at political relevance. She also believed that it was unlikely anything had been accomplished in the short weeks since they had last spoken.

"Well Lisa, we're very excited to announce the addition of Speaker Trent Kennedy to our ranks in addition to more than forty other members of Congress."

Lisa's mouth dropped open. Behind the camera, you could hear Lisa's producer's mouth drop to the floor. There were no actual audience members, but you could feel the surprise from the crew members.

"You managed to pull the Speaker of the House, a Republican for almost thirty years, to your party after existing for a few short weeks? How, may I ask, did you accomplish such a remarkable feat?"

"Well, Lisa. Speaker Kennedy is a close personal friend of mine. We have shared many conversations concerning political ideology and belief throughout our time in Congress. We think a lot alike. Concerning this President, we feel the same. The man must be removed from office under any circumstances." Luther delivered the lines in a cool, composed manner. His poker face had been developed over time, but he was a master at it now. It successfully masked the internalized screaming that was happening when he was speaking.

"Well, he's not the Speaker anymore, right?" Lisa had connected a couple of dots while Luther was talking.

"Actually, he is. The Constitutionalist and Democratic parties have a temporary political alliance in order to effectuate the removal of President Harold Drum. Part of that agreement is that Kennedy had to remain the Speaker of the House." Luther's words were essentially treason in this world. Openly calling for the President's job was a one-way ticket to committing suicide, yet Luther felt that it was his duty to keep walking down the path.

Lisa was beyond being shocked. She stared at Luther for a moment. She had thought that this was a stupid kid and just another cog in his father in law's political machine. This was no child. This was a crusader. A person with a clarity of purpose that resonated with her.

"So, assuming all of this is true - and for our viewers out there, we have no way of verifying it currently – what are your grounds for impeachment?"

This is it. No coming back from this. Luther thought to himself. He took a deep breath in, and he began to speak.

"Hello, my name is Trevor Stewart and I'm coming to you live from Wolf News. Today, our headline story is a false accusation by a Congressman against our beloved President. The Congressman, the infamous Luther Washington, has attempted to spin a tall tale about government involvement in the Lincoln Memorial Attacks just two years ago."

The camera panned to a different side of Trevor, the lights dimmed and a loud ominous tone played underneath his words to make the message appear menacing.

"I'm here to tell you today that the President had no involvement in these heinous crimes, and the mere suggestion that he may have is simply un-American in every way. In the studio today we have White House Chief of Staff, Rick Young, here to discuss these allegations with us."

Rick walked onto the stage. There was a time that this was all Rick ever wanted. He wanted the attention and the love of the people, but it was never his to get. Clearly not himself, Rick walked onto the set where Trevor was sitting. Rick sat down in the chair across from the desk, his shoulders were slumped and his hair was messy. No longer the spitting image of the real politic, Rick looked more like the drunkard down the lane that had an amazing story to tell you if you'd buy him one more drink.

"Mr. Young, are you feeling okay?" Trevor said to him. Trevor was a Caliphate member and had met Rick hundreds of times. They were acquainted with one another, and Trevor immediately recognized that Rick was not himself. Rick didn't say anything in response before Trevor started again.

"Here today is Rick Young, White House Chief of Staff," Trevor turned to Rick, "Mr. Young, is there any merit to these allegations?"

Rick sat there blankly. He stared into the camera, half hungover and half terrified. He had only taken this interview because Harold had drunkenly demanded he do so. Washington had hit them so hard so fast yesterday that the entire plan was in danger of falling apart. The top players in the game were struggling to keep pace, and Rick felt like he was drowning under the constant pressure of running the country and running Harold's life for him. Not to mention running interference with the Caliphate to convince them that their leader, who they had risked everything in backing, was not a disordered alcoholic who could barely stand the sight of responsibility.

Rick's thoughts came at a bad time. His silence was not golden, and he had no answer. Continuing his dumbfounded stupor, Rick finally snapped out of his own head long enough to answer the question.

"N-no there is no merit to any of it. Does that sound like a logical thing?" Rick could barely bring himself to say it. The screams all came back to him at once. He was there that day at the Lincoln Memorial, he had given the order to proceed. Rick had stood side by side with the other members of the army as they had torn through an innocent mob of people. The image of a little girl still holding her mother's dead hand flashed into his mind. His mental blocks around the atrocity began to crumble. The stream of guilt flooded into his mind, and he was struggling to hold it back. He had tried for so long to forget what he had done on that day.

Trevor looked confused, clearly this was not what was on the teleprompter for Rick to say. Going off message was not something Rick was prone to do. Trevor reached out his hand and put it on Rick's shoulder. Rick began to sob uncontrollably. For the world, this was proof enough. The mask was off, and so were the gloves.

Elizabeth was standing at the doors waiting to go into the Congressional Chambers. The impeachment vote was scheduled for the next day, but the President had insisted on giving the State of the Union Address. It was already approved prior to the revelation about the Lincoln Memorial and Drum's alleged involvement in it. National opinion remained stagnant. The people were so divided on the believability of the accusations. It seemed beyond reason that a sitting President would have harmed his people, but the proof was undeniable for the majority. Impeachment seemed inevitable; removal was likely after Trent's defection skewed the balance of power in both chambers.

President Drum was desperate. When an animal is cornered, and the option for retreat no longer exists, the animal becomes dangerous. An inherent aggression that worships at the altar of survival at all costs reveals itself at the times of the highest desperation. In some people, this instinct is a meaningless whimper that travels to the ears of the inflictor and no further. But for others, this instinct undermines the course of time so much that humanity is irrevocably altered. For President Drum, the coin was in the air.

Attempting to assuage her terror, she went back to her office. The State of the Union wasn't scheduled to begin for another hour. As she returned to her office, she saw Speaker Kennedy walking into his from across the way. She pivoted and went down the long marble hallway into his office. He was visibly shaking, obviously nervous.

"Trent, are you okay?" There was genuine concern in Elizabeth's voice.

"I made Luther the lone survivor in case something happens tonight." Trent's voice was raspy.

"What do you mean? You don't think he's going to do something drastic do you?" She was skeptical that all of the accusations against President Drum were true, they seemed genuinely far-fetched. Elizabeth thought it was much more likely that Trent was just out for a power grab and used a contrived story about a tragedy to throw the party into chaos. *Choosing his puppet, Washington, as the lone survivor is likely just a publicity stunt,* Elizabeth thought.

Trent didn't speak again. He went into his private office and shut the door without speaking to Elizabeth again. Thinking herself quite the detective, Elizabeth walked triumphantly back to her office to await the State of the Union.

Sober, Harold stood at the window of the Oval Office and stared out over the lawn. His navy suit was buttoned up top and his hands were stuffed into his pockets. His hair was styled with a large swoosh to the left. There was a visible imprint in his jacket pocket of a book, the Bible. His blue eyes had dark circles under them, turning their once peaceful appearance into one of exhaustion. His hair remained perfect.

The door opened behind Harold, and James walked into the office. James had taken to his role as Director of the Secret Service quite well. Systematically, James had removed the career Secret Service agents and replaced them with soldiers from the Caliphate. There were no holdovers left, and what remained was a force of secret police that were absolutely loyal to the President. The entire operation had been Harold's idea, but James executed it with unexpected amounts of success. *He is truly the most valuable of all of my lieutenants. He must have an expanded role in the new regime*, Harold thought to himself.

"We are ready, sir." James spoke exactly the right way and exactly the right amount of words for Harold's wishes. The perfect soldier.

"Does everyone understand what is to happen?" Harold raised an eyebrow. James nodded.

"Anything of note?" Harold asked. James shook his head, everything looked as expected.

Harold stepped back behind his desk and grabbed a pen and paper. He began writing on the piece of paper and signed it at the bottom.

"Get this to Kennedy. Before. I want to speak with him." Harold gave the note to James who handed it to a lesser agent who was standing outside the door. James was many things, but he was not a messenger boy.

"Dismissed." James nodded and walked out the door.

"Letter for you, sir." Trent took the letter from his secretary's hand.

Trent read the letter to himself. His heart began pounding. He pulled out his phone and sent a text message to Luther. *Get in your car and disappear, right now.* Trent sank down in his chair, there were only ten minutes until the State of the Union started.

The Chamber of Congress was filled completely with people. The entire government was there. The Speaker of the House, Trent Kennedy, walked up to the podium. Noticing the significance, the room quieted. All of the members of the government sat down, and Speaker Kennedy began to speak.

"Tonight, we welcome the President of the United States, Harold Drum, into our Chambers to address this great body on the State of our Union. This is one of the storied traditions of our great Republic, and we are honored to welcome the President into our chambers this evening. Mr. President." Trent gestured towards

Harold, who was seated just below, awaiting to be called upon to speak.

Harold walked up to the podium. His demeanor had shifted. Where he had addressed the people during his campaign and the majority of his term with warm smiles, tonight he wore a stern line across his face. Surrounding him was an aura of anger and frustration. He placed a three-ring binder on the podium and opened it.

"Thank you, Mr. Speaker, the House of Representatives and the Senate of the United States for inviting me to give the State of the Union Address this evening." Harold paused as half of the room erupted into thunderous applause.

"The State of our Union is weak." The chamber gasped. A deafening silence descended over the entire room, even the Republicans.

"I stand before you today as a President who has been accused of murdering his own people for political power. Of orchestrating a false flag operation in order to gain control of the political power of the country." He paused again. There was no applause, the tension in the room was palpable. It tasted like fear.

"There are those who support these false accusations despite knowing fully that they are contrived political machinations. There are those who truly believe these heinous falsities. Both are offensive to me, and both are offensive to God. I will not mislead the American people and tell them that the Union is strong when it is not. The House of Representatives and the Senate seek to grab power themselves and overturn the results of an election. I! Will! Not! Have! It!" Harold slammed his fist onto the podium.

As the fist slam landed on the podium, the Chamber doors opened. Harold's Secret Service funneled into the Chamber. They lined each side and aisle of the chairs, completely disabling any exit from the Chamber. Harold smiled.

"My fellow Americans, I hope that you will understand that each and every action that I take is in support and defense of our Great Republic, under God! I feel that it is inexorably my duty to protect this great and enduring body at all costs. I believe that my God put me here to save this nation from itself, and thus I must do as God commands. I must save the Republic, for ALL!"

Harold raised his hand into the air, half clenched, towards Heaven. When he raised his hand, the Secret Service raised their guns. They began to fire into the Congressman and Senators on the left. Part of the right side that had been a Constitutionalist seating area was also fired upon. The bullets ripped through the pack of unsuspecting politicians. Their panicked screams filled the room, as the bullets drowned out their sorrow. The metallic cacophony rang out like a great orchestra crescendo. A moment in time, singular in its importance, marked by a bitter symphony of industrial wrath.

The death toll was vast. When the orchestra halted, all the members of the Democratic and Constitutionalist parties were dead. All that remained were the members of the Republican party who had been part of the Caliphate. They were informed prior of the events and sat in very specific seats for a reason.

Harold was still at the podium, and the world was still viewing in full sight the atrocity that had been perpetrated. Harold continued.

"Brothers and Sisters, I am sorry that this was the path we were forced to walk. Know that I did this for all of us. The Republic was too important to risk, and I had to act against those that would destroy it. There will be a new order after this, and we will not stop until this country is safe from those who mean it harm." Harold walked down the aisle of blood and out of the main doors, escorted the entire time by the Secret Service.

At certain points in history, some men commit acts of violence that define a generation. The reaction to these acts vary. Sometimes, the people react with violence, overthrowing the regime that committed the heinous act. Other times, the act itself is so heinous that the terror it produces shocks people into compliance. Harold was becoming familiar with the fateful coin toss. Absolute power was within his grasp, and he intended to hold the baton in his hand as long as he could. *I will never go back in the box.*

Part IV: The American Dream

"No one reigns innocently." – Louis de Saint-Just

Chapter 21: Past the Rubicon

Luther checked his phone. There was a text message from Trent Kennedy. The phone flipped open. *Get in your car and disappear, now.* Blood began to rush to Luther's face. His hands began to clench at his side. His heart pounding, he began to panic and rushed to his bedroom to start to put some clothes together.

A clock started ticking in his head, his time was running out. He threw a random assortment of clothes into his bag and zipped it up. There was a toiletry bag that he had packed normally for when he left for North Carolina, so he grabbed that. Luther grabbed his keys and raced out the door.

The car roared to life as if it knew that they were going somewhere, fast. He didn't know why he was running, or who he was running from, but Trent said to run. Luther couldn't wrap his head around what was happening. More terrorists? Another attack? It was the night of the State of the Union address, and Harold Drum seemed desperate.

Gliding down the road, trying not to draw suspicion, he plotted his next move. He had to stay off the grid. After he had received the text from Trent telling him to run, he had to find out what happened. *Drum must have done something.* Luther's heart began pounding in his chest and the hair on the back of his neck stood up.

195

After Luther had been driving for what seemed like only a few seconds, he found himself outside of Richmond, VA. He had made it out of Washington unmolested and went to check into a motel. The motel was old, the floors smelled like they had been wet and moldy for a few years. The counter was thin plastic laminate that had chipped and cracked in many places. Thin, plastic sheeting was peeling off of the top layer. Sitting behind the desk was a slender Indian man with an untucked, short sleeve, collared shirt. The shirt was decorated with pineapples and was a deep blue. He set down the book he was reading and walked up to the counter.

"Hello, welcome to Motel of Richmond. How can we help you, sir?" He spoke very clearly and had obviously been raised in the United States.

"I need a room." Luther was very quiet when he spoke.

"Okay, I'll need a form of payment and your ID." The man looked half asleep as he spoke. It was late, and he obviously did not want to be here.

"Look, I don't have either. I have cash that I can pay in. I'll give you some cash, too, if you don't need my ID." Luther took out his wallet.

The man held out his hand to take the money. Luther put $500 in the man's hand. He began counting out the bills and looked at Luther with a raised eyebrow. After pausing for a moment, the man held out his hand once again. Luther put another $100 in his hand. The man smiled, and without saying another word grabbed one of the small brass keys from below the desk and handed it to Luther.

Luther spun around quickly and left the small office. He looked at the key, it was for room four. The key slid into the door lock, and Luther turned it. He entered the room and went immediately to the bathroom. The bathroom was disturbing. It was very clear that it had not been cleaned within the last year. *How does this pass health codes?* He mused in his head about reporting them. Still, Luther used the toilet and tried not to breathe.

He washed his hands and then walked back into the bedroom. Luther had a habit in hotels of checking for bed bugs, and he didn't change his habit on this particular occasion. The sheets looked clean enough, which was a shock after the condition of the bathroom. *I might actually get some sleep tonight.* Luther smiled and laid his head down. When he put his arms down on the bed, his left hand struck something hard and plastic. The T.V. remote was right next to Luther's hand. He grabbed it and turned on the T.V. He changed it to ABS news. He expected to see a re-run of Lisa's earlier segment. It was around 1 a.m.

Instead, it was a new person that was still doing live coverage. *Strange, most networks stop live coverage at 11,* Luther was genuinely perplexed. He pressed the volume button and listened intently.

"We bring you back to the breaking live coverage of the attempted Democratic coup during the State of the Union Address yesterday evening." A small screen appeared beside the news anchor, and the screen focused in on her face. She had sharp features and wore black rimmed glasses. Her blonde hair was curled slightly at the end and hung down to around her shoulders.

"Late yesterday evening, Democrats in both the House and the Senate conspired to overthrow President

Harold Drum. In conjunction with the renegade Constitutionalist Party, they had published Articles of Impeachment based on the false allegations levied against the President concerning the terrorist attacks on the Lincoln Memorial. The President was forced to react to the situation and has declared martial law in the District of Columbia."

They switched to a different camera, marking the end of that segment. She shuffled her papers and continued.

"We have just learned that one of the conspirators, Luther Washington, has escaped custody and is a fugitive on the run. Authorities are asking anyone who has seen Congressman Washington to report him to the nearest local law enforcement agency. He was last seen at his townhouse in D.C. and is believed to be driving a blue sedan."

Luther sat stunned, watching the screen as they replayed the State of the Union address. *They killed them all, because of me.* The guilt and shame began to creep into Luther's mind. He could barely breathe. He stood up and took off his shirt. It was so heavy. Sweat began to pour down his face profusely. His entire body was clammy and cold. His pants became drenched, soaking in his sweat. He took off his pants and curled into a ball on the ground. Rocking back and forth uncontrollably, Luther began to weep.

It is often said that what doesn't kill you makes you stronger. While sometimes it is true that pressure makes diamonds, when the material upon which the pressure is applied is not on solid foundation, it can also crush anything in its path.

"Where is he, Trent?" Harold was inches from Trent's face. Trent was tied to a chair in a cell in the basement of the White House. The cell was used from time to time by the Secret Service.

Trent sat in the chair, blood streaming down his face from the abuse that he had taken. He looked back up at Harold and spat that blood in his face. Harold struck him again with an open palm on the left side of his face.

"You're not leaving this room until you tell me where he went." With that, Harold walked out of the room. Rick and James followed closely behind him. When they got back to the Oval Office, there was a host of Congressional members waiting for them. They all shuffled out of the way of Harold who had blood splatter all over his face and hands.

Harold sat at the desk and poured a glass of whiskey. He put his feet on the desk and leaned back. The entire room sat there in silence, waiting for him to speak. The tension in the room was palpable. Harold sat up in his seat.

"Director Farnsworth?" Harold shouted angrily into the crowd.

"Y-y-yes, Mr. President?" The fear in his voice was palpable. It was like a whimpering dog who had no choice but to obey his master.

"What is the status of our national security?"

"Well, the District of Columbia is on total lockdown, but we've found a lot of protestors trying to come out after curfew. The rest of the country doesn't seem to have had any reaction as of yet."

Harold swirled the whiskey around in his glass. The coin had landed, and it came up with fear.

"Find Washington." Harold drank his whiskey.

Passed out on the floor, Luther's eyes were swollen and red. The guilt and the shame of his political game causing the death of all of those Senators and Congresspeople was weighing on him. Originally, Luther didn't believe the Lincoln Memorial accusations, but now he did. How could he not? The country was now living under the rule of a tyrant. The Republic had fallen.

Cracking his eyes a little bit, Luther saw that it was light outside now. *Have to keep moving,* Luther thought to himself. He grabbed his bag which he hadn't unpacked and went back to his car. Luther sat in his car for a moment before starting the engine. Looking behind him, he saw a black SUV with the windows tinted. It immediately made shock go through Luther's body. Driving by the office again, Luther looked in and saw three men in black suits talking to a different Indian man in the office. He looked a bit older.

Luther sped away in his car; his heart was beating out of his chest. *They found me. They are looking for me.* Fear creeping into his mind, Luther began to piece together where to go. He just kept driving south, careful to use cash wherever he went. *Thank you, Sam, for telling me to always have cash.* He never thought that he would be thanking his wife for anything again.

Eventually, Luther made it down to North Carolina. He began to head to the western portion of the state, it was a heavily mountainous region. The idea that he could hide out in the mountains was on the forefront of his mind. *I can survive, but I'll need some gear.* He got to a small cropping of civilization, there was an old sign that read "Highlands, NC."

Luther drove in circles around the town and eventually saw a store called "Snow Goose Outfitters." He walked into the store. There was a teenage girl at the counter. Luther breathed a little more easily, *she probably doesn't watch the news.* Walking around the store, Luther grabbed a hatchet, a hiking pack, a tent, and a sleeping bag with a pad. He also grabbed a pack of lighters with lighter fluid and two large water bottles. There was a large selection of camp stoves and pots, but Luther didn't think that he could get any more stuff into the pack he had picked out.

He walked up to the counter and purchased the items. The girl at the counter kept staring at him. She almost recognized him. She was staring at him like she remembered who he was, like a phantom memory trying to bring itself to the forefront. Despite the lurking phantom creeping into this girl's mind, she rang Luther's purchase up. Luther gathered everything up and went back out to his car. He stuffed the clothes into his bag and put the items he had purchased into the bag.

Unscrewing the screws that fastened his license plate, Luther took the license plate and put it in the bag. He then walked up to the front panel of the car and scratched out the VIN number. Next thing Luther knew, he was walking straight into the forest, leaving his car behind in that parking lot.

Sitting at the same bar she was at yesterday, Lisa held up her hand for another drink. The bartender came over and poured some gin into her glass and then put some ginger soda in it. Lisa took a sip of the cocktail and swirled it for a second, watching the carbonation bubble up to the surface. She could barely think straight between the booze and the sadness. The network fired her because of Washington's accusations on air as if she knew what he was going to say.

As soon as a thought about work crept into her head, she finished her drink. Once more, she held up her hand for another drink. The bartender came back over. "Sorry miss, can't give you anymore. You're toast. Walk it off."

Lisa gave the man a thumbs up and walked out of the bar. She tripped over her barstool and stumbled forward for a bit. Managing to regain her balance, she made her way to the train station. *I have to see Trev,* she kept thinking to herself. She needed to feel something other than what she was feeling, and she knew where to go to get it.

Taking out her phone, Lisa punched his address into her GPS and waved down a taxi. After a minute, a yellow cab pulled up and asked where she was going. She held out her phone for the address and then hopped into the back of the cab. The driver kept checking on her during the drive. Lisa figured he just didn't want her to throw up in his cab. Which was a legitimate concern she didn't blame him for.

After about twenty minutes, they arrived outside of Trevor's building. Lisa threw a generic amount of money at the cab driver and then stumbled towards the bellman for his building.

"Hey Tony, can I go up?" Lisa asked, managing to not slur her speech too dramatically.

"Um, was Mr. Stewart expecting you, ma'am?" Tony was a native New Yorker, so it was strange to hear ma'am come out of his mouth like some sort of southerner.

"Tony, you've known me for years. Let me up." Tony sighed and let her through the door.

Lisa entered the elevator and rode it to the twelfth floor. 12A was Trevor's apartment, Lisa knew exactly where she was going. She had been there so many times that she knew the path. She arrived at Trevor's door and knocked.

"Trevor? It's me, Lisa," she knocked again, "Trev?" She waited for a moment, but she didn't hear any movement. So, she took out her key and opened the door. All of the lights were off, Trevor wasn't there. Lisa went to his bed and fell asleep.

Lisa awoke to the smell of coffee and bacon. Leaving the warm confines of the blankets that she didn't remember putting on herself, she made her way towards the beautiful aroma. Once she entered the kitchen, she saw Trevor cooking a breakfast of eggs and bacon.

"Good morning sleeping beauty. Are we recovered?" His voice was so loud, why was his voice so loud? Lisa put a hand up to her head and felt a dizzy spell come on.

"I guess not quite recovered, ha." Trevor chuckled to himself. Lisa walked over to the coffee pot and poured herself some of the sweet nectar of the gods. The smell of coffee had a way of curing her of any ailments. She always remembered sitting around the table with her mother and father when they were still alive. Drinking coffee, reading the newspaper. It was the boring times that she remembered the most about them.

Thinking of her parents brought her back down to Earth. While her head was still splitting, she was fully conscious and her memories roared back to life.

"Did you know?" Lisa asked as she sipped her coffee.

"Did I know what, Lisa?" Trevor stood straight backed. He stopped focusing on the eggs in front of him, "What are you asking me?"

"Did you know that Drum and his cronies were responsible for the Lincoln Memorial?"

Taking the eggs off the burner, Trevor turned towards her, "That didn't happen, Lisa. They made that up. Liberals make up a lot of things, you should know that."

"How dare you?! HE SLAUGHTERED CONGRESS TREVOR, WHEN WILL YOU OPEN YOUR EYES?!" Her headache became unbearable, she sank down to the ground. Her stomach churned and she tried to locate the trash can. She began to vomit uncontrollably into the trash.

"I-I… Look, there's no evidence that he did the Lincoln Memorial. There's nothing. I know these guys personally. They swore to me they weren't involved. So, what is he supposed to do? Just sit back and let them impeach him on lies?"

"How can you even say that, Trev? He slaughtered innocent people!" Lisa began to weep while still clutching the trash can for dear life.

Trevor sighed, "I'm not sure they were innocent, but I know. I don't agree with his actions, but I don't know what to do."

Lisa stared at him. Rage, confusion and love all wrapped up into a single emotion. Trevor stooped down and sat down beside her on the floor. She put her head onto his shoulder and began to weep.

"I'm scared, Trev."

"I know. Me, too."

Chapter 22: Phoenix Down

The Vegas air was still and dry. It was frigid outside, but it still felt like a desert. The dust had finally settled after almost a week of intense winds. The air smelled new like the dust had cleaned the environment. *Ironic how dirt can be a cleaning agent*, Nida thought to herself.

She was sitting outside holding Tahir in her arms. He was crying because he was hungry, but Nida had nothing left to give him. The guards barely supplied enough food to survive, and that was not enough to produce enough milk for Tahir. Abdul and Nida had begged the guards for some formula or anything to help with the baby. They had not obliged.

It had been eight months since they arrived at the internment camp. Over time, it became clear that wealthy Muslims were targeted first and foremost. Most of the families that had arrived at this camp had come from wealthy backgrounds. They were likely targeting those with assets and power to make it easier to go after the rest according to Mahmoud, another prisoner staying in their barracks. Mahmoud was a bit of a conspiracy theorist in Nida's view. She still believed that this was all a big misunderstanding, and that they would be back home one day.

It was about midday. The men had not returned from their internment labor requirements yet. Mahmoud said it was just slavery with a twist. Abdul agreed with him, but Nida again thought he was just being an alarmist. It made complete sense to help the government sustain the cost of feeding them, Nida thought. She was still angry at the guard who had accosted her, though. The feeling of helplessness overwhelmed Nida at times, causing random bouts of crying and a catatonic state.

There was a doctor that had been taken away about two weeks ago that had told her she was suffering from PTSD. He had told the guards that Nida needed to be hospitalized and observed for a time, but once the guards figured out he was a doctor, they took him away to their hospital. Nida was still suffering.

She went back inside the barracks-prison that they had come to call home. The older couple had been moved out about a month prior. Supposedly, they had been set free to return to their home. Mahmoud suspected that they were simply killed for being useless. Again, Nida just believed him to be a conspiracist. *We are all Americans, after all*, Nida thought.

Mahmoud had arrived approximately three weeks after Nida's attack. Abdul and he became fast friends as they shared common political and religious beliefs. They spent many nights debating philosophy and the world. Nida listened but they did not allow her to speak very often. When she did, Abdul dismissed her as uneducated. She was used to these dismissals. It was how women were treated where she was from. Mahmoud would always listen, though. He was raised in America by Christian foster parents.

Mahmoud's parents had died during the initial Iraq surge. The soldiers there put him up for foster care in America. Mahmoud was only three when he came to America and was adopted by the age of four. He went to a Catholic high school and then attended university in Chicago. To his core, Mahmoud was a conservative. The Republic was the core of Mahmoud's identity. He was horrified at the actions of President Drum and would spend his evenings going on political diatribes about how offensive his actions were to the dream of the Founders. Nida listened intently to every word he said, even if she believed it to be a bit extreme.

He was compelling and intelligent. Nida loved him. It was a different type of love, like that of a mentor to a student rather than a lover. Nida had never been to school. It wasn't allowed for women when she grew up in Saudi Arabia. Listening to Mahmoud was the only education she was likely to ever receive. So, she hung on his every word. She began to believe in the idea of what America could be through Mahmoud's eyes.

She laid down on her bunk and began to write. It was strange that the guards refused to give them food for their baby, but if you asked them for paper and pencil, they were happy to oblige. Unfortunately, it was out of these strange green notepads that they carried on their person. The Army was apparently adamant about soldiers' abilities to take notes at any time.

Nida began to try and write down what Mahmoud and Abdul had been saying last night. She started to try and write down and read what they discussed each and every night. This was how she learned. She began:

> *"The Founders created a system of checks and balances to ensure that power could not concentrate too much into the hands of the few. They harnessed the need for conflict that is at the heart of every man into a system of government. The large assumption that they had made was that the selfishness of each man would inhibit their desire to be unfaithful to the Republic for the benefit of another.*

They miscalculated though. They misunderstood the scope of personal loyalty, and the ability of people with an agenda to act in concert. The structure of the government could not survive the advent of mass communication and the ability for a single person to dictate the message to millions of people simultaneously.

The result of their miscalculation led to Drum. He was the perfect storm of deep personal loyalty and charismatic enticement that fooled the masses. It was like he was created in a lab for this exact purpose."

Nida was still writing when the doors of the barracks opened. Abdul and Mahmoud walked in with a few of the other men that had been working. Nida was the only woman left in the barracks. They had tried to move her to a separate barracks, but Captain Winters had intervened on their behalf. The Captain was a nice man. He was just about the only nice man that they had encountered at this camp.

Behind the men walked three guards. One of them was Sergeant Harrington, the one who had attacked Nida. He looked at her and smiled, almost as if he reveled in the fear that he caused her. Nida couldn't bring herself to look him in the eyes. She was mortified that they had let him out of his cell and cleared him of any wrongdoing. The court martial found that Nida had provoked the attack despite having no evidence. Captain Winters indicated he was barred from testifying by his commanding officer, Lt. Col. McAdams.

Lt. Col. McAdams walked in behind the three guards and scanned the room. Once he saw where Nida was with Tahir, he walked over to them. He gestured for the guards to follow him into the barracks, and they filed into a line and gripped their weapons.

"Ma'am, with authority of Executive Order 13307 signed by President Harold Drum, no children may stay in the Terrorist Internment Camps. We are required by law to send your child out of the camp for its own safety. Please give us the child."

Nida was in shock. *No, no, no, no, no.* Her mind was a fog of swirling confusion. She would not give up her child. She pulled Tahir away from the man and crawled further into the corner of her bunk.

McAdams turned to the guards accompanying him and waved. They stepped forward and began to grab at Nida. Abdul and Mahmoud began shouting, "LEAVE HER ALONE!" They rushed forward to try and peel the guards off of Nida. McAdams took out his pistol and shot both of them. They both slumped down to the ground, Abdul was shot in the leg and Mahmoud was shot in the chest. Their blood began spreading out over the concrete.

Nida screamed, terrified. McAdams walked over to Mahmoud, put the pistol to his head and pulled the trigger. Nida screamed again as she watched the only person who had ever taught her anything die in front of her. McAdams walked over to Abdul, looked into Nida's eyes, and repeated the action.

By this time, the guards had been able to pry Tahir from Nida. McAdams took the child in his arms and began to walk out of the barracks. Tahir was screaming and crying furiously, the noise had woken him up from a nap.

Nida was catatonic. Sergeant Harrington grabbed her by the ankles again and pulled her to him. This time, nobody was coming to save her. He began to unzip and pull down his pants.

He leaned over Nida and pulled up the dress she was still wearing. Nida reached up to her hair bun and pulled one of the pins out. When Sergeant Harrington's face got close to hers, she stabbed the pin into his eye. He yelled out in pain and landed a right hook on Nida's jaw. She immediately went unconscious, but Sergeant Harrington withdrew, more concerned about keeping his eye than raping a lifeless body. How noble.

Nida awoke in a different place than when she had gone to sleep. She tried to reach up and touch her face where Harrington had hit her, but she could only bring her hand about halfway up to her face. There were shackles on her wrists and ankles. She was in a much smaller room; it looked like a cell. The chains that were attached to the shackles had their opposite end attached to small circles on the wall. She was completely restrained.

A flood of memories came back into her mind. She began to sob uncontrollably. Her entire world was gone. Her husband was dead. Her child was taken from her. Her teacher was dead. Her barracks were gone. Her house was gone. Her life was shattered into a million pieces. Gone was the idea that she could go home one day. She couldn't hold back the well of darkness in her soul any longer. So, she wept.

She heard footsteps coming down the hall. There were two or three sets of steps, she had learned to count the guards by footsteps during her time in the barracks. There was a rap at the door and then a loud clank. The door swung open. It was the same three guards who had attacked Nida previously. Harrington was the middle one, and he was sporting a new eyepatch. They stepped into the cell and closed the door behind them.

None of them seemed interested in the carnal pleasures they had been previously. They were here for revenge. Harrington took his guard stick off of his belt and swung it at Nida's arm. She screamed in pain. The two other guards followed suit. They began to strike Nida in rapid succession and in perfect concert. This was not their first time doing this as a team.

Nida's screams gave way to exhaustion. She lost consciousness. The guards left her there. Broken, bleeding, defeated. She looked like an ash heap on the ground, cold and lifeless.

Chapter 23: Behind the Curtain

Trent was laying down in the small, metal bunk that had been provided to him by the Secret Service. One of his ankles was chained to the bunk. They had given him books to read, a small concession to an otherwise high value prisoner. One of the guards had told him that he was reported as dead to the world. Everyone thought Trent Kennedy had been killed during what was being called the Democratic Insurrection. The country had largely bought into the lie.

I'm going to spend the rest of my life in this cell, and nobody even knows that I'm here. Trent was distraught at his fortunes. He had been in the cell for what seemed like an eternity. Nobody would tell him how much time had actually passed, and there was nobody seemingly authorized to talk to him. The guard that told him he was dead hadn't shown back up again.

He began reading *Julius Caesar* by Shakespeare. They had only given him classics. Trent had never slowed down to read that type of book. For the most part, Trent had really never read much at all. At school, they had tutors just tell them what was in the books. As a criminal prosecutor, he had paralegals do the same and used his charm and charisma to sway juries. As a Congressman, he had aides break things down and give him presentations. Reading wasn't really Trent's style, but it was the only thing he had left in this purgatory.

Suddenly, he heard the door start to open. Harold Drum walked into the cell. Trent didn't move, he just kept reading. He did not want to give the impression that he was surprised in any way. The instinct to play politics still raged on in his mind. *Optics matter*, Trent thought to himself.

"Good Evening, Trent. I hope your stay here in the White House has been pleasant enough." Harold chuckled under his breath.

"Oh, it's been right pleasant. Hope yours has been, as well." Trent still hadn't looked away from his book. He was trying to act like this was a normal conversation. The shackle around his ankle belied his best efforts for nonchalance.

"It has been nice as of late. Much better without all of these annoying liberals trying to get in my way. We have been able to accomplish so much in recent weeks." A Secret Service agent brought in a chair for Harold, and he sat down. Trent looked at the man, and he noticed that the American flag had been altered on his pin. Instead of the 50 stars in the blue block, there was a circle with a trident through it.

"You changed the flag?" Trent blinked, utterly bewildered. Harold boisterously laughed at this, down to his belly.

"We've changed the entire government, my friend. No longer are we the United States of America, we are now the Christian States of America. We felt a new flag was important to establish a symbol of our new found freedom." Harold sat back in the chair, clearly pleased with himself.

"But, how? How is there not rioting in the streets?" Trent was shocked. *How long have I been in here?* He thought to himself. There were no windows to count the days. Trent had completely lost track of the concept of time.

"There was at first, but they were dealt with. The rest of the people fell in line quickly enough. The majority were more than happy to finally have the Christian nation we all felt was intended by our Founders." Harold got up from the chair and began to proselytize.

"You see, Trent, fear is the strongest motivation of the masses. If they fear you as they fear God, there is nothing that you can't do. I'm still the President, but that's just an illusion." Harold paused and looked at Trent, staring into his eyes, "I'm God, now. Or, at least, as close to God as one human can get." Harold smiled.

"You're insane. I can't believe that I helped you. If I would have known that this was your goal, I never would have gone along with this. You said that you just wanted to move us toward a religious revival, not a theocracy!" Trent was mortified. He could barely contain his sorrow. The Republic had collapsed on his watch, and he helped make it happen.

"Insane? Hmm… nobody has ever suggested such a thing. It's perfectly possible. I don't think I am, but I'll yield to the judgment of the psychiatrists on my staff," Harold chuckled softly, he thought he was very clever, "You see, Trent, you've lost. Your world is shattered, we live in my world now." Harold continued his pacing back and forth.

"Once I'm finished rounding up all of these Muslims, I'll turn my attention to the Catholics, Jews, homosexuals, and Mormons. It will be difficult to uproot them, but it must be done. The Christian church must win, and humanity must stay obedient to God. Do you

215

understand, Trent?" Trent looked as if he was just informed his family was murdered.

"W-why? Catholics and Mormons are Christian, just like you!" Harold walked over and slapped him in the face.

"They are nothing like us! They are evil fiends who worship Lucifer himself! The only thing that separates us from the animalistic savages we used to be is our belief in the one true God. If we continue to allow humanity to move away and pledge their loyalty to false Gods, we will be ruined." Harold was rubbing his hand. It was not easy to slap a man that was much larger than you. Trent had lost a considerable amount of weight in captivity, but he was still an imposing figure.

"Don't you understand? If we continue to allow scientists and intellectuals to control the world order, we will destroy ourselves. Sometimes curiosity opens doors that can never be shut again. The goal of the Caliphate is to keep humanity within its proper confines. Devotion to God, subservience to God's will on Earth. This is the path forward."

"You mean subservience to you and your cronies." Trent spat back at Harold. Harold raised his hand to strike Trent again, but Trent didn't react. "Hit me again, you hit like a child."

Harold smiled and looked around the room. He saw the book that Trent was reading and laughed. He walked over and picked up the book. Leafing through the pages, he began to scan some of the lines of the famous play. Closing the book, Harold breathed in deeply and closed his eyes. Then, Harold walked back over to Trent and handed him the book.

"You know, I'm our era's Caesar. I was forced into a corner, and I made a decision that would change the structure of my world forever. I did not want to destroy this country, I wanted to give it a new life, a new purpose. You and your cronies pushed me over the edge. You tried to end my work before it could be complete." Harold walked over and placed his hand on Trent's shoulder, he clapped his shoulder a few times.

"Ironically, you made it easier for me to implement my vision. A process that would have taken years and possibly would have never been complete. Your little puppet, Washington, let us win in a way that we never thought possible. Your insistence that we get the media into the Caliphate was even more helpful. The mouthpieces convinced the country that WE were the ones under attack."

Harold crouched down to where he was directly level with Trent's position sitting on the bed. He pulled out two cigarettes from a pack he had in his coat pocket. He put one in his mouth and handed one to Trent. He lit both and took a drag. He sat back down in the chair and leaned back.

"In fact, the only reason you're alive is because of how instrumental you were in all of this. It seems a great waste to get rid of such a shrewd political mind." Harold dragged on the cigarette again and exhaled, "I'm here to see if you will serve me willingly."

Trent cocked an eyebrow and looked up at Harold. His pulse accelerated and his mind raced with possibilities. *It's either stay in here and rot or help a madman continue his power grab.* Wrestling with the prospect of aiding the man who had slaughtered the world's most powerful government, Trent couldn't bring himself to agree. Something inside of him resisted the pull to survive.

"I will never help you. My loyalty is to the people you murdered. I will not be the puppet of a butcher." Trent whispered this in a quiet recalcitrance, loud enough for Harold to hear.

"You misunderstand, Trent. I was giving you the option to help willingly. You're still going to help me, but you will not like how we get there." With that, Harold stood up and walked out of the room. Two men walked in with an empty 50-gallon drum and a basin of water. One of them was carrying a pitcher. They began to set up. Trent sighed in defeat because he knew what was coming.

Chapter 24: Into the Wind

It was turning into fall. The lush North Carolina mountains began to turn into a brilliant rainbow of impending loss. Light shown down through the canopy in solid beams, creating a bright but shadowy effect. The bite of the fall chill nibbled at your face and made you clutch your arms into your stomach to stay warm. The breeze rushing through the trees created a peaceful sound that brought one closer to serenity.

Luther was tending his fire, smoke slowly rising out of the pit into the sky. He was careful not to build a fire too big in the event that someone was around, he didn't want to be found. He reached his hand up to scratch his face and encountered a scruff beard that had begun to grow out significantly. It had been several months since he fled into the woods. He had survived initially by going into the nearby town at night and getting what scraps he could out of the trash cans. Eventually, he built up enough materials and supplies to start a camp.

He had created a small little hut for himself by a secluded lake. There were no paths that Luther could find around the lake, and there was plentiful wildlife. He had set up a number of fish traps in the lake and lived handsomely from their fruits. At first, he cooked the fish on a stick and ate them that way but kept getting bones with the fish. About a month in, he found a fishing knife that someone had discarded in one of the trash cans. It was old and rusted, but Luther could make it work.

He began to cut the fish into clean filets and then smoke them. There was a feeling of fulfillment in continuing to survive in the wild. Every day, Luther thought of his grandfather, Marcus. Marcus had been the one to teach Luther everything he knew about survival, hunting, fishing and camping. Each day that Luther defied capture and avoided death in the wilderness was a day he felt he honored Marcus's memory. He bit into one of the smoked trout filets he had made the previous week. *Smoked meat lasts so much longer, but I don't know why,* Luther thought to himself.

When Luther was young, he would ask Marcus the "why" behind everything. Marcus would always reply the same way, "The 'why' is not important, all you need to know is that it is." Luther never stopped wondering why.

The fire began to die, so Luther got up and threw another log onto it. The log was a bit damp, so it took time for the heat of the coals to dry it out. Luther's wood pile had begun to diminish, it had been about two days since he went and collected any wood. He got up and retrieved his hatchet from the hut where he kept it. Then, Luther went looking for good dead wood on the forest floor. He had to find something to fuel the fire before it died, there was nothing dry to start another fire. If this one went out, it would be several days before Luther could start another one.

The lake gave way to a small creek that trickled down the side of the mountain. Luther used the creek as a guide in order to travel around this area of the woods effectively. Once you went down the creek about four-hundred feet or so, there was a great valley. Four mountains peaked on the horizon, and the trees sprawled in their orange and red majesty as far as the eye could see. The great sprawl of humanity hadn't quite made it out to this remote area. So, nature remained uninterrupted.

There were a great many birds singing, and tree frogs could be heard croaking. Sounds like these calmed Luther and made him feel at home.

About three miles down the creek, Luther found what he was looking for: a large branch that had fallen from a nearby pine tree. Pine didn't burn very well, but it was better than nothing. Luther began to drag the large branch back up the creek. The intent was to drag the branch all the way back to the hut prior to cutting it into smaller pieces. It took about two and a half hours to drag the branch back to camp, and Luther was exhausted from the effort.

Luther stopped a while to rest after he had returned to camp. He had set up a water evaporator system that gave him clean water to drink. So, he took out his recycled bottle and began to drink from it. Taking a bite out of the smoked fish he had left out prior to leaving, he relaxed his shoulders and began to drift off into a joyous slumber.

In the corner of his mind, something awoke Luther. He heard voices and rustling in the distance. His hut was concealed, but the fire was still smoldering so anyone could easily figure out where he was. In the months he had been at this lake, nobody had even come close to him. He didn't expect anyone to ever come out here, and Luther didn't know what to do. Stamping out the fire, Luther elected to hide as best as he could.

Luther moved slowly out of the hut and closed the door behind him. He took his hatchet with him. There was a series of taller trees on the opposite side of the lake that made a much thicker wall. Luther went and hid behind those trees, trying to escape the voices by running away from their source. He watched the lake for what felt like forever, and out of the tree line on the far side of the trees, two figures emerged. There were two women in hiking gear. Both had white skin, but one had dreaded hair that was pulled back and tied up with a bandana.

They stayed for some time at the lake's edge, admiring the beauty that Luther had grown used to. Each of them took off their packs and set them down. They started to take their tent and sleeping bags off of their packs. Eventually, they got their tent set up and put their stuff in it. Each of them stripped down to their underwear and went to swim in the water.

"Freaking cold!" One of them shouted so loudly, Luther could hear it clearly from where he was hiding. Luther was terrified, he didn't know how long these women intended on staying, and he wouldn't be able to get back to his hut without being noticed. The choice was between staying behind these trees until they left or introducing himself and hoping they didn't know who he was. Although, he didn't know how they would receive the news that there was another person in a secluded lake area near them. He also had no idea what he looked like, so he was scared that he might frighten the two women even if he did say something.

Paralyzed by indecision and the specter of being caught, Luther stayed behind the trees. The two women got out of the lake and dried off, putting their clothes back on. Curiosity got the best of them and they began to explore around the lake.

"Hey, there's a hut over here, and it looks like there's a fire that hasn't been put out." Luther could hear them talk to each other; the stillness of the mountains made the sound carry more than usual.

"Strange, do you think there's someone up here? I thought you said nobody knew about this place?" The one with dreads said to the brunette she was with.

"I mean, I assumed nobody knew where it was, but we have satellites in the sky and stuff. I'm sure someone could figure out where this was if they really wanted to." The brunette had a squeaky voice.

Luther figured this was the best time to approach them since they already figured someone was here. He made his way back around the lake, trying to be as loud and conspicuous as possible to let the women know he wasn't trying to be stealthy.

"Wait, I hear something... be quiet." The dreaded one said to the brunette.

"Hello?!" she shouted.

Now or never, I suppose, Luther thought to himself. "Hello!" Luther shouted back.

"Who are you? What's your name?" She shouted back in response.

"My name is Marcus, what's yours?" Luther shouted back.

"My name is Olivia and my friend's name is Patricia. Are you a weirdo?" This brought out an audible laugh from Luther.

"No, not a weirdo. Just a man who's down on his luck. I live here." Luther was uneasy about being so honest, but figured it was the only way.

"Oh, well, we like your hut. Can you come out and show yourself?" Luther put the hatchet into the back waist of his pants and covered it with his shirt.

"I'm coming out." Luther walked from the tree where he was hiding into clear view of both of the girls. Now that Luther could see them, they were middle aged. They seemed to be together, and they were standing very defensively. Despite their kind overture, they were still incredibly nervous about meeting a strange man in a secluded area of the woods. Often, natural instinct rather than reason is what guides the initial reaction in any setting.

Finally, Luther made it up to the edge of the clearing where he had made his fire and set up his hut. The girls were essentially face to face with him, and the clear sight of his face made them recoil. His appearance was that of a wild man. His face was smeared with mud and grime, his beard scraggly and untamed. The clothes he had were mostly taken from the garbage and were tattered and worn in addition to being stained by the filth. Several months in the wilderness will turn any person into a savage.

"Holy shit, dude. Are you okay? How long have you lived out here?" The brunette was plugging her nose with her left hand as if she could smell him. In her right hand was the unmistakable canister of pepper spray. These women were fighters, and they weren't stupid, Luther could surmise that much from their precautions.

"I'm not really sure, to be honest. Being out here has a way of making time meaningless." Luther walked past them into the hut and grabbed some of the smoked fish. Grabbing one of the skewers that he had made, he put the fish on the skewers and handed it to the girls. The blonde one with dreads took it from him and smelled it. She frowned, but in a way that made Luther think she expected it to smell worse.

"Thank you. This is very kind." She took a bite of the fish and then handed the skewer to her friend.

"Consider it a token of good will. What are your names again?" Luther walked to the edge of the lake and began to splash water on his face. He hadn't thought to wash himself in weeks, so he figured now was as good a time as any.

"I'm Patricia, and this is Olivia." The brunette spoke and gestured towards the blonde when she said the second name.

Luther smiled, "Well, my name is Marcus. It's a pleasure to meet y'all. Gotta be honest, it's nice to talk to people again. Being out here alone, well, it's lonely as you might imagine."

The civility and softness of Luther's voice relaxed Patricia and Olivia. Patricia put the pepper spray that she was holding in her pocket. She was still gnawing on the fish that Luther had handed her, she seemed to enjoy it.

Patricia spoke up again, "Well, if you can't tell us how long you've been out here, can you tell us why you're out here?" She seemed honestly interested, as if she was fascinated about why someone would choose to live alone in the wilderness.

"Society left me behind, so I felt like I had to leave society. Just had no place anymore." Luther was being sincere if extremely veiled and vague. He felt like he could never go back. After hearing the news of the crackdown in Washington, Luther knew that if he was ever discovered he would die. *Hopefully my face is obscured enough that they don't recognize me…* Luther thought to himself. Patricia seemed to accept that answer, nodding along as he spoke.

"I get that. We run away into the woods more often than we stay at home. We're both teachers, so we spend our breaks in the woods no matter what." Patricia was doing most of the talking, Olivia was just staring at Luther. *She knows,* Luther thought to himself.

"Is something wrong Olivia?" Luther asked.

"I just… I feel like I know you. Like I've seen your face before. I can't put my finger on it." Her face twisted into a crunch. She was trying to remember a ghost, and her mind couldn't pull out the image. "Ah well, I'm sure it's just my imagination."

"Well, if you figure it out let me know, I'd like to know who I look like." Luther chuckled but glanced sideways towards Olivia to see her reaction. She was still trying to figure it out.

Luther turned towards rebuilding the fire. First, he needed to chop the large branch up that he had retrieved the previous day. The weather had been bright and sunny today, so the fire was easier to start back up with the dry wood. *Thwack, thwack, thwack,* Luther chopped at the wood. *What if she knows who I am?* Luther's mind was racing. *Thwack, thwack, thwack. What if she tells someone I'm out here?* Luther's mind began to be overwhelmed with a paranoia that hadn't existed before the arrival of the girls. *Thwack, thwack, thwack. I can't let them leave. Thwack, thwack, thwack.* Luther stacked two pieces of freshly cut wood into the stack. The girls were still sitting at the camp chewing on the fish.

Olivia's eyes widened. The prolonged exposure jogged her memory. She leaned over to Patricia and whispered something into her ear. Patricia's eyes lit up the same way. Luther knew that there wasn't much time left. *Remember who you are.* He heard Marcus in his head, but this time there was a different voice that he hadn't heard in a long time. It was his father's. A memory so old that it wasn't something he consciously remembered. *At the end of the day, son, the only choice we have is to live or die. Survive.* Luther looked over at the girls. They were unsettled and were clearly starting to get up to leave. *Survive.*

"What's the matter?" Luther said in a soft but imperious tone, as if he expected an answer.

"We're just going to go back to our camp. Nothing's wrong." Patricia was obviously the talker of the two.

"Why? I'm just about to get the fire started, why don't you stay a while?" Luther couldn't let them leave, but he'd prefer the easy way.

"Well, we're actually going to camp somewhere else, we don't want to crowd you. This is your home." Patricia was backing up slowly.

"You can't leave. I know you know who I am." Luther stood up and grabbed the hatchet. Patricia pulled out the pepper spray and sprayed it at Luther. She missed as Luther dashed to the left and rolled on his shoulder. Something in Luther snapped. All he could see was red. Patricia tried to spray him again with the pepper spray, but Luther sidestepped the stream and closed on her quickly.

He knocked the pepper spray to the ground and brought down the ax into Patricia's head. Blood squirted from the wound and she fell limp to the ground. Olivia had already begun running after the first miss. She was screaming for help in a shrill, desperate panic. Luther chased after her, primal instinct moving him through the forest with the swiftness of a hunter. Luther began to gain on her. When he was about two feet from her, Luther leaped and tackled her to the ground. She clawed at his face and tore ribbons into his skin. Luther roared in anger, but he brought the hatchet down into her skull. Her body went lifeless.

Swelling with primal fury, Luther reveled in his kill. After a moment, the bloodlust of victory began to wane. He looked below and saw what he had done. *Oh, God. What have I done?!* His stomach twisted and he puked all over the ground next to him. His mind was rejecting this action, and it was taking it out on the body which had done it. Inside his head was like a circus. The two parts of him were clashing for control and it was ripping Luther apart. *Remember who you are.* Luther vomited. *Survive.* Luther vomited. *Survive. Remember. Survive. Remember. Survive.* Luther let out a primal roar and clutched his stomach. He fell to the ground and passed out. Blackness.

Chapter 25: The Beast Awakens

Luther arose from his stupor. He put his hand on the ground and the ground was wet from the blood that had poured out of Olivia's head. The grim reality of what had passed dawned on Luther's fresh mind. He went to the edge of the lake and washed the blood off his hands and face.

They knew who I was. Luther began to wrestle with his feelings. *If I had let them go, they would have told someone that I was out here. I would have been found, and they would kill me. I had to do it. Oh, God why did I kill someone? How could I have done this?* Luther couldn't control the tempest that swirled inside of him. His mind was fracturing, and he could not stop the schism.

Luther's mind snapped to the conversation he had with his father. It seemed like an incomplete memory, barely on the cusp of Luther's consciousness. He was young, no older than six or seven. Luther's mother had just died, and he was sitting in the car in the cemetery after they had just buried her. His father got into the car. He was a slender man, but tall. He had gaunt, drawn features on his face. The defining feature of him was his deep, black eyes. He was in a black suit with a black tie and his hair was slicked straight back like a mafia don.

They both sat there for a time. Neither of them said anything, allowing the collective sadness to be unspoken. It was like a putrid moisture that they could taste, but they didn't want to open their mouths to make it any worse.

"Son, you may not remember this, but you need to listen to me. Sometimes the world acts in ways that we can't predict. The only thing that we can do is choose how to react to the circumstances at hand." He took out a cigarette and lit it. He took a long drag from the cigarette, then rolled down the manual window and ashed it outside of the car. It was raining, so some of the rain droplets got in the car and sprayed them both with the ricochets.

"Your mother's people believe that growth and life are the way of things, but my people have always seen things differently. See, we understand the truth, that death is part of life. The two are a necessary balance to each other. Yin and yang. Push and pull." He took another drag of the cigarette.

"Reality is, you're either fighting or you're dying. There's no in between. The only choice that you have, son, is to decide. The only decision that you must make is whether to fight or die." There were tears rolling down his face. He was suffering. A man broken by the reality of chaos that existed all around them. This man had created an entire life, gathered allies and power, devoted himself to the system that his parents had created; and yet, his happiness was taken from him in an instant. One careless driver, one second of indecision, and his wife was gone. When a man cracks, and the thin armor he has against the sorrow of reality breaks, what is left is dangerous.

"Live or die. Survive. You must always survive. Death is the enemy, but it will always win. Fight as long as you can, as hard as you can, but we all inevitably fail." Luther's father took another drag of the cigarette.

Suddenly, Luther was back at the edge of the lake. The ache of nostalgia washed over him. He hadn't seen his father in years, and Luther was unsure of whether he was alive or dead. He hadn't thought of him in even longer. After his father had dropped him with Marcus and Joanne, Luther spent decades resenting the man. It seems that Luther turned out more like his dad than he cared to. *Survive.* Luther couldn't drive the thought from his head. Looking down at his grim harvest, Luther knew what had to be done. He began to dig a hole with his hands.

After several hours of digging, Luther's hands were thrashed and bloody. He barely had dug deep enough to fit both of them in the hole, but he was fairly certain they would fit. He dragged Olivia in first since she was the closest, and then went to get Patricia next. The sand covered both of them by about an inch, but it did cover them. Luther stood up and stared at the fresh mound.

He walked over to where they had set down their packs originally. Rummaging through the packs, Luther found two cell phones, money, a Swiss-army knife, water purification tablets, a water pouch with a hose on it to drink out of, fresh socks, a large box of matches, pots and pans, and Luther took one of their far superior backpacks for himself. He loaded the other pack and the items Luther did not need with rocks and tossed it into the lake. Turning back towards his hut, he grabbed all of his fish and put them into his new pack. He rolled up his sleeping bag and lashed it to the side of his pack. Finally, Luther knocked the support beams out of his hut and it collapsed to the ground.

With one last look at the lake that Luther had called home, he set off to find a new one. *They'll be looking for these girls sooner rather than later, I can't stay here.* Luther sighed and turned away. He began walking. He didn't know where he was going, but he knew he couldn't stay here.

So, he walked. For several days, he walked during the day and camped at night. He didn't have much fish left after the fifth day, and started to ration it. His stomach grumbled and ached. His legs began to get shaky as he continued to move forward. He came to an uphill climb. The terrain was rocky, and the way forward wasn't clear. Putting his left leg onto one of the rocks, he tried to hoist himself up. The leg gave out and he slipped. Luther tumbled down the ledge. As he rolled, he hit a few trees, but his momentum didn't stop. There was a cliff that Luther got glimpses of when he was rolling. There was no way to stop himself before the cliff. Accepting his fate, Luther closed his eyes.

He launched off the cliff. Luther felt the oppressive pull of gravity leave momentarily. He was floating. In that moment, he felt a clarity he had never felt before. A clarity that only comes when one has accepted their death. Then, he felt water. Then, blackness.

The light stung Luther's face. There was sand under his head and he cracked his eyes open to witness what had befallen him. His right arm felt a sharp stabbing and his body ached. There was water at his feet, Luther tried to sit up but the pain was too great. He collapsed back onto the ground. *Survive.* Luther kept hearing his father's voice. *I can't, I can't fight anymore.* Luther accepted his defeat and laid his head down to rest.

Hours passed and the warm embrace of death hadn't yet welcomed Luther into its waiting arms. He heard a slight jingling in the distance followed by a slight patter of footsteps. Suddenly, Luther felt warm breath on his face, and then some licks. Luther cracked his eye open to see what was going on and saw a large German Shepherd standing over him.

"TITUS!" Luther heard someone yell. The dog stopped licking Luther and walked over to where the voice had originated. "Good boy Titus, where did you get off to?" Luther could hear the man talking to him, and then Titus barked.

"Oh my god!" Luther heard the man exclaim. Then the man began to walk towards Luther. The man began to shake Luther, "Wake up!"

Luther opened his eyes and groaned but couldn't muster anything else. The man pulled out a radio and called to someone, "Hey boss, we got a bit of a situation here." A voice over the radio came back, "What's up, Raul?"

"I just found a guy on the side of the river up here at the foot of the falls. He's got a tree limb through his arm and looks like he's about to die." Luther moaned again.

"What's the problem then? Leave him there."

"Jar, I think this is that guy the feds are after." The man said back. Daggers of fear struck into Luther's heart. *He knows.* Luther tried to react, but his body didn't respond.

"Who?" The man replied.

"Washington." There was a long silence.

"We're on the way." The man, *his name is Raul,* Luther remembered from overhearing the conversation, reached down towards Luther's arm. He tugged at the branch that had pierced through his arm. It didn't move. Raul reached into his pack and pulled out a tourniquet and placed it above Luther's wound. He wound the tourniquet and Luther screamed out in pain. Luther passed out from the pain.

Luther awoke on a bed. The bed was soft, but he could feel the springs like it was a cot. He looked around and saw a few cots around him with some belongings strewn about the room. The room looked like an old congregation building for a church. There was even a large crucifix at the far end of the room. The entire place had been converted for… something. Luther almost thought it might be a business of some sort.

He looked down at his arm. It was still there, but heavily bandaged. *Strange. Where am I?* Luther was totally out of sorts. He began to panic. *They knew who I was, I have to get out of here.* He began to look around for his pack and couldn't find it. Losing his cool, Luther began to grab all the items around him that he thought could be useful. If he couldn't find his own pack, he would at least get enough to survive and rebuild.

In his mad dash to abscond with as many supplies as possible, he had stopped paying attention to his surroundings. "Excuse me, what do you think you're doing?"

There was a tall black man standing at the far end of the room. Luther didn't know how long he had been watching, or if he had been there the entire time. Frozen, Luther began to place things back on a table that was close to him.

"W-Where am I? Who are you?"

The man smiled. He had a drink in his hand and pulled the cup up to take a swig. After he was done, he placed the drink in front of him. Luther had barely noticed the desk in front of the man. There was a computer on it. He had been working there the entire time and had probably seen Luther wake up and start rummaging around.

"My name is Jartavius Gaston. You're in the High Falls Baptist Chapel near Brevard, North Carolina. We found you half dead on the side of the Nantahala."

Still in North Carolina... Okay...

"You know who I am?" Luther asked the man timidly. Jartavius nodded his head and took another drink.

"Yeah, only reason we saved you. Thought we might get a reward from the feds for turning you in." Luther's eyes widened. *Survive.* The word rang in his head like an alarm bell. Luther began to survey the room for an exit or a weapon. Flight or fight were both options, but he had to do one.

Jartavius gave a huge belly laugh, "Calm down there. We ain't turnin' you in. You think we'd call the feds? Man, I'd sooner shoot one dead than deal with them." Luther looked at him confused.

"Follow me." Jartavius waved for him to follow. *I guess I have nothing to lose*, Luther thought to himself and began to follow him. Jartavius led Luther down a flight of stairs to a basement area. Once they got down there, Luther's jaw dropped. From floor to ceiling were racks of marijuana plants and lights to grow them. There were a few men cutting the plants and a few others watering and trimming the leaves. Luther counted four total men and one woman.

"You see, we don't deal with the feds too much round these parts." Jartavius laughed again. Luther was stunned.

"Why would you show me this?" Jartavius looked at him after he spoke and smiled.

"Well, we talked for a bit when you were out. You were asleep for 'bout three days, ya know? Anyways, we was talkin' and figured we can't turn you in cause we can't bring no light to ourselves, and you can't turn us in cause they'd pick you up on the spot and kill ya. So, we figured we'd give ya the chance to help us out. Figure we could trust ya cause you dead either way, ya know?"

Luther steeled himself. *They'll kill me if I say no, and the government will kill me if I run.* Luther held out his hand to the man, "I'm in." Jartavius shook his hand and smiled.

Jartavius leaned in and whispered into Luther's ear, "Don't get it twisted, I own you." *Survive.* Luther heard his dad in his head. *Never forget who you are.* He then heard his grandfather's. Luther's shoulders sunk, *I don't know who I am.* Jartavius waved for him to follow, and Luther followed behind dutifully.

Lisa was perched in a local cafe. She was typing some notes on her laptop. After losing her network job, she had devoted herself to investigating the Lincoln Memorial. So far, she had found nothing but redacted files from her information requests. The government wasn't very forthcoming with information which made her even more curious. *Anything the government doesn't want you to know is generally worth knowing,* Lisa thought to herself.

She started scrolling back through news articles on her laptop about the attack. It was hard to look at. Back then, she was just really getting started as a primary anchor. The Lincoln Memorial was one of the highlights of her career. She won an award for staying on air for twenty-eight hours straight covering the story. It put her on the map and gave her the right to dictate what she reported on.

She kept scrolling, but something caught her eye. More specifically, someone. One of the pictures that the Herald article used had the candidate that was speaking that day, Michael DeLauer. Behind him was someone she thought she recognized. A man with jet black hair and a nice suit, but it was his eyes that set him out. Jet black eyes with a coldness to them stared back into the camera with disdain.

Lisa tried to use the credit lines to see if they identified the person in the photograph, but he was either uncredited or such a small part of the photo nobody ever looked into it. She couldn't shake the feeling that she knew him, though. A waiter came over to her table and poured some more coffee into her mug.

"Hey, do you know this guy?" Lisa asked and pointed onto her screen. The waiter leaned over to look at the screen.

"No, but those eyes are mean. Never seen him before." The waiter shrugged and walked away.

Undeterred, Lisa kept looking into the man. *If he was on the stage, he must have been someone important to the campaign,* Lisa felt like that was her best lead. So, she began to search for the old campaign pages for DeLauer. Hopefully, some of them were still up.

After about an hour or so of mindless scrolling through search results, Lisa was ready to give up on this guy. It was likely a useless endeavor anyway, there weren't many survivors from the Lincoln Memorial. This guy was an unlikely exception if he made it out.

Lisa decided to go watch Trevor's show to take her mind off things and pulled it up on her laptop. She had been watching him lately since she lost her job. It made her proud. They were able to be more together now since she wasn't so publicly opposed to him anymore.

"My next guest is a man who will help set the record straight on the Lincoln Memorial, the director of the Secret Service, James Callahan."

The man walked onto the stage. Lisa knew at that moment that everything Luther Washington said was the absolute truth as she watched those cold dead eyes look back at her from the camera.

Chapter 26: Veritas

Trent was laying in his hard cot. He was breathing slowly and staring at the ceiling. His clothes were dry now, but they had stiffened from the process. The passage of time was imperceptible. Trent was grasping for some concept of when he was, or whether he was.

When the human condition is removed from its monotonous charge forward, what remains is disillusionment. Time moves forward but the husk remains suspended in eternity. Life appears to be an echo, ringing hollow down the endless abyss towards the infinite horizon. Meaningless.

There was still water on the floor from where Trent had been tortured earlier that day. Another day in the endless stream of it. The water had ripples running through it showing that the moon's gravity was pulling at the edges. Even locked down in here, the moon's pull commanded the water to move. Trent's head began to pound, a headache overtook his senses and he couldn't see straight. Unsteady, Trent tried to sit up to gain his senses, but it just made the pounding worse. He vomited in front of him from the pain.

Looking to the left out of the cell, he saw a man sitting there. The man was wearing a simple untucked white button-down shirt and jeans. He looked benign, like he was emitting light and warmth. The man looked up at Trent and smiled. He was tall and lanky. White hair adorned his head, pulled back into a tight bun on the back of his head. His face was adorned with a thin, white beard peppered with some remnants of black. His eyes were steel blue, and they gave off a slight emanation.

"Ah, so you're awake." The man closed the book he was reading and stood up. Walking towards the bars of the cell, the man got right up to them and smiled again. He held his hand out, offering it to Trent. Pounding overtook his senses as he tried to get up, he felt compelled to walk towards him. Resisting the pain and walking forward, he stumbled towards the bars and grabbed his hand. Trent felt better almost immediately, the pain evaporated from his body. It felt like an icy release, but the pain was gone.

"W-w-what is this? What just happened?" Trent looked down at his hands and began to breathe heavily, unable to accept what just happened.

"Sit down, Mr. Kennedy." Trent went back to the cot and sat down. A guard came in and opened the gate and the man stepped through, and he brought the chair he was sitting on with him. He sat down. The guard shut the gate but looked skeptically at the man before doing so.

The man spoke, "You may call me Brother." He handed Trent a book. *Veritas,* it read on the front.

"You've met an agent of mine. His name is Harold. Do you know whom I speak of?" Trent laughed audibly.

"You mean the mad man that just spent forever torturing me? Yes, I'd say we're acquainted." Trent immediately began to distrust Brother, or whatever his name was.

"Good. You must understand that Harold is a means to an end, not an end. He will fall as many tyrants have fallen before him." Brother sounded so sure, so absolute. It sounded like he spoke from knowledge, not from learning or history.

"Why would you do all of this just for him to fall?" Trent was so confused, and his heart was beating out of his chest.

"You misunderstand. You see such a small view of the truth. Harold is an agent of chaos, a necessary fire to burn down what is to rebirth what may be." Brother stood up and touched Trent's head. Trent saw a vision of Rome in its golden age, and then the fires that burned it to the ground. He saw the fall of Constantinople, the destruction of Baghdad by the Mongols, the guillotines falling in Paris, the destruction of Napoleon, the blood of Verdun, and the fires of Dresden. He saw the scope of human history, the push and pull of empire and freedom. Coiling around each other in an eternal dance, never capable of staying in balance.

"What are you?" Trent was in shock, he didn't know what was happening.

"I have been called many things. The reality is that I am none of these things." The man tapped on the book in front of Trent, "this will explain more, but suffice it to say that I am the original human on this planet. I came here from a distant planet known as Tarsus."

He began pacing back and forth. As he twisted back, he began to speak again. "You see, my people destroyed themselves. We were a peaceful people, we lived and died just as you do. One day, a scientist from our world developed a vaccine against aging. Our planet became immortal." He sighed and looked at the ground. "We thought this would be the cure to the downfalls of our society. A cure for the selfish reality we lived in. This was wrong. It made it worse. Once people knew that they would exist forever, they began to want even more of their existence."

He sat back down. "My world destroyed itself with weapons so powerful that the planet died. The only reason me and my compatriots survived was because we were scientists on an expedition to another planet. Our society had made the decision to colonize the universe so that we could give people a new purpose. We didn't realize that our world was gone until years after the sky started to fall."

He raised his hand up to his hair and smoothed it back. This was not information he shared very often, and it almost seemed as if he was telling it for the first time. He sat back in the chair and held out his hand again. Trent took it. He saw a vision of a world on fire, volcanoes erupting and churning.

"This is how we found Earth originally. Wild and untamed. Uninhabitable. We searched the cosmos for other planets. There were several that we tried to settle. We had the genetic materials to reproduce a perfected gene pool, and so we'd produce a tribe of humans and settle worlds. Twelve worlds in total. Their societies flourished and grew, civilizations rose and fell. Eventually, they found the cure as well. Once they gained their immortality, they went the same way. They destroyed each other just like we did. It's ironic, as soon as humanity finds the cure to their shared pain, they end everything permanently. Over and over again in an endless cycle."

Trent wanted to call the man crazy, but he didn't sound insane. He sounded despondent, sad. Like an engineer who kept trying to build something the right way but kept getting it wrong. Like a father who tried to raise a son, only for the son to be just like him.

"My compatriots gave up after Primus, our last planet, fell. They launched themselves down to the planet to die. I couldn't give up. Humanity's existence hung in the balance of my resilience. So, I resolved myself to try one last time. I returned to Earth to find that the planet had become dominated by large, aggressive reptiles. A few of them had shown signs of developing into something more, but they were a necessary sacrifice. I directed a nearby meteor with a gravitational tether towards the planet and wiped them out. It took many years for the environment to calm for humans to inhabit. But, one day, it was ready."

He took the book from Trent's hands and opened it. "This is when the book begins. At the dawn of the last gasp of humanity's existence. The last chance." A tear ran down his cheek, and his eyes had something to them Trent hadn't noticed at the beginning. He was tired, an exhaustion of the spirit borne by eons untold of torment.

"I made a change to the experiment this time though. Instead of perfecting the human condition and then allowing them to grow, I gave them disease. I put them back to the state that we had come from originally back before Tarsus had ever existed, before the great empire of Atlantis conquered our world. It has taken Earth much longer to settle than I had anticipated. The greater fears of death from this world have made people even more aggressive than we had been. It's strange, by trying to make people care for each other more, I made their violent natures even more exacerbated."

"While with the past planets, I had refused any form of intervention, this time I took a different path. I resolved that, if the human race's pinnacle would always lead to destruction, I would keep humanity from ever reaching it. No longer would the goal be to have a settled society based on utopian ideals of peace and tranquility. The only ethic I would ever embrace would be to keep the pendulum swinging, humanity must not discover the cure to aging ever again. They must never reach the pinnacle. So, I've created this little organization whose purpose is to destabilize and subvert progress."

"You're probably wondering why I've told you all of this, aren't you?" Trent nodded, visibly confused.

"I've told you this because you will never leave this place. Harold wanted to incorporate you into his scheme, but you're too shrewd to allow to regain power. You can't be allowed to live." Placing the book on Trent's bed, he stood up and placed his hand on Trent's shoulder. "Goodbye, friend."

Brother walked out of the cell. He turned back once more and looked at Trent. "My name is Altarian." Then, he walked out of the room.

Trent clutched at his chest, something felt wrong. There was a tightness in his heart. He began to spasm, and fell to the ground, cracking his skull open. The guard stared at him, unmoving. Trent looked up and saw the circle with the trident through it. That was the last thing he ever saw.

"Trevor!!" Lisa was banging on the door to his apartment. She had forgotten her key at her apartment, so she couldn't get in, "TREVOR!!" She was shouting at this point, but she knew he was here.

Eventually, he came to the door. It was clear that he had been asleep, his hair was all messed up and his eyes were sensitive to the light. He was only wearing underwear which distracted Lisa momentarily, but she barged in past him and opened up her laptop.

"Look! Look at this!" She pointed onto the screen to James at the picture at the Lincoln Memorial.

Trevor looked at it and then blinked. He then turned his head towards Lisa and cocked an eyebrow.

"What am I looking at here, babe?" He didn't see it.

"Look at that man on the left part of the stage towards the back. Right there." She put her index finger right under his face.

"Huh, that looks like James. Just had him on the show. That's wild, what a resemblance."

Lisa smacked Trevor on the back of the head, "You moron, that IS James Callahan. He was there!"

Trevor took a deeper look at the screen. Lisa could see the wheels turning in his head.

Trevor took a breath and began to speak, "Why would James Callahan be at a political event for a socialist? That doesn't make any sense."

Apparently, the wheels didn't turn that quickly for her handsome acquaintance. She breathed in and breathed out slowly. Her heart had been racing the entire time.

"Who was the Secret Service director during the State of the Union?" Lisa asked, already knowing the answer, but wanting Trevor to come to the realization for himself.

"James, of course. He was appointed about five months before. Why is that relevant?"

"What actions did he take during the State of the Union?" She knew he could figure it out.

"Are you seriously suggesting that it was James who ordered the attacks that day? I don't think he's capable of something-" Lisa smacked him in the back of the head again before he could finish his sentence.

"Are you serious, Trev? The man is a cold-blooded killer. He's the muscle behind Drum."

Trevor sat for a moment. "I don't know, babe. I'll look into it and see if I can find anything. It is super weird that he was there, admittedly."

"Okay, be careful. These people are dangerous." Trevor nodded and went back to lay down. Lisa left and began to make her way back to her apartment.

Once Lisa left, Trevor picked up his phone and called James. After a few rings, James picked up the phone.

"Hey Trevor, what's up man? Couldn't get enough of me earlier?" James chided over the phone.

"No, I couldn't. Needed to ask you a question." Trevor was hesitant.

"Sure, what's up?" James' tone turned serious very quickly.

"Lisa has been looking into the Lincoln Memorial a bit and found a weird photo on the Herald report of it. Were you there?"

"What? Was I at the Lincoln Memorial? No, absolutely not. Where's this picture?"

Trevor breathed a sigh of relief, "Oh, I didn't think it was you, but I had to ask. The guy had a real resemblance to you. It's one of the Herald articles in their archives, I'm not sure which one. Lisa had it up on her laptop. She went back to her place, though. I'll ask her tomorrow."

"Oh, makes sense. Lisa Young? The old ABS anchor? I didn't know y'all were a thing?" James sounded intrigued.

"Well, it's sort of just a physical thing. You know how I am with blondes, haha." James laughed on the other end.

"Good, good. Hey man, thanks for calling. I'll talk to you later, okay?"

"Later dude." Trevor was relieved. He knew there was nothing to the story, but it was good to hear it from James.

There was a bath running in the other room. Lisa needed to relax, so she poured some salts and bubble bath into the tub. She was getting a bottle of white wine from her fridge that she had left chilling earlier. Taking that and a glass into the bathroom, she dipped her feet into the scalding water. She took out her phone and snapped a picture. She sent it to Trevor with a message, *Wish you were in this bath with me. Maybe later. Love you, see you tomorrow.*

The warmth took over her body as she submerged into the water and she felt the instant comfort of the water's warm embrace. As much as the human

247

condition has changed throughout history, the unmistakable joy of bathing never changed. She could feel the echoes of her ancestors in her skin. Closing her eyes, she let herself drift off.

Crrrrk, Lisa heard the sound of a door opening and popped awake. There were three men standing above her. One of the men pushed her head back under the water.

Chapter 27: From the Ashes

They're gone. They're all gone… what is the point? Nida held a thin piece of metal in her hand, her palms were sweaty. There was perspiration running down her back, she was shaking. Rocking back and forth and sobbing uncontrollably, she held the thin piece of metal to her wrist. *Push it in!* She screamed to herself. *Push it in! Go to your loves! Go to your son! WAKE UP!!* She tried to make herself take the final leap, but she couldn't.

The guards had finally taken her back to the barracks after several days of torture. They had beaten her senseless several times over and her body still ached. Her arm felt like it was broken in at least two places, but she was so numb to the pain she didn't care. She tried to feel something more, but all she felt was numbness. Nothing mattered any more. The reason for her existence had been extinguished at the hands of hateful men. She had believed that the world was good, and that good things were on the horizon. How naïve she had been.

She sat on her bunk and stared at the wall. The other inhabitants of the barracks were still asleep, it was early morning. The work bells would sound soon and the walking zombie shuffle of the captive slaves would begin. Recently, they had been put to work mining lithium out of an underground mine in Nevada. The lithium was a fairly recent discovery, and apparently modern mining techniques were not necessary due to the amount of available cheap labor. The guards had loud mouths, so Nida was able to hear their conversations. Her numbness allowed her to work without thought, just going through monotonous actions without regard to the outcome.

The bells finally sounded, and the workers began making the trek towards the mines. *Clank, clank, clank.* The mining pick railed against the stone. *Clank, clank, clank.* The pain in Nida's arm radiated into her chest, causing her body to spasm uncontrollably for a moment. Nida steadied herself and began her work anew. Mindlessly mining the resource that she is being exploited to extract. She began to think of all of the people who suffered like this throughout history. In her head, she pictured her ancestors working in the salt mines, pulling carts, and digging trenches at the end of a sword.

Eventually, the work bells sounded again signaling an end to today's exertion. The subdued cretins shuffled back to their quarters where they received a lukewarm bowl of oats. Today, they had a little sausage in the oats. In a state of freedom, Nida would have been greatly offended by the insult of including pork in a Muslim's dish, but Nida felt that her god had abandoned her in this place. She would not turn down the nutrients for a god that no longer cared.

She sat in her bunk and began to mindlessly shovel the food into her mouth. Eating was the last thing that made her feel the warmth of life, despair had taken the rest of her senses. The rest of the people in this barracks were eating their meals without complaint as well. It was very strange when they started bringing in the Catholics and the Jews, but Nida understood now that the government was specifically for Protestants and Evangelicals; at least, that's what the newcomers kept saying.

It was hard for Nida to see them come in with the same look of resonant hope that she had, only to watch the soldiers beat it out of them one by one. The conditions had worsened over time, and the soldiers began to take more liberties with the people. Assaults and rape became commonplace among the camp, and everyone had to listen to the cries of their neighbors with horrified resignation.

Nida laid her head down on the pillow, desperate to escape her reality for just a few hours. Perhaps she could see Tahir and Abdul's faces once more in her dreams. She closed her eyes and tried to sleep. The door to the barracks opened and two guards entered.

"Everybody up! Random inspection!" Nida panicked, knowing she had the thin piece of metal under her pillow. She grabbed it and held it in her hand, hopefully concealing it.

The guards walked through the barracks, unmaking beds, checking pockets, and physically searching each of the prisoners. They came to a young girl, barely twenty-five years old and began to search her. She was new, they had just brought her in a few days ago. From the looks of her, she was Jewish. She had olive skin and deep black eyes. Her hair was pulled back into a bun, and she had that defiant look of a people defined by oppression and persecution. This would be another chapter in her people's sad legacy. Another victory for ignorance.

When she squirmed and started to resist their search, they began to get more aggressive. The guard who was watching stepped up and slapped her in the face. The original guard, who Nida quickly recognized as Sergeant Harrington by the strap on the back of his head from his eyepatch, began to strip her clothes off. The woman shrieked, "No, PLEASE NO!"

Harrington slapped her across the face again, "Shut up, jew!" He began to strip off her pants, and she continued to resist. This prompted her other guard to get his night stick out and begin to strike the woman. She began to scream in horrifying agony, "HELP ME!! PLEASE NO!!"

What do you have to live for? Nida thought to herself as she watched the woman go through what she had gone through. *Who am I to do nothing when I have nothing to lose?* Nida felt the metal in her hand and her heart began to beat wildly. *They have taken everything from you. Take something from them.* A cold resolution settled over Nida. Her heart rate slowed, the world came into focus. The numbness that had been her reality for the past several days receded and she began to stride forward.

Harrington had begun to pull down his pants to violate the woman as he had so many others as she lay unconscious on the ground. The other guard had moved on to another prisoner and the room stood there silently watching. Nida walked up behind him and without hesitation put the thin piece of metal against his neck and pushed into his throat with as much force as she could muster. Blood spewed forth from the carotid artery, covering the unfortunate girl in the blood of her attacker. His body fell limp on the ground.

Nida grabbed his pistol out of its holster and pointed it at the other guard. Without heed of the consequences, she pulled the trigger. The bullet went straight into the guard's head and his lifeless husk fell over onto the concrete floor. There Nida stood for what

252

seemed like forever with the gun extended parallel to the ground. The numbness crept back in now that the thrill was over. She looked around her at the awestruck faces of the other prisoners.

A young man walked up. He was black but very light skinned. His eyes were green, and his hair was wavy, thick, and brown. Nida felt that he looked Arabic, but definitely with some African heritage. Nida had always found genetics fascinating, even when she was a kid. Nida knew him as Leon, "Why have you done this? You've brought ruin to all of us! They're going to kill us all!"

Nida looked at the man. A few weeks ago she was just like him. Obsessed with preserving the last vestige of a life of suffering. So afraid of death that she cowered in fear while evil was perpetrated in front of her. Nida no longer was chained by that fear, she welcomed death, welcomed the chance to see her son one more time. She slapped the man across the face and looked at the rest of the people.

"I have made a choice for all of us. Leon is right, they will kill all of us. We only have two choices: live on our feet or die on our knees." Nida handed the gun to Leon and began walking up the hallway between the bunks.

"I have been raped, I have been beaten, I have watched them murder my husband, my son, and all of my friends. They have taken my home and my future. I refuse to stand by and do nothing any longer! You all have a choice to make, follow me and give them a taste of fear, or stay here and die as slaves for your oppressors."

A woman who was near the young Jewish woman who was attacked stepped forward. She looked like an older version of the woman. Nida guessed it was her mother. The woman stepped over to the guard whom Nida had shot and pulled his gun out of its holster. She walked over to Nida and handed her the pistol. She then embraced Nida and began to shake.

"T-t-thank you for d-doing what I could not...I will follow wherever you go." She was speaking through her tears, barely able to make out the words.

Nida pushed her away and put her hand affectionately on her face. She looked into the woman's eyes and nodded. She then looked around the barracks to see what the reaction of the room was. To a person they all gave her a nod. The time was now, the die was cast.

"I won't lie to any of you, I don't have a plan. I didn't intend this, but I could not stand by and watch anymore. I would rather die than hear any more screams in my dreams. We should try and storm the command tower. I know they keep more weapons there. I saw them when they took me there to torture me. We should wait a few minutes though. They will be sending a second patrol soon to investigate the gunshot."

The people nodded. They began to hide behind their bunks and Nida and Leon took up positions on either side of the doors to try and surprise the incoming guards. The thrill that had overtaken Nida before surged forward again, drowning out the numbness in her soul. Her arm ached, but it didn't matter.

About three minutes later, there was a knock on the door of the barracks. "Harrington, you in there? We heard a shot." The guards didn't enter.

"HARRINGTON! YOU IN THERE?!" They sounded furious and desperate at the same time. About three seconds later, the door exploded open as if kicked with tremendous force, it hit the back of the barracks. Five guards rushed in, not noticing Nida and Leon inside the door. They opened fire. *Pop, pop, pop, pop, pop, pop, pop.* Nida emptied her clip and so did Leon. All five guards lay dead on the ground before they even realized what happened.

Nida waved for the rest of the prisoners to come forward and began to relieve the guards of their firearms. She handed one pistol to the mother of the Jewish woman. The woman smiled, "My name is Irene, by the way. You saved my daughter Marissa's life. I can never repay you." The woman hugged Nida again. The numbness stayed away.

Nida spoke with Leon and inquired about how many guns they had acquired. Two of the men had rifles and pistols, the other three just had pistols. *Nine total guns, that's a good start.* Nida thought to herself. All at once the anxiety started to set in, *I don't know anything about fighting, I didn't expect this to actually work.* She began to panic and in the back of her mind she knew she was in way over her head. She placed her hand on the wall as the waves of panic washed over her, *I have nothing to lose.* Taking stock of the room, all of the prisoners were looking at her waiting for a command. Whether she liked it or not, she had a group who would follow her. It was time to lead them.

"Does anyone have any idea on how many guards are on duty at one time?" Nida polled the group, hoping someone had paid attention.

"I don't know how many are on duty at a time, but I know we've killed seven here tonight. I think we should attack the armory now while we still have the element of surprise." Leon seemed invested and sincere.

"Okay, I agree. I know where a door is that might be unlocked, but there's going to be a guard there. We'll need to distract him somehow…" Nida began to think through what to do. *What could distract this guard without him raising an alarm?* Nida immediately had an idea.

"Here's the plan: most of you, go to the other barracks, let them know what's happened here. Spread the word, we're breaking out of here. I need eight volunteers with me. We're going to the tower."

Leon, the young man who spoke up earlier, and five other men stepped forward. Finally, Irene also stepped forward, pistol in hand. The other five were Travis, Alar, Prateek, Nitin and Rono. They all had the guns in their hands and then followed Nida when she led them towards the tower. It was dark outside, but there was enough light to make out the pathway towards the tower.

The nine of them made the final approach to the security door where they had taken Nida originally. Just as she had remembered, there was a guard there. He was a young man, barely over twenty from the looks of him. He was sitting in a chair scrolling mindlessly on his cell phone. Nida looked back at Irene and handed her the pistol she was carrying. Irene looked at her with a gaze of confusion. Nida just smiled and took off her shirt, before she made any move, she checked her pocket to make sure the thin piece of metal was still there.

Feigning intoxication, Nida stumbled drunkenly up towards the guard. She came into the light, wearing only a bra and her jumpsuit pants. The guard called to her.

"You there! Halt!" Nida stopped and jokingly put her hands in the air while blocking out the light.

"I'm stopped!" She chuckled as she said it.

"What are you doing here? You should be in your barracks, it's after curfew." Nida kept walking towards him with her hands in the air.

"Well, I was drinking with one of your buddies… what's his name… Harrington?"

"Oh, you were with Jerry? Did y'all have a good time?" The soldier smiled at Nida, she finally put her hands down, but she kept advancing.

"Not as good of a time as you could have. He just got me a little drunk. I've seen you around the camp." Nida walked up to the soldier and put her hand on his face. He smiled.

"Oh yeah?" The soldier looked all around him to see if there was anyone in eyesight. There wasn't. He turned to open the door, and Nida walked in behind him. He stooped down to kiss her, and their lips met. Nida returned the kiss and slipped her hand behind her back, acting like she was going to unclasp her bra. She grabbed the thin piece of metal and thrust violently upwards into the soldier's throat. His blood covered her in a crimson shower. Her entire body felt like it was singing.

She came back out and waved for her group to come in. They tried their best to imitate a sneaking pose and darted into the open door. Once they entered the door, they saw the guard lying on the ground and Nida covered in his blood. Their eyes reflected fear and respect simultaneously. When Irene finally entered and saw the guard, she smiled and handed Nida her shirt back.

"Nice," she said under her breath. They started trying to find their way through the tower. They found a map of the first floor posted on a bulletin board. Down the hallway to the left, it was marked "Armory." They went that way, there was a closed gate in front of a counter. There was a sleeping guard behind the gate, and he hadn't noticed their approach yet. Nida motioned backwards with her hands and the group retreated down the hall.

She whispered to the group, "Check that other guard to see if he has any keys." Leon bent down to inspect the guard and came back up with a key card. It seemed more like an access card. *Better hope this guard has access to the armory or this won't work out.* They walked back to the armory and swiped the card. The door opened.

Nida burst through the door with speed beyond what she thought herself capable of, instinct had begun to cloud her thoughts. There was something inside of her that had taken over and she was surrendering herself to it. Before the guard even woke up, Nida had slit his throat with the thin piece of metal. Taking stock of the guard, Nida noticed he had a knife on his belt. She took the belt off of him and put it on her own waist with the knife and its sheath.

There was a large vault door that was slightly propped open. The soldiers didn't even bother to close the vault when not in use. *Sort of defeats the purpose of the vault,* Nida thought to herself. Thankful for her luck, they walked into the armory and began to arm themselves even further. They found bullet proof vests, a large stockpile of ammunition and assault rifles, and finally they found extra radios.

"Leon, go get the others and lead them as quietly as possible back here. The camp is still asleep. It's time to take this compound from them."

Chapter 28: Who Am I?

Luther was walking up and down among the cannabis plants. Jar had told him they used the scientific name because they were running a professional operation. They were part of the United Sanguine Nations, and that gang had started using old, abandoned churches as fronts for their production operations, which is how they had ended up here.

For the last several weeks, Luther had been put on plant duty. One of the other guys, Joe, had been showing him the ropes on cultivation. How to cut the leaves, when to cut off the flowers and package them for distribution. The work was a kind reprieve from the trials of his time in the woods. He still saw the faces of the girls, but he couldn't remember their names anymore. They were lost to him after the fall, many things were. He remembered a lot, but the recent past was fuzzy in his mind. Quatrell, another one of the guys here, had some medical training from his time in the Army. He told Luther it was likely short-term amnesia caused by head trauma.

The memory of his father was blazed into his head as if it had happened yesterday. The vision he had seen in his desperation of that day after his mother's funeral kept haunting his dreams. He heard his grandfather less and less. He couldn't remember what it meant to even be himself. It seemed like a dream. He was a congressman, but that no longer mattered. Across the entire world, his name was marked for death. Of all the people in this country, his name was at the top of the most wanted list. Ironically, it gave him a ton of cred in the gang.

They continued to give him a place to live and food to eat, so he kept working without complaint. This was fine.

The door to the upper walkway opened and Jartavius and Quatrell walked in. They had a pretty serious look on their faces and were clearly heading towards Luther. The grow house was down in the basement of the church. There were ten triangle stacks of plants that could be lifted off the rack if necessary for re-planting or harvesting. These stacks were placed approximately five feet apart in even rows. On the ceiling were rows of halogen light bulbs. There was an upper walkway made of corrugated metal, and it stretched around the entire upper reach of the room with staircases on each length to get down to the grow area.

Jartavius and Quatrell walked down the stairs and came over to Luther. Jartavius clapped Luther on the shoulder and then lightly raised a leaf of a nearby plant, like a father showing affection to his children. Quatrell nudged him a little and Jartavius turned back towards Luther to speak.

"So, Lu. We got a bit of a mission for you." Jartavius had a habit of giving everyone around them nicknames. Nobody really seemed to mind, so Luther had just let it go.

"What's up, what can I help with?" Luther had no illusions about needing to continue to work for safe harbor, and it was a fair trade in his mind.

"There's a fucking snitch named Jimmy Potts that is threatening to talk to the feds if we don't forgive some debts of his. He owes us about twenty grand, so obviously we can't just let that go." Jartavius looked Luther dead in the eyes, "We need you to take care of him."

Luther was stunned into silence. *They want me to be a hitman?* He stood there for a moment. On one hand, he didn't believe in violence for the sake of violence, but on the other he didn't really have a choice. *Survive.* His dad's voice echoed in his head. Luther held up his hand in a fist and Jartavius touched his fist to Luther's.

"Tell me where and give me a gun." Jartavius and Quatrell smiled. Luther got the sense that this conversation had gone much better than they had anticipated, but Luther knew the score and valued his own life above someone who might sick the feds on them.

Luther was riding in the passenger seat of Zip's black muscle car. He had tinted the windows to be basically black, so nobody could see who they were. This made Luther breathe much easier, he knew he'd be recognized no matter where they went. So, nobody being able to see him was just fine.

Zip and Luther were cruising down the highway, not saying a word. Some hip hop was playing on the radio. Zip had his phone synced to the speakers, so Luther couldn't really control what they listened to. Which was a shame because Luther did not like this type of music.

Growing up, Luther wasn't really into music. He preferred not to waste a ton of time on artistic pursuits. There was always a sense to him that time wasted was time he could never get back. It was ironic now, though. He spent so much time investing into his future and now his future was gone. Tending to plants and running odd jobs for a local drug lord was probably the rest of Luther's life. It was oddly satisfying to have no ambition. Luther had just succumbed entirely to his situation. Nothing was left of the social climbing congressman.

They had been driving for about an hour at this point, Luther had zoned out almost entirely. Staring out the window at the trees that ran by the car, and watching the blur of nature zoom past was mesmerizing. Time seemed to slow down in the car, but eventually they pulled up to a small trailer park. Luther knew they were somewhere outside of Charlotte, NC, but he had no idea where they were. Although he had asked where they were going, the only response that he got was that Zip would take him there. Which was just fine by Luther, the less he knew the better. The cold steel of the 9mm pistol was heavy in its holster around his waist.

Zip pulled up to a trailer with a blacked-out luxury car outside of it. *I guess this is it,* Luther thought to himself. The quality of the car was a dead giveaway for the type of business that the owner of this trailer was into. They both got out and walked up to the door. Luther raised his hand to knock, but Zip caught his hand. Zip never really said much, but he held his finger up to his lips to silence Luther.

Zip pulled out a credit card and slipped it in between the crevice of the door. After some brief jimmying, the door flew open. Zip walked in and Luther followed behind. In the middle of what Luther assumed was the living room of the double wide trailer was a man. He had a heroin needle in his arm and the rubber tourniquet was laying on his lap. The man had passed out and had not stirred even with Zip and Luther's entrance. Luther heard a kid crying in the bedroom. Raising his hand high, Zip slapped the man across the face. He woke up, startled and out of sorts.

"W-w-w-what's g-g-going on?" The man managed to get out.

"Jimmy, you remember me?" Zip got down on his level by squatting slightly. Jimmy nodded his head.

"W-w-why are you here? Does... does Jar need something?" Zip smiled at this question.

"He needs to know why you're talking to the feds, Jimmy. You know you owe us a lot, and you're going to talk to them? What gives, man?"

Jimmy looked pale and frozen like he had seen a ghost. "How'd Jar find out about that? I didn't mean to, they picked me up on some charges and offered me immunity. I haven't said anything yet – I was going to come to Jar and talk it out, I swear."

"Yeah, course you were, bro. 'Cept that was two weeks ago, wasn't it? You've had a good long time to come talk to Jar. So, where were you?"

"I – uh – uh – I – I, swear I was gonna come talk to Jar and square up. Look I got your money!" Jimmy dashed into his bedroom and came back out with a wad of cash. Zip grabbed the cash and began to count.

"This is eight grand, Jimmy. We gave you twenty worth of product. Where's the rest?"

"The feds took it, man! I swear!" Zip looked at Luther and motioned his head. Luther knew that was the sign. He took out his pistol and pointed it at Jimmy's head but held his shot for the moment.

"I SWEAR! I FUCKING SWEAR! I'M SORRY, I DIDN'T SAY NOTHIN'!" Luther looked back at Zip and Zip nodded his head. Luther steeled his gaze back at Jimmy's head. *Pull the trigger*. He kept repeating to himself. *Survive*. His dad's words echoed in his head. *Never forget who you are*. His grandfather's words made him freeze. *Never forget who you are*. Luther began to shake uncontrollably. He wanted to pull the trigger, he knew he had to, but he couldn't. *Never forget who you are*.

Zip shouted at Luther, "Fucking do it and let's get out of here, come on man!" Luther tried to pull the trigger, but he just couldn't do it. His grandfather's words echoed in his mind, overshadowing every sense and desire that he could muster. The recent reality of Luther's existence began to flash back into his head. Feeling the shame of killing the girls in the woods, feeling the fear he had felt rolling headlong over a cliff, feeling the sense of peace he had tending the plants. *I DON'T KNOW WHO I AM ANYMORE*. Luther's mind felt like it was shattering.

Survive. Was the last word that Luther heard in his mind. He closed his eyes and squeezed the trigger. The gun rang out like a macabre anvil, and the sound of death persisted in his ear drums for several seconds. Jimmy laid on the floor and Luther could hear the baby stirring in the bedroom. A half-naked woman wearing nothing but a thong came rushing out of the bedroom.

"JIMMY! OH MY GOD! WHAT THE FUCK HAVE YOU DONE TO MY BABY?!"

Zip looked at Luther and whispered, "No witnesses." *Survive*. Luther turned the gun to the woman and pulled the trigger five times. She joined her lover in eternity. Zip turned to leave, but Luther grabbed him.

"We can't just leave the kid, man. He might die." Luther's conscience had cracked into a thousand pieces.

"Not our problem, bro. Social services will pick him up, but we gotta go right now before the cops show." Zip wrestled free from Luther's grasp and walked out of the door, "I'm leaving whether you're with me or not."

Luther followed. The man who walked out of the trailer was not the same one that had entered. He was hollow now; the last vestige of his previous life had left his body. *Who am I?* was all that Luther could think to himself. *Survive.*

"Power is not given, it is taken." – *Caesar Augustus*

Chapter 29: Flames Anew

A full moon sat overhead, peering over Nida as she twirled in the office chair that had previously been occupied by the commander of the base. She was drenched in blood, sweat and dirt. The thrill of victory was still singing in her veins, and she was taking in the sweet nectar. Every breath was exhilarating, a new day had dawned in Nida's mind.

Taking in this moment alone, Nida began to reflect. How long had it been since she'd been truly alone? How long had she been in this camp? Her old life felt like a distant memory. She closed her eyes, and she was back in her house again. Tahir's brown ringlets flowed through her fingers as she caressed his head. The sunlight poured through the blinds creating a web of sunbeams that made the entire room feel light and pure.

Suddenly, there was a knock at the door and Nida's blissful daydream came to an end. Irene and Leon walked in with rifles hanging on their arms; Irene had a clipboard in her right hand. She handed the clipboard to Nida before speaking.

"We've rounded up twenty-eight guards in total. None of the guards escaped, and to our knowledge the alarm was never sounded to the main supply depot in Las Vegas. However, the commander of the base had previously left after some prisoners were reassigned to a

267

base somewhere else in the country. But, we're clear at the moment."

Nida looked over the list for the only name she cared about. *Winters* was second to last on the list, but it was there. She looked up from the clipboard, "Bring me Captain Winters." She had switched off the young girl that came to the camps and switched on the nihilist woman she had become. Through torment, enslavement and loss, Nida had become something more.

Leon nodded at her command and walked out of the room. Irene remained and she put her rifle down next to a chair that was in front of the desk Nida was sitting at. She then sat down, crossed her legs and leaned her head back. Her eyes were closed. For a time, Nida and Irene sat together saying nothing. Basking in the total silence around them.

A breeze rolled through the open window to the commander's office. The breeze was dry from the intense heat of the Nevada desert, but there was something in the air that made it seem like something more. A slight hint of salt that carried in the wind from the Pacific to where they were. To Nida, that salt smelled like freedom. It smelled like summer afternoons spent on the beach listening to the waves with Abdul and Tahir. A world gone by.

Standing up, Irene walked over to the desk and put her hand on Nida's. She didn't say anything, she just stared into Nida's eyes. It felt like when Nida's mother used to grab her hands to pray; a familiar calm settled over Nida. She had protected Irene's daughter - Irene was now going to protect her. No words needed to be exchanged.

After a few heartbeats, there was a knock on the door. Leon walked in with two other men Nida hadn't met, but she recognized that they were from a nearby barracks. Leon had gone about organizing those who wished to fight into something resembling what they had seen from the soldiers in the camp. Most had chosen to stand with Nida which had come as a shock to her.

Behind the two men was Captain Winters. His hands were shackled, and he had been stripped down to a white t-shirt and underwear. His shoulders were dirty as if he had been laying on the ground for days. Bloody and cracked lips framed a sad smile as he looked up and saw Nida.

"W-why did you bring me here? Are you going to kill me?" Once a strong, proud figure now seemed a small child. His spirit was broken.

"No, I am not going to kill you, Captain. I am going to offer you a deal." Irene and Leon exchanged troubled glances.

"When Harrington came for me the first time, you protected me. You used what power you had to protect someone who you didn't need to, and that cost you a lot. When Harrington and his cronies beat me half to death, it was you who put an end to it." Nida stood up and walked over to Winters.

"Now, you are rewarded for your humanity with your life. I need something in exchange, though. Will you help me?" A single tear rolled down Winters' face. His voice failed him, but he managed to croak out, "*Anything…*"

"I need you to tell me how to save these people." Winters looked up into Nida's eyes, and Nida noticed something she hadn't seen earlier. *Hope.*

"I will help you, but I'm going to need some clothes." Leon interjected, furious.

"We don't need him, Nida! We can do this on our own! He's going to lead us to ruin and death, right into the waiting arms of Drum. He is our enemy! We should kill him now like the rest of them."

With that, Leon took out his pistol and pressed it against Winters' temple. Winters pissed himself and began to cry. There was nothing left of the career military officer, something had happened to him before he came before Nida. Holding up her hand, Nida signaled Leon to stop.

"We do what I say, Leon. Not what you say." Nida was trying to exert authority on a group of people whose religion generally excluded female authority. It had only been a day and it was already getting difficult to get these men to listen to her.

Leon spat on Winters' face and looked at Nida, "I should have known better than to let a woman take the lead. You are weak." Leon turned to walk out the door.

"Guards, arrest Leon. Handcuff him and put him with the soldiers." The guards looked at each other and then to Leon. They didn't move, unsure of what to do. Their nominal leader had given an order, but thousands of years of cultural pressure made them unable to move against Leon. They stood there.

Nida didn't know what to do. If nobody followed her orders, was she really in charge? Was she really ever in charge? Winters was still on the ground, and he had finally stopped sobbing. He was looking at Leon with ill intent but couldn't do anything from his position on the ground.

Locking eyes with Nida, Winters mouthed, *Kill him*. She nodded.

"Leon, either you follow me, or you die. Those are your choices. This is your last chance."

Leon laughed and then pointed his rifle at Nida. Her heart began pounding in her chest. She was frozen in time. Leon drew in breath to steady his aim, and then Winters swept his legs out from under him. The rifle discharged as Leon fell backwards to the ground, and the bullet struck the ceiling and ricocheted out the window.

The rifle slammed on the ground, causing another round to discharge that grazed Winters' left arm. He screamed in pain and then quickly coiled his handcuffs around Leon's neck. The guards ran up to stop him, but by this time Irene and Nida both had their guns drawn and pointed. Walking over to where Leon was starting to lose consciousness, Nida laughed and kicked him in the groin. She waved for Winters to stop before he killed him, but Winters was in another world - his survival instinct had taken over. Nida eventually slapped him in the face, and he released his grip. Leon lay unconscious on the floor, but Nida could feel a pulse.

She turned towards the so-called guards and looked at both of them. They didn't have rifles because there were only one hundred allocated to the camp, and these two weren't lucky enough to get them. Nida bent down to pick up the rifle that Leon had threatened her with and handed it to Winters. Then, with her own rifle she pointed it at both guards.

"Tell me why I shouldn't kill you both?"

"P-p-please… we just… we just…" The guards were stammering. They knew they had crossed a line when they hesitated to follow orders, and there was no coming back.

"Get on the ground." The guards got on their knees. Nida uncuffed Winters using the keys that Leon had on his belt. She then cuffed the two guards together. It was only then she noticed that Winters was bleeding profusely out of his arm from where the bullet grazed him. Nida took off her jacket and began to use it to apply pressure and soak the blood. The social norms of her youth still made her feel uncomfortable with not being covered, but the old Nida was dead now.

"Who is your leader?" Nida's tone was pure venom. She never knew that she was capable of this, but she had never been in this position before.

"Y-y-y-y-ou…. are?" The other guard managed to stutter out.

"Whose orders do you listen to?" Nida looked at both of them but grabbed the guard on the right by his cheeks.

"Yours!" They were pleading at this point. Begging for mercy like sobbing children. *It is a pity how quickly men become nothing more than sheep once they are shown strength.*

"Stand up." Both of the men stood up, clearly shaken. "You will remember my generosity in letting you live. You will always follow my commands. Do you understand?" They nodded their heads.

"Good. Grab Leon and come with me. Irene, have everyone assemble in the courtyard outside of the control tower." Irene nodded and moved her hands towards the PA speaker controls that were on the back part of the room.

Her voice came over the loudspeaker, "Friends, please come to the control tower. Nida would like to address everyone." She said this three times, and then Nida left with the two guards carrying Leon and Winters following behind. The blood had stopped pouring, but he still had the jacket pressed against his arm.

They finally made their way out to the courtyard, and a crowd had started to gather. According to Leon's initial reports, the total prison population was somewhere around twelve hundred. They had used a collection of fifty armed guards to control that population and had about double the amount of equipment for their outfit.

Nida stood on the stage that the guards would stand on when making announcements to the group. Behind her were the two guards holding Leon and Captain Winters. The sight of the scantily clad man standing behind a furious Nida made people start whispering. She hadn't really thought through bringing him down here with her, but now she needed to address it.

"Friends, I bring unfortunate news. Today, Leon threatened to kill me with a rifle that was entrusted to him by all of us." The gasps in the crowd were audible. "If it weren't for the heroic actions of Captain Winters, I would likely be dead. He is the one who subdued Leon and saved my life for the third time."

"Captain Winters is a good man. Many of you have interacted with him and know him to be a man of character and kindness. Today, I ask two things of you. First, that you accept Captain Winters as our friend and

273

ally. Second, that you condemn Leon to die for his crime." The crowd hushed entirely. The intermittent chatter ceased, and Nida had their full attention.

Someone yelled out from the crowd, "How do we know you're telling the truth?"

Nida waved the guards forward. "These two guards witnessed the whole thing. Isn't that right?" The guards nodded their heads dutifully. "Did you witness Leon point his gun at me?" The guards nodded their heads dutifully. Nida held out her hand to the side as if to present the two men to the crowd as proof of her claim.

"Show of hands, who will accept Winters with me?" The crowd almost unanimously raised their hands. A few religious hardliners did not, they were still not okay taking orders from a woman regardless of what happened.

"Show of hands, who believes that Leon must die?" Many hands went up, but there was no clear consensus. It was impossible to tell from looking if the majority agreed or not. Nida was surprised by the result, but she wouldn't be like the leaders that she so despised.

"Well, it had to be unanimous. Leon lives, but he will be imprisoned for the time being until he has served a proper penance." The crowd seemed to relax and breathe a sigh of relief. They were not following a bloody tyrant; they were following a leader whose instincts were to be fair and just. People can recognize that almost implicitly in a leader, and people will follow that leader to the ends of the earth so long as they remain just and fair.

Without even trying to, Nida had solidified her position as leader of the insurgent band. She had descended the tower to deal with Leon, but by showing restraint she had proven to the group that she was worthy of their trust. Nida's instincts had served her well so far, but there was much work to be done.

Chapter 30: Phoenix Rising

The next day, Nida, Winters, and Irene were sitting in the commander's office. It was mid-morning, and the dust was swirling outside. The entire camp was locked down due to the dust storms. According to some of the locals detained in the camps, the dust storms had started getting worse in the past few years. Global climate change was beginning to affect the wind patterns over the desert area, and the conflicting air streams stirred up these storms.

"What's the strategy here, Nida? Are you going to fight the entire U.S. military with a band of a hundred prisoners? You're no Spartacus and he still lost with much better odds." Winters was looking over the lists of prisoners and the available supplies, "Not only that, but our supply situation is incredibly dire. We have enough food and rations remaining for about three weeks. No more shipments will come unless they are ordered from the Army depot." Winters stroked his now scraggly chin. He had let his military discipline lapse since being a captive.

"Where's the depot?" Nida asked, an idea was forming in her mind.

"The depot is about 30 miles south of Las Vegas. It's about a two-hour drive from here if you take the highway." Winters replied.

Nida walked over to the table where there was a map of the camp and the surrounding area. The map included most of the state of Nevada and had lines that ran vertically and horizontally on the page. The lines formed a grid system, but Nida didn't know what that was for.

"Can you mark it here?" Nida asked while pointing at the map. Winters walked over to the map and marked it. Both of them peered down at the map.

Nida started to speak again, "How many men are at the depot?" Nida turned toward Winters, expecting a response.

"I'm honestly not sure. They don't keep the interior supply depots very densely garrisoned. They are mainly just storage facilities, probably no more than twenty or thirty soldiers. Why?" Nida smiled.

"We are going to take the supply depot. We have vehicles here. I think we can take enough people to successfully take it." Winters looked shocked, but Irene, who had been quiet thus far, interjected.

"A bold plan. I like it. We have two trucks that can take about twelve people each and one Humvee, at least, I think that's what they're called.." Irene was only addressing Nida as she did not think too highly of her once captor.

Winters was shaking his head, "It's not going to work. Nellis Air Force base is a two-minute jet flight away. As soon as those men inside the facility send out the SOS, we're toast."

Nida thought intently about what to do. They needed the supplies, that much was obvious. She was no military strategist, though. Clearly, Winters was right as Nida could see Nellis on her map just centimeters away from where the depot was marked. It was not a long distance.

"Look, Billy, it's either sit here and die or attack the depot and maybe win. I don't see what other choice we have. Do you have another idea?"

Winters, who was still shaking his head over the plan, was taken off guard when Nida called him by his first name. He didn't remember ever telling her his name, but it made him drop his guard. She was trying to bring him into her confidence, continuously guarding himself and shielding his thoughts was just going to make things worse.

"I don't. I have no other ideas. Let's focus on how to make yours work." Winters hoped his deference would demonstrate that he was trying to meet her halfway.

They began to strategize together. Nida and Winters thought of every scenario they could imagine for how to attack and seize the depot without alerting the guards. Irene stood guard, hawkishly protecting Nida despite Winters' capitulation to her leadership. She had two daughters now. One was still a broken shell from her attack and the other was a broken shell that was filled with unquenched vengeance. She was unsure which one needed her more, but she would stay with Nida until Marissa was ready to rejoin the world.

Eventually, they settled on a plan that would first attempt to knock out a communications relay that Winters thought may control the entire Las Vegas military chain. It was at a seemingly innocuous power station about three miles outside of the depot. Hiding in plain sight was one of the military's favorite strategies.

They brought what they were now calling the central council into the commander's briefing room and laid out the plan for them. There were eight people in total on the council. Nida, Irene, and six other men that were picked from the major housing areas. The men were all older, generally more conservative Muslims. It was obvious from the beginning of the meeting that they were uncomfortable with Nida's leadership. When Winters talked, they listened intently to his strategic advice, but when Nida spoke, they talked incessantly amongst themselves for long stretches. The disrespect was not lost on Nida.

If Nida was truly going to lead these people, she needed to convince these men that she was capable of leadership. It was a hard line to balance for her. On one hand, the cultural pressure she felt to let a man take over the reins was immense. The group of men she was attempting to lead clearly had no time to listen to the military thoughts of a woman. Their attitudes greatly frustrated Nida. *Winters wanted to throw his hands up and do nothing*, Nida thought to herself, *it was my idea to take the depot, but they only listen to him.*

Looking at Winters, Nida decided that she had to make him subordinate in public. She had to be sure that when the people of the camp that *she* liberated thought of who was in charge, the first thought in their minds was Nida. While she was processing all of this, the meeting continued. The men on the council were consistently asking questions about the plan to Winters, not a single question had been directed towards Nida during the entire meeting.

Nida had enough, "Winters, who came up with this plan?" she asked.

Winters paused for a moment, "Well… you did Nida. Why?"

Nida continued, "I just find it interesting that you wanted to throw up your hands and quit. I came up with this plan, and now we present it to these men, it seems like it's your plan. Why is that?" The men shifted uncomfortably in their seats. They were not used to a woman openly questioning a man.

"I… you.. uh.. you… told me to present to these… these… men." Winters was nervous. Nida made him nervous like few people ever had. Perhaps it was that he understood how far she was willing to go, or perhaps it was something else, but when she spoke like that to him, he was helpless.

"That's right. I ordered you to present the plan. I am now ordering you to stop presenting the plan. I will take it from here." Winters sat down at the table in the chair Nida had gestured for him to occupy. He was red-faced and flustered; he hadn't expected the sudden dressing down. Nevertheless, he sat.

"You will now address your questions to me and only me." The men looked at her wide-eyed. They had just witnessed a male insulted in their presence so greatly that it was an affront to their honor.

The man at the far end of the table, one of the elders who had refused to vote in the previous day's pardon of Winters or the execution of Leon, named Artur, rose out of his seat, "How dare you speak to any man in such a manner, even an infidel like him." He walked over to Nida and pulled his arm back as if to strike her in the face.

Without thinking, Nida grabbed the knife she kept permanently on her belt and held it up to Artur's throat. Their eyes met. When Artur rose, his demeanor was angry and aggressive; however, when the cold steel of the knife reached his throat all Nida saw was fear. Nida began to walk him slowly backwards while keeping enough pressure on the knife that one false move would be the end for Artur.

They reached his chair, "Sit. Down," Nida growled. Artur sat back down. Knife still drawn; Nida looked at the other men in the room. "Anyone else?" she asked with a tinge of unhinged aggression on her tongue. Nobody moved or said anything.

She went back to the head of the table where Winters was previously presenting and continued outlining the finer details of the plan including personnel and equipment. Ultimately, it was decided that there would be three teams. The first team would consist of five people, they would ride with the main column until the electrical station and then break off. They would be given four sticks of C4 and the necessary detonators to destroy the power station. The second and third groups would continue on to the depot.

Once at the depot, the second group would secure the parking lot and the main entrance to make sure that nobody left, and nobody entered. The third group would be led by Nida personally. She would lead them to a security door on the far side of the building. According to Winters, when he had spent a few weeks there doing a supply audit, one of the soldiers would go out there to smoke quite often. The plan was to hope he was still stationed there and that they could catch him opening the door. This way, they could sneak inside without being noticed and take everyone out without alerting the wing detachment at Nellis.

The men agreed with the plan and said that they would support it among their people and bring the best warriors forward. As they were leaving, the men started to talk amongst themselves. Nida did not like them talking amongst themselves much at all. *They're probably hoping I die in the assault*, Nida thought to herself. *I'm hoping I die in the assault, too.* Tahir and Abdul flashed into her mind. *I'm coming my darlings, wait for me.* Nida prepared herself for the task ahead.

Nida was up before dawn. She got out of the bed that she had taken up using in the commander's old quarters. Taking a liberty that she had not had in several months, Nida showered. The caked blood and dirt that had been her constant companions since the night that they took over the prison camp rinsed off of her. She got out of the shower and noticed that there were several clean Army uniforms in the commander's footlocker. She took them out and tried them on, desperate for any type of clean clothing.

The jacket was long enough for her as Lt. Col. McAdams was not the tallest of men, but the shoulders were absolutely huge. Nida took out her knife and cut off the sleeves of the uniform and then tore the sleeves into thin strips, making a single band of cloth. Then, she tied the cloth around her waist to make the jacket fit better to her form. Similarly, the pants fit length wise, but she had to cinch the waist down dramatically in order to wear them. Threading the friction belt that she had found in the footlocker through the knife pouch, Nida was finally ready. She picked up her rifle and went outside.

When she arrived into the main courtyard area outside of the command tower, there was only one other person there, Irene. Irene saw her first and began to approach her. They met with a hug and Irene kissed her on the cheek.

"Good morning, Nida." Her love made Nida feel whole again for the first time in a long time. The torturous months spent in this hell had made Nida forget what kindness was. Nida thought of her own mother, and whether she was still alive all the way in Saudi Arabia.

"Good morning, Irene." Nida dipped more into the hug, grateful for the closeness.

One by one, the ex-prisoners began to filter their way into the courtyard. Some were wearing only rags, some brandished rifles and pistols. Others weren't actually included in the plan but wanted to come send these brave souls off. Everyone in the camp knew the stakes, they would not survive the month without the supplies. That was assuming that their seizure of the camp wasn't discovered before that. The only choice they had was to fight.

Eventually, the entire camp poured into the courtyard. Some people began to stand on boxes to get a glimpse of Nida on the raised steps where she was awaiting her fighters. Everyone began to quiet down, it was getting close to time to go. Nida, still not exactly sure what she was doing, took the silence as an opportunity.

"Brothers and Sisters, today we dare to strike back!" Nida stopped for a moment, but everyone just stared. *A little more build up*, Nida thought to herself.

"We are united in our common pain. We have toiled in this prison for months and years, we have had our freedom taken from us, and we have been abandoned by those who we thought were our friends." Nida began to look around at the despair on all of their faces.

"But today, we are doing something entirely different. We seized this camp which was our prison. We ate the tyrant's food, we took his weapons, and we slept in their towers. But today, well, today we take even more." The mood of the crowd shifted from despair to resolve. Nida could feel the collective energy and took it as her opening.

"Today we take the first steps towards freedom once more! No longer will we be slaves to be tread upon! No longer will we allow ourselves to be a subject people of those who seek to destroy us! Today, yes today, WE WILL LIVE FREE ONCE MORE!" The camp exploded, they began to chant "NI - DA! NI - DA!" The rabid energy of the oppressed striving to be free once more infused Nida with a sense of purpose.

Once the chanting died down, Nida shouted once more, "Fighters, let's go." Those designated for the three groups began to move toward their vehicles. Group 1 in the Humvee, groups 2 and 3 in the personnel carriers. Much to her surprise as she entered her truck, Leon was sitting in her vehicle.

"What are you doing here?! You should be in chains!" Nida was furious and pulled her pistol out down by her side. She flipped the safety off.

"I'm sorry, Nida. I should not have challenged you. I wish to make amends with my life." He sounded sincere. *Well, we need fighters. I at least know he's got fight in him.*

Without any more words, Nida stepped up into the truck and the column departed. They were driving for about two hours when Nida heard Winters over the radio.

"Group 1, take the side road that's coming up after the next exit. Over."

"Got it," came the reply from the Group 1 driver, a man named Ahmed.

"Is that it? Over." Winters replied.

An audible snort was heard over the radio, "Got it. Over," came the reply. Winters was insistent on the use of proper radio etiquette. Nida found the whole practice quite silly, but the man decided to draw a line in the sand on that one.

Group 1 eventually broke off from the column and drove down to the power station. The other two vehicles pressed on towards the depot. At about 2 PM, the column arrived approximately a mile outside of the depot, exactly as planned. Over the radio, Winters called to Group 1.

"Group 1, are you in position? Over."

"Yes." There was radio silence for about 30 seconds, and then the channel opened, "Over." Nida chuckled softly with the people beside her.

This time, Nida came over the channel, "Alright everyone, get into your positions. We attack at sundown. Radio silence until we are in position. Over and out."

Over the next several hours, the groups moved into a ring of people around the depot. They had every entrance and window scouted and locked down with arms fire if anything went wrong. Nida and Irene went around to the far side of the building where the side door was. Just as Winters had remembered, a guard came outside about once every hour for a cigarette break and propped open the door.

Eventually, the sun went down. It had been about twenty minutes since the last time the guard came to the door, but Nida decided it was time to knock out the communications. She called over the radio once more, "Group 1, go. Over."

About five minutes later, the power flickered at the depot. About six of the soldiers that were inside came out the side door and left it propped open. They were attempting to fix the communications lines on the outside box. Nida saw a golden opportunity.

"Group 3, advance and take them out." The group of fighters advanced across the open terrain, masked by the complete obliviousness of the guards and the darkness, they crossed unnoticed. Nida snuck up behind one of the guards that had stood by the door to make sure it didn't close. Before he could even sense her touch, she slit his throat and guided his body to the ground.

The others went similarly except for the one Leon attacked who noticed his compatriots dropping like flies. He began to shout and tackled Leon. There was a struggle on the ground where the soldier continued to shout for help. Nida quickly closed the distance between them as the soldier got the upper hand and was on top of Leon. Leaping the final distance, she dug the knife into the soldier's spine and his body fell limp to the ground. The soldier landed directly on top of Leon who began to flail and eventually kicked the soldier off.

Over the soldier's radio, a call came out, "Thompson, everything alright out there with the transformer? Over." Nida chuckled at the decorum.

She nodded to Leon who took the radio, but before Leon could speak, Nida whispered into his ear, "*See if you can get more to come out here.*" Leon smiled and nodded.

Leon responded, "Everything is okay, sir. We may need a few more hands out here, need to lift this transformer." Leon paused for a second, believing himself to be done. Nida made a circle motion with her hands implying that he needed to say more, Leon quickly chided into the radio, "Over." It took everything Nida had not to explode into laughter, but she managed to hold it together.

"Okay, we'll send Bravo squad out there. Maybe Jones can lift it by himself. Over." Leon looked at Nida expecting her to tell him what to say. Nida shrugged. So, Leon chose to improvise.

"Copy that. Over." Leon waited for some response, but none came. The group got into attack position around the door. About five minutes later, they began to hear voices coming out of the hallway through the door.

".... those pansies can't even lift a transformer, haha. Don't worry boys, Stoneleg Jones will help you out!" The voice got louder towards the end of the sentence, and a few seconds later a titan of a human stepped through the door. The man stood, to Nida's reckoning, about 6'8" tall. He must have been well north of 300 lbs. For a second, Nida was truly afraid. Then, she felt the familiar weight of the knife in her hand. *He'll die just like the rest of them.* Nida leaped onto the colossus's back and dug her knife into his spine before he could react. Wordlessly, breathlessly, the giant slunk to the ground.

Behind him, the other four members of the squad looked on in horror as a blood-soaked Arabian woman with a long combat knife stared at them while standing on the back of their strongest soldier. Before they could run or scream, they were seized and slaughtered by the other members of the group.

Nida called over the radio, "Winters, we've got twelve down over here. Anything out front? Over."

"Nothing, no alarms have been sounded. Over."

Nida motioned to Leon to come closer and whispered in his ear again, "*Call that man again and tell him we got it taken care of, shouldn't be too much longer until communications are restored.*" Leon smiled and nodded. He repeated her message over the radio to the Captain.

"Great. Thompson, get a hospital pass tomorrow, you sound awful. Over." Leon looked at the radio as if he was insulted, but there was no time to dwell on such things.

Nida called back over the radio, "Group 3 is going in. Over."

Winters called back, "Godspeed. Over."

The group entered the depot, but the layout was not at all what Winters had drawn out. The hallways were in different places and different directions than Nida had memorized from the diagram. She was completely lost, so she began to look at the signs on the walls to give her some sort of direction. Luckily, military bases were made to be navigable for the soldiers, so there were signs everywhere.

Eventually, the group found a large bulletin board with a map of the facility depicting the fire escape routes for the inhabitants. *Strange that they are so unguarded at a military installation like this.* Nida had always imagined that these bases would be impossible to penetrate, but here was a massive storehouse of military supplies and hardware and they walked into it like it was somebody's house. Nida ignored the reality of the slaughter she had enacted to gain entrance to this particular abode.

They cleared the entire building but were unable to find any additional personnel until they finally found the commander's office. They opened the cracked door to find a fully uniformed military officer watching videos on his computer. Quickly standing up and attempting to re-dress himself, the officer reached for his weapon.

Nida pulled her rifle up and leveled it at the officer, "One more move and you die." He put his hands in the air and his pants fell back to his knees. Trying her best not to look down, Nida motioned with the rifle for the man to pull his pants up. Once that bit of business was cleared up, she motioned for Leon to tie him up on the chair.

Nida stooped down to him, "Where are the rest of your soldiers?" Her voice was low, whispered and immensely threatening. She was learning quickly and her instincts began to take over more and more.

"Uhhh… about half the garrison was re-deployed to Las Vegas last week." The officer was immediately compliant without need for enticement, which Nida found incredibly strange.

"Why would troops be deployed to a city? What's happening?"

"Oh, you haven't heard about the riots?" The officer looked surprised.

Chapter 31: Puppet Master

Harold sat alone in the Oval Office. The moon shone brightly through the glass windows behind him. There were no lights on, just a fire burning in the fireplace. Grabbing the perspiring glass on the desk, Harold put the scotch back up to his lips once more.

The scotch was simply today's escape. Time had been cruel to Harold, in his mind. Never was he given a choice, every moment since that day in the desert has been one unchosen path after another. Locked in a cage that he was trying to escape, he wound up running right into a different one.

"Everyone serves a master, Harold. Everyone." On the couch in front of him was his captor.

"What are you doing here? I told you never to come here, it's too risky." At this, Altarian laughed.

"What is risk when you cannot die, Harold? What is risk when there is nothing to risk?" Harold never quite believed in what Altarian claimed to be, but when he was offered power, he grabbed it.

"To what do I owe this honor, Brother? It has been years since you've stooped so low as to visit me." Harold's disdain for his cage was palpable.

"It is time to move our strategy into the end game."

Harold paused. *The end game? I thought this was the end game.* Standing up, Harold walked over to the fire and stared into the embers for a moment. Fire was chaotic and wild, but you can contain it. When properly contained, that same chaos creates massive engines of order and

291

control. Harold always imagined that's how the world really was - something to be controlled. Without control, the chaos would run wild and burn everything down. For years, Altarian convinced him that in order to obtain the type of control necessary to build a great society that the Christians had to seize control. So, he did.

Harold had built an army, trained them, extended political influence across the country and globe, and ultimately toppled the greatest democracy in the history of Earthen civilization to fulfill that vision. This was the end game, this was what they had envisioned and planned. It was unfathomable that now, after decades of working together, that Altarian would have a different strategy waiting for him.

"What end game?" Altarian smiled.

"You have done well, Harold. I'm honestly impressed. Even young Julius didn't quite have the political acumen to pull off such a massive coup. Out of all the agents I have employed throughout my years, you have by far been the most successful. I am truly in awe of your accomplishments." Altarian was pacing back and forth in front of the desk. Harold had never heard him give a compliment, or be kind in general for that matter. It made him uneasy.

"Now, it is time for you to extend your control further. You must purge this planet of any race but your own."

Harold turned suddenly towards Altarian, eyes wide. His knees were weak and his mind was already blurry from the scotch, but he could not believe what he just heard.

"WHAT?! You told me we were doing this to build the greatest civilization in the history of the human race! I have done everything that you asked because you said that the true God would understand what we did in his name. You swore that he would understand!" Harold was foaming at the mouth now. His anger was untamable.

"I WILL NOT ORDER THE MASS SLAUGHTER OF ANY MORE PEOPLE! I'M DONE!" Harold's shoulders were moving up and down rapidly. He was hyperventilating and in shock. His mind was racing. He began to cry and shake uncontrollably, "I... I... I wish I would have died in the desert... I can't ... I can't do this..."

Altarian looked down at his puppet and sighed. They always seemed to break eventually, these weak-minded, half humans. Stooping down, Altarian put a hand on the wretches' shoulder. *Calm.* Altarian thought, and Harold stopped crying and looked up. The serenity that He had seen so long ago returned.

"Ah, there he is. How are we feeling?" Altarian asked with a voice so kind it sounded degrading.

"I'm fine. I'm fine. What would you ask of me?"

"Good. You must begin by rounding up any non-white person into the prison camps. I intentionally saved this one for last, as it is likely to meet the most resistance." Altarian was staring out the large glass windows now.

"Once this is done, you are to exterminate any person remaining in the prison camps. We must purge this land of the unworthy. Then, we shall be truly united. Then, we can move into the end game."

Harold nodded slowly. He tried to take in the gravity of what he was being asked to do. At first, he was happy to defeat the enemies of God. He believed in that goal. This wasn't that, though. Growing up in the urban south, Harold ran across black people all the time. Many of them were his friends, coworkers, members of his clergy and flock. This felt wrong on a level that none of the previous atrocities felt to Harold.

"I - I don't think I can do this, Brother. I'm sorry." Harold's shoulders dropped. There had never been a time in their entire relationship that Harold had said no. Over thirty years of work, careful planning and coordination, and Harold had been a willing, eager participant in all of it. However, this line he could not cross. He would not order the death of innocents. Even the Lincoln Memorial had been difficult for him, but he justified it because it was necessary to do what must be done. This wasn't necessary to accomplish Harold's goal, in fact it was the opposite. It was detrimental to everything Harold had accomplished.

Altarian sighed. He walked over to Harold and placed his hand on his shoulder once more. *Obey.* He released a small amount of energy into Harold's body. Harold's back stiffened and his pupils shrank.

"I am at your command, Brother." Harold's voice was mechanical, as if he was no longer in control.

"Good, now begin the task that I have assigned you without delay."

"Yes, Brother." Harold turned and walked into Rick's office to begin the necessary preparations for the new order.

Curious, I've never had to use such strong compulsion on him before. Altarian looked at Harold with an air of concern, perhaps he had misjudged the man. *Oh well, all tyrants must fall some day.* With that, Altarian disappeared.

Harold walked into Rick's office and looked at him with a strange gaze. Rick, drunk and disheveled, stood up to meet Harold. Sticking out his hand, Harold took it and shook it. Harold's pupils came back to normal and his demeanor shifted.

"Brother came to visit me today." Harold sounded drained, like he was straining against a great weight.

"Oh. It's been a bit, right? What did he want?"

"He wanted us to commit racial genocide across the entire country. Purge any non-white person. He says this is preparing for the 'end game.'"

Rick's jaw dropped. They had been following Brother for years, and he was always ruthless. This was the first thing that was just demonstrably cruel and evil without purpose. The Lincoln Memorial strained all of their moral compasses, but this was different. This wasn't even in the name of expanding the power of God, this was just cruelty.

"What do we do?" Rick asked.

"I don't know. Will our soldiers even comply? None of their training ever talked about racial hatred. We aren't the KKK." Harold was visibly disturbed again. This was never part of the plan.

"Who did we get into bed with, Harold? How is the guy still even alive? He was ancient forty years ago!" Harold looked at Rick. It was time to tell him.

"He claims to be an ancient being from another planet." Rick stared at Harold with an eyebrow raised.

"Look, it's hard to explain, but he can put visions in your head. He can show you things that are inexplicable. He showed me a vision of Earth with dinosaurs, and he showed me how he hit the planet with a meteor to kill them. I'm not sure if he's just some sort of mad scientist, but the man seems to be, if he is to be believed, millions of years old."

Rick just continued to stare, Harold continued, "He told me that we had to unite the world behind a single religion in order to save the human race. He showed me the future if we don't unite. It was terrifying, Rick. A nuclear wasteland with mutated humans attempting to survive by feeding off of each other. That's why I followed him. I thought he was an agent of God, and that I was, too."

"Harold, I just…"

"I know, Rick. I can't do this either." They both slumped down in their chairs and drank scotch in silence. Neither wanting to address the massive elephant in the room.

Harold sat down at his desk. The new immigration reform package was finally rubber stamped today. Only a few people knew the actual target of the bill, but it had already drawn a lot of media attention because of the wording. Leaning back in his chair, Harold turned on the news.

"Good Evening, my name is Trevor Stewart, and this is Absolute Truth from Wolf News. Tonight, our top story is a new immigration law passed by the intermediary Senate that creates a new class of people that can be deported. The new class is known as 'non-conforming people' and takes aim at those who refuse to follow our laws. It is unclear how this will be administered, and so our guest tonight is Homeland Security Director Farnsworth. Director, thanks for being on the show tonight."

The decrepit shell of the Director held up his hand and gave a wave to the camera. "Thanks for having me, Trevor, it's good to be here."

"Director, can you tell us what this bill means and how it will be enforced?"

"Well, Trevor, for a long time in American politics, there has been a counterculture that prevents us from doing what is necessary to keep America strong and united. These people continuously protest every action of the government and prevent us from governing as we need to in order to make a great society."

"Excuse me, director, did you just suggest this bill will be used to deport protestors? That seems very un-American."

"I didn't say that, I said we will use it to ensure that we can govern appropriately without people interfering with what needs to be done."

Stewart leaned into the table a little bit, "And what needs to be done, director? The President has already murdered half of Congress and the proof that we were promised that they were in some sort of conspiracy magically hasn't turned up. So, I'm asking you, what needs to be done? What is the point of this bill?"

"The point of the bill is to allow our government to remove seditious individuals who would challenge the rule of law in this country." The Director was struggling to maintain the lines that he had been given, he was getting too old for this. He was a statuesque relic, well past his prime, but he refused to release his grip on the small power he had gathered in his career.

"So, if a person is protesting on the street against the religious internment policies that the President has told us are necessary for national security, would this bill allow them to be deported?" Trevor pressed.

The Director was taken aback, this was supposed to be a puff piece supporting the bill, he had not prepared for an actual interview. He began to scan the faces of the production crew and they seemed to be panicked. It became obvious to the Director at that point that Stewart was going off the reservation. The Director began to feel anger swell in his chest, he was being ambushed on live TV. His skin became clammy, and his hands started to tremble. There was no way out and he was not prepared.

"I - uhhh - I, look, I, don't think that's what -errr we're about neces-"

Trevor interjected, "Look, it's a yes or a no question, will you arrest and deport protestors who are demonstrating against these religious internment policies?"

"Trevor, that's not the type of people that these measures are intended for." Farnsworth managed to choke out that answer, but Trevor didn't seem deterred.

"Okay, so what type of people are these measures intended for?" Time seemed to stop for that moment. Farnsworth could hear his heart beating out of his chest for the first time in a long time. It had been so long since he had felt alive that he almost forgot that he had one.

"Well, I can tell you that they're not for you and me." Farnsworth chuckled. He thought that was a very clever dodge.

"So, you mean to say that these provisions specifically don't target white people?" Trevor's face was red. He was holding back a pent-up rage that he didn't realize was there. A tool that had finally woken up to the abusive nature of its use.

Farnsworth froze with his mouth open. He looked back and forth between Trevor and the production crew, scanning for some sort of shut down signal or something; however, the panic that had been prevalent at the beginning had subsided. The production crew seemed to want to see this through to the end.

"Do you not have an answer to this question, Director? Does this bill target minorities for deportation?"

Farnsworth couldn't answer. There was nothing coming to his mind, he was too old for this game. This was supposed to be a layup, Stewart had been a loyal mouthpiece for a decade. It appears that he grew a conscience at the worst possible time.

"I- I- I don't know…" He choked out.

299

"What do you mean? That should be a very simple no answer, sir." Trevor was not backing down - this was personal.

"This bill protects this country, that's all I know. We will do what is necessary to achieve that end." Farnsworth had recovered himself a little, but he was still shaken.

"Protects this country, how?"

"God, I am so tired of you liberals attacking this great nation. We finally put God and his representative back in charge, and all you want to talk about is how evil we are. I'm tired of it." The Director smiled. *Blame the liberals, that's always a winner with the people,* he thought to himself.

"Sir, I am not a liberal. I've been a conservative all my life, and in this Republic, we have freedom of speech and the right to protest. I don't like what these people have to say, either, but I'll defend their right to say whatever it is they please." Trevor was seemingly on fire. An energy surrounded him that was almost visible.

Farnsworth laughed, "You don't have any rights, haha, the Republic died when the Democrats did." He continued to laugh, but Trevor recoiled in disgust. A slip of truth from an old liar.

"You heard it here first, ladies and gentlemen, the Republic is dead. Long live King Drum." With that, Trevor took off his microphone. He then unpinned the American flag from his lapel and hurled it at Farnsworth. The cameras cut off, the broadcast went off the air.

300

"That was for Lisa." Trevor took one last look at the cameras he had spent his life trying to stay in front of and walked off the set.

Harold put down his drink. He knew Farnsworth was old, but this was a total catastrophe. It didn't make any sense. Stewart was a member of the Caliphate, he had been loyal for almost twenty years and nobody had sold him out. *How could this have happened?* Harold was scrambling for any explanation, but none came. Hopefully this would all blow over by the morning as insane ramblings by an old fool.

Chapter 32: Meeting of the Dons

"The sun came up over the horizon, bathing the valley below in a golden light. The trees had started to turn in the mountains, creating a blissful portrait of the earth. In a way, the only real peace that people get is from nature. The food that we eat, the materials that we use to build, and the place where we finally rest, humans are as much a part of nature. Separated only by the fact of our observance, humans ignore their natural beginnings. Accepting that reality creates an end. People would rather conceive of any other concept than the end.

Watching nature, watching the leaves change is a constant reminder of the truth of our existence, it is a cycle. There is an end. Living within this cycle is the true beauty of the human condition. There remains only one choice available to any of us, live or die."

Luther closed the journal he had begun to keep. He hoped that it would be something that would keep him grounded. *If I write them down, maybe I can remember who I was*, Luther pondered the nature of his captivity. Safe, but bound. Luther couldn't help but feel that it was a strange dichotomy.

A knock on the door disturbed Luther's thoughts. He got up to open the door to his room, it was rare to get visitors. Jartavius was standing at the door. He was dressed differently. Still with familiar red accents, but he was now wearing a black tuxedo, a red bowtie, red shoes, red pocket square and a black hat with a red band wrapped around the top part. In short, he looked fabulous.

Luther noticed that Jartavius was also holding what looked to be a suit bag. As he approached, Jartavius held the bag up towards Luther. Luther moved to grab the bag that was being offered.

"What is this, Jar?" Luther questioned why he would be getting dressed. He couldn't leave.

"We're going down to Atlanta tonight. You're coming with us." Jartavius seemed serious.

"What? What's happening?" Luther's concern crept up on him.

"Look, people are freaking out right now man. The Homeland Security Director just told the entire country that they were rounding up non-whites and that the Republic has fallen. There's riots everywhere. We're driving to Atlanta to meet with the other dons of the Sanguine Nations to see what we can do about it." Jartavius seemed passionate, inspired almost, like he had found a purpose or a cause worth fighting for.

"Why am I coming? I can stay here with the plants like always." Fear was palpable on Luther's lips.

"So, we kept you alive because one of the dons, Horace Birch, see he's a lawyer. Basically, the way he saw it, is if they made a new country, the whole 'Christian States of America' bullshit, anyway, he said if it's a new country, and everyone remaining from the old United States joined up, you'd technically be the only remaining member of the United States Government." Somewhere in that incoherent rabble, Luther figured out what Jartavius meant.

"You think I'm the President?" Luther scoffed.

"You are. You have to be. I saw you on TV man, you were smart and a leader." An admiration that Jartavius had not shown before tinged his words.

"I…. I'm not that man anymore. I'm changed." The words fell out of Luther like a raging river. It had been years since he talked to anyone about his feelings. He didn't remember the last time he had spoken to anyone about anything other than growing weed in this church. That was his life, and the plants kept him occupied. There was a simplicity that distracted him from his pain, from his hatred of himself.

"Look man, you don't have a choice. You're the only person on the planet that can calm this down, we need you to be that guy. People use your image as a symbol of hope, the last guy who was willing to stand against Drum." The admiration woven into Jartavius's words stirred something in Luther. A storm that had been lying dormant in his soul began to brew once more.

"I'm not sure I can but give me the suit. I'll try my best." Luther took the suit bag from Jartavius. Inside was just a plain black suit with a red tie. The suit jacket had an American flag lapel pin. *Nice touch,* Luther thought to himself.

"Hey, Jar?" Luther saw him walking away and was trying to get him to stop.

"What's up, Lu?" Jartavius turned back around.

"Do you think I can get some stuff to shave my face? If I'm going to be that person again, I should probably look like him."

Jartavius smiled and nodded. Luther turned back to the suit and began to undress out of his familiar gardening clothes. A t-shirt with a light, but thick shirt over top and cargo pants. Luther began to unlace his boots, and as he was finishing, Jartavius appeared again with a razor and shaving cream. He put his hand on Luther's shoulder without saying anything and walked back out of the room.

"Hey, Jar."

Jartavius came back into the room with an annoyed look on his face, "What, Lu?"

"Do you think God will ever forgive me for the things that I've done?" The storm brewing in Luther's soul was causing a torrent of emotions that he had buried since the State of the Union. *They died because of me,* Luther couldn't get the thought out of his head again. *They died because I pushed too hard.*

"I don't know, Lu. I don't believe in that shit." He tossed Luther a piece of gum and walked out of the room. Somehow, that was exactly what Luther needed to hear. He walked over to the mirror and began to shave the beard that had taken over his face. His beard was probably twelve inches off of his face by this point, he hadn't shaved since he fled from DC two years ago. Luther had lost track of time for those months he spent in the woods. Zip had helped him figure it out a few months back, but he tried not to think about those times.

The beard finally left his face, and Luther continued to shave his head. He had gone bald years ago, and time certainly did nothing to change that. So, he shaved off the remainder of his hair on the sides of his head. Then, he opened the suit bag and began to get dressed. Putting back on the suit did something to Luther. There was something familiar about the ritual of putting on a suit that brought forth more of the storm that Luther thought he had put to rest. *Never forget who you are.* Luther's heart began to race and he clutched his chest.

Sinking down to sit back on the bed, Luther began to weep. *I'm so sorry, grandpa. I tried, I did. I had to survive.* The suit brought back memories of a different person, a man of honor and integrity. *I'm a murderer, I killed those girls and that man and his wife, I don't deserve to lead.* Luther was on the floor now, rolling back and forth. Removing the mask of his captivity ripped open the floodgates that he had built in his soul. The memory of what Luther had lost ripped him apart.

After some time had passed, Luther gained control of his emotions, or perhaps he just ran out of energy to feel them. He stood up and straightened out his suit jacket. Once more he looked in the mirror to see the drawn and gaunt man who he had become. Before his ordeal, he had a smooth and healthy face. Now, his skin was cracked, his jawline was extremely defined and his eyes had sunken. Like a soldier who had gone to war only to come out the other side a changed person.

At the end of the day, son, we all only have one choice, Luther heard his dad's voice in his head as he straightened up his tie. *Live or die,* Luther heard his own voice this time, not his dad's. He pulled the jacket forward to fit it to his form and turned to walk out into the greenhouse floor that had been his home. Walking through the plants which had become his constant companions, he wondered if he would ever come back to this simple cycle.

"Hey Lu! Looking good my man." Zip walked up to Luther and dapped him up. "Haven't seen you in anything but rags man, I forgot what Congressman Washington looked like, haha. Come on, Jar is waiting with the car." Luther followed Zip outside and saw the black SUV waiting outside for him. He opened the door and ducked his head inside the car. Jartavius was inside the car in the backseat and Zip got in the passenger seat. A person who Luther didn't recognize was driving the car. He looked to Jartavius to get some idea of who this guy was, but Jartavius just shook his head and handed Luther a pistol. It was a 9mm, standard issue police sidearm. The steel felt heavy and dangerous - just like Luther.

After a six-and-a-half-hour drive, the car pulled up to a large office tower in the heart of Atlanta, Georgia. It was a massive glass and steel building. A group of bellhops came out to the car to open the doors for the men and Jartavius, Zip and Luther all stepped out of the car. A rotund black man waddled out of the building. He was wearing a deep purple suit with golden suspenders and was bejeweled in a display of jewelry that Luther found distasteful. He also walked with a deep black cane that had a golden skull adorned on the top.

Jartavius approached the man and they performed an elaborate handshake and then embraced. After a brief moment, they separated once more and Jartavius motioned towards Luther and the two of them approached.

Jartavius spoke first, "Lu, this is Walt Piper, he's one of the dons we're here to talk to."

Walt piped up at this point, "As I live and breathe, it is him. I didn't believe you, Jar. I really didn't." Walt didn't stop to shake Luther's hand, he pulled him in for a full on embrace, "I have never had more hope than I do right now. Our boys are being rounded up and murdered by Drum and his cronies. We need you more than you know."

Luther was confused and out of sorts. These were supposed to be seasoned killers and drug dealers, not weepy men looking for hope. It was at this point that Luther began to look around. He was in the heart of downtown Atlanta, one of the largest cities in the entire country, and there was not a soul walking the streets. The city felt abandoned and hopeless. The normal hustle and bustle of cars, bikes, trains and planes ceased and all that was left was the sound of silence. It was eerie and terrifying.

"What happened here?" Luther had been in the dark for two years. Jartavius had kept him there. He had thought Jartavius kept him hidden because he was a prisoner, but more and more Luther felt that it was more likely Jartavius was protecting him from the truth of what the country had become.

Walt looked up at Luther, "Drum happened." Walt waved the group in and they all followed. The lobby of the building was ornate, decorated in marble and gold lining between the tiles on the floor. The elevator was at the far end of the lobby tucked into a small side hall that ran up the length of the building. Once they got in, Walt pushed the button for the top floor. They rode the elevator in silence. Once they got to the top, the doors opened into a similar hallway as the bottom floor.

But once Luther stepped out into the hallway, he was awestruck by the view. They must be fifty stories up, and he could see the entirety of the city. More importantly, he could see the large military installation that was set up on the outskirts of the city. Luther realized that things had become far worse than he ever imagined.

The room was an entirely open conference room surrounded by windows on all sides. In the middle was a long rectangular table with seats lining each side of it. There were approximately twenty people in the room, but only a handful of them were seated at the table. When Luther entered the room, everyone went silent. *Never forget who you are*, Luther heard the words again, but they were again in his own voice.

He walked to the head of the table and sat down. Nobody moved to stop him or said anything. He clasped his hands in front of him and bowed his head for a moment to gather his thoughts. Breathing in and out slowly, Luther poised himself for what was to come.

"Hello everyone." Luther picked up his head and smiled. There was no reaction from the people seated at the table.

"Everyone, this is Luther Washington." Walt finally broke the awkward silence that had permeated the room.

"Wow man, you look terrible." The youngest looking of the seated men spoke up, and everyone laughed as he said that. "Where have you been?"

After the laughter died down, Luther responded, "I've been through hell, truly. Seems like maybe that experience has been mutual."

The young man spoke up again, "Yeah, you could say that. My name is Daquan Hightower, I rep the Eastside Crew." The table went around and introduced themselves. Luther forgot most of their names as soon as they said them, it was too much information. He would remember Daquan though.

"Well, it's very nice to meet all of you, but I gotta ask, why am I here?"

Daquan seemed to be the most vocal, "Drum has been rounding up black folk and putting them in those camps with the Muslims, Jews and Catholics. Even Christian black folk. He's killing us."

Luther was shocked, "I knew the man was insane, but I didn't think he'd ever sink to this. How'd this happen?"

Another man at the opposite side of the table spoke up, Luther tried to remember his name, "After the State of the Union, Drum imposed martial law. He moved military garrisons into most of the major cities. Police played right along, everyone was on board when they were just rounding up the Muslims."

"I'm sorry, what's your name again?" Luther asked, embarrassed.

"You can call me August. Name is August Hayes."

"Okay, so August, they're rounding up Catholics, too?" Luther was so confused.

"Shit Jar, did you not tell him anything?" The entire room looked towards Jartavius.

"Look, the man was great at growing plants and I didn't want to mess that up. You didn't see him when he came to us. He was not right." Luther looked down into the table and saw his reflection in the wooden sheen. The group shook their heads.

August spoke up again, "Look, son, there's been some real bad shit going down. Drum rounded up all the Muslims, then he rounded up all the Catholics, and now he's rounding up every minority in the country. We used to have twenty thousand people working our distribution networks, and now we've got half that number. Any person caught protesting or committing any sort of criminal act is just being thrown in those camps without any second thought." The macabre echoes of August's words stuck in Luther's mind.

"The UN has watch dogs in place for this type of stuff, are they not doing anything?" Luther asked, the entire room looked down again.

"The UN can't do anything because of the war in Europe. About a month after Drum created his fancy new country, Russia and Turkey began a full-scale war against western Europe. Those krauts are holding out so far, but nobody is sure if it'll escalate or not."

Luther sighed. He thought about what to do. *Never forget who you are. Survive.* The echoes of his ancestors reverberated with what he was being told. *At the end of the day, there's only one answer for tyrants,* Luther thought to himself, a steel resolve descending into his mind.

"Gentlemen, I don't know much anymore. What I do know is that the answer to this riddle is very simple: we're going to kill Harold Drum."

Chapter 33: The City of Fire

The dry air blew into the window of the commander's office as the decrepit odor of the deceased soldiers lingered. The taste of the horror stung Nida's lungs and occasionally made her cough from revulsion. They had not had time to bury the bodies of the men at the depot, and Nida didn't want to abandon the position given the immense amount of supplies they had access to here.

She had given the order to start bussing people from the internment camp to the depot, but it was taking a significantly greater amount of time than Nida had originally assumed. It seemed a common theme that whenever someone told her how long something would take, that she should double the estimate at a minimum. *At least then I won't be so consistently disappointed,* Nida thought to herself.

Lost in her thoughts and planning, Nida didn't notice when Captain Winters walked in. He shuffled through the door and put some documents down on Nida's desk. He then sat down in one of the chairs arrayed in front of the desk that Nida had acquired for herself.

"These are some of the news dispatches received by this station over the past few weeks. It appears that mass protests have erupted across the country. They've been able to militarily lock down most of the east coast, but the western cities are still burning." Winters was talking very bluntly, as if he was briefing a superior officer.

"Are there any openings for us to get more recruits?" Nida asked. The need for more muscle was at the forefront of her mind.

"Well, there are two national guard armories on the periphery of Las Vegas that have apparently refused orders to move into the city. Perhaps they would be willing to defect?"

Nida paused for a moment. "Two armories? How many men at each?"

"Well, from all reports their battalions responded to the all hands call, but didn't deploy. According to the service records that I was able to obtain using this site's previous commander's credentials, there are four hundred and eighteen guardsmen at the first and a contingent of two hundred and seventy-six at the second. The larger armory consists almost entirely of transportation and engineering personnel, but the second one is an infantry brigade." Winters had initially laid the documents down on the desk for Nida to review, but had picked them up and was reading the data out to Nida.

"That many men could help us get into the city, right?" Nida began to form an idea.

"What are you thinking?" Winters was still reviewing the documents, but had an eyebrow up towards Nida.

"These people are rioting against the government. If we can get enough weapons and convince them that we're going to take down the government, that would be a lot more soldiers than just the six hundred from the armories. We need to go to the armories, convince them, and then take our forces into the city."

313

"Nida, you're talking about a rebellion. I don't think I can sign on for that." There was a sadness to Winters' voice. He was being forced to choose between two things that he had come to love.

"The revolution is here, Billy. The only choice we have left is whether to join or die when the reaction comes. We've killed dozens of soldiers and guards, stolen military equipment and have taken over two military outposts. Exactly how do you think that they will treat you if they win?" There was no path backwards for Nida, she was committed.

"Maybe you're right, Nida. Maybe you're right." He didn't move, but reached up to scratch his chin where a whiskered beard began to grow in.

"Look, if it will make you feel more comfortable, we'll try to reach out to the leaders of the city to see if they'll meet with us peacefully. Okay?" Nida was trying to compromise. Winters considered it for a moment and then shrugged his shoulders, continuing to read.

Nida moved over to him and sat down in the chair next to him. Winters kept reading the documents and eventually turned towards Nida again.

"Hey, I went to college with the commander of the transportation battalion. Small world." Winters chuckled to himself, but Nida had alarm bells ringing in her head.

"We need you to make the introduction! You're the only one who can do this, they'll kill us on sight if we roll up with an armed band of rebels." The path forward was obvious, but Nida had lingering doubts about Winters. His earlier statements mixed with his strangely docile demeanor since they pulled him out of his cell at the camp gave Nida tremendous pause when considering the plan.

"I haven't spoken with the guy since college, I don't know if I can do that, but I'll certainly try." His tone changed to carry a tinge of hope to it.

"Good, we leave at 8 am tomorrow." Nida began to leave the room, but Winters grabbed her by the arm. Nida turned towards him, shocked by the contact.

He looked her in the eyes, "If we do this, I need to know that we are fighting for democracy."

Nida took his hand off her arm. Taking his hand in hers, she leaned down to kiss it. She smiled at him and said, "That will always be what we're fighting for." Nida turned and left the room.

The road stretched on for several desert miles. The dry air made it oppressive to breathe but was somehow still tolerable. For whatever reason, the U.S. Army apparently did not outfit its humvees with air conditioning. Nida could feel the sweat starting to coat her inner clothing, and it became uncomfortable to sit for very long.

Nida checked her watch. It was 11:36 am, the sun was high in the sky and the heat was getting worse. Winters sat beside her in the driver's seat. Nida had never driven a vehicle, Abdul always drove her wherever she needed to go. So, she let Winters drive.

"How much longer do we have?" Nida moaned.

"About ten minutes to the armory, it's on the northern route heading out of Las Vegas, we've had to go around the city to avoid eyes."

Sweat was pouring down Winters' face. He was clearly as uncomfortable as Nida, so she took out one of her water bottles and handed it to him. He gleefully took the bottle and began to chug the sweet nectar. Water poured out the sides of his mouth as he struggled to contain the flow.

Handing it back to her, he spoke up again, "When we get there, just let me talk. I know how these guys operate." Nida nodded to mask her skepticism. Many people had expressed doubt to her about how far she could trust Winters. She held her own doubts, but he had been steadfast so far. The worst part to Nida was that even if he wasn't trustworthy, she still needed him.

After a few more minutes, Nida began to see the outline of barbed wire fencing. *We're here*, she thought to herself. She sat upright in her seat and began to adjust the outfit that had quickly become her permanent uniform. Still wearing the cut off army jacket and wrapped belt, Nida had added a ballistic plate carrier to her outfit. They found a lot of extra ones at the depot. They had found a few uniforms that may actually fit Nida, but she liked the one she had.

Eventually, they came to what looked like a gatehouse. The gate was closed and there were a few guards posted outside. Winters began to slow the truck down as they approached, but the guards primed their rifles and pointed them at the truck anyway.

"STEP OUT OF THE VEHICLE WITH YOUR HANDS UP!" Shouted the guard closest to the truck.

Winters spoke up, "We're getting out. We're on your side!" Winters opened the door, and Nida followed his lead. They both stepped out of the truck with their hands held up. Another guard approached and they proceeded to search Winters and Nida. They then searched the truck.

"They're unarmed." The first guard said to the one that arrived after.

"Take them to Col. Miller, pull their vehicle in through the gate and then close it up."

"Roger that, sir." The first guard waved for Winters and Nida to follow him.

"What's your name, soldier?" Winters asked the guard that was escorting them.

"It's better if we don't talk." The soldier replied dismissively. The three walked in silence as they approached a large brick building. *It's so strange how plain and unimaginative all these military buildings are. This could be a shopping mall,* Nida thought to herself. They walked into the armory and were astonished at what they saw. The entire building had essentially been turned into a hospital. There were soldiers and civilians lying in cots that lined every room that they could see, and some of the hallways. The smell of death lingered in the air.

"Wh-what happened here?" Nida cried out.

"Drum happened." The soldier replied, impatiently waving once more.

They continued into an elevator. The soldier pressed the button to go to the fourth floor. After a short while in the magic metal box, the three stepped out into a clear hallway. It was staggering how quiet it was on this floor compared to the first. They made it to the end of the hallway and entered into a very average looking doorway.

Sitting at a desk with his dress uniform on was a smaller, white man. He was completely bald but sported a robust black mustache. His face was adorned with black rimmed glasses that had circular rims. Nida figured he couldn't be more than 5'6", but he was still sitting down so it was hard to tell.

"Private, did you knock before you came in here?" The man said.

"No, sir. LT told me to bring these two to you. They came in the main gate in a humvee, sir."

At this, the small man finally took his eyes off of what he was working on long enough to observe who was in the room. His eyes were very blue, which combined with his mustache gave a very serious look. There was a black oak leaf embroidered on his shoulder's lapels, and what looked to be a huge stack of award ribbons on his chest. This man did not let complete chaos dampen his military decorum.

"To what do I owe the pleasure, Captain Winters?" The private turned around and looked at the gaunt man he had been escorting.

"Sorry, sir. Didn't realize." The private said to Winters. Winters clapped him on the shoulder.

"Don't mention it, not sure I'm technically still in at this point." Winters then turned towards the small man, "you owe this to the circumstances at hand, my friend. It is good to see you."

The small man pursed his lips and shot a glance towards Nida. "Who's she?"

Nida spoke up at this point, "My name is Nida Muhammad. I am the leader of a group of people who broke free of imprisonment at the hands of Harold Drum. We are here to discuss cooperation with your outfit."

Winters' shoulders dropped and he shot an annoyed glance towards Nida. Nevertheless, she continued, "What has happened with all of these wounded people here?"

"Well, Ms. Muhammad-" Nida interjected, "You may call me Nida." The small man shuffled in his desk a little bit, very clearly not used to being interrupted.

"Well, Nida, my name is Lt. Col. Jacob Miller. This is the 391st Engineering Battalion headquarters. We've been tasked by the governor of Nevada with providing medical and transportation services for the injured street fighters in Las Vegas."

Winters spoke up, "You're still in contact with the governor?" He sounded hopeful for the first time in a while.

"We were until about five days ago. Something knocked out our communications in the area, and we haven't been able to get in touch with them. I sent some scouts to receive orders, but by all reports the governor's mansion was burned to the ground." The cold reality of military life allowed Lt. Col. Miller to speak plainly, but each word stung.

"Burned down? What's going on, sir?" Winters' hope turned into shock and anger.

"It's a total cluster. Drum passed some immigration act and then his cronies started rounding up blacks and hispanics. The backlash has been violent. Protestors are burning government buildings to the ground, and every attempt at intervention has been met with immense violence. The entire eastern seaboard is on military lockdown, and they've committed almost every military asset that they have to keeping order over there."

"So, what's the situation here?" Nida asked.

"We've got armed bands of insurgents attacking and destroying military outposts and government buildings. We aren't even attempting a presence inside the city, it's mainly been taken over by gangs and street muscle. We tried to slowly set a perimeter up, but they have enough small arms to hold out long enough for us to be forced to retreat."

Nida sat down in a chair in front of the desk and crossed her legs. She stared out of the window for a minute, contemplating what to do now. To her right, Winters sat down in another chair that was placed against the wall.

"Well, shit." Nida sighed and leaned her head back.

Miller spoke up, "Why did you two even come here?"

"Uhh... we were hoping that you'd join us." Nida responded.

"Not quite, Nida, not quite. We want to help restore order in the city, and we wanted to put our forces together."

Miller's eyebrow raised dramatically, "Forces?"

Nida gave him a chilling smile, "Yes, we have around eight hundred people in our camp ready to help…. uhh… restore order."

Miller turned towards Winters who just gave him a nod. This made the old colonel lean back in his chair for a bit. He twiddled his mustache as he considered the implications of a battalion sized independent militia in the area.

"What do you want from my unit?" Miller asked.

"As much personnel and equipment as you can spare." Nida replied.

"And if I refuse to help you?" Miller asked.

"We'd prefer not to discuss that option. We'd prefer it much more if you would just help." Winters interjected. He knew Nida was just going to overtly threaten him, that had been her modus operandi of late.

"Well, I can't spare many. Most of my people are helping with the triage unit, but I can spare vehicles and the 2nd Platoon of Delta Company is a Sapper unit, so they could be helpful to you. I'll have Lieutenant Bedard come find you and walk you through the vehicles we have here. Take what you need. We're certainly not going to help the President at this point, the Governor gave direct orders not to listen to DC before we lost contact."

Nida was pleasantly surprised. She had fully expected to have to take this armory by force. She wasn't getting quite the influx of people she had expected, but the vehicles alone were likely going to be worth the trouble.

"I've got to ask, how'd you get a militia together with that many people?" Miller seemed genuinely curious.

"I killed our captors and seized control of our prison. I then successfully led a raid into a supply depot that will allow us to eat and supply ourselves for several months." Nida spoke flatly.

"Ah, that explains why our communications have been down. Well, victory is a great legitimizer, I suppose. What do you plan to do if you're successful?" Miller was nervous. Nida's answer gave him a feeling of trepidation about continuing to assist her.

"I want to restore democracy to this country. It was such a beautiful place before Drum. I just want that back." Nida was sincere, she believed in what America was supposed to be.

Miller nodded and looked towards Winters, "Billy, take whatever you need. I can see why you're helping her. Please close the door on the way out."

Nida and Winters got up and went back down the hallway. Their guard was still standing outside the door and began to follow them once they exited. Nida wheeled towards the guard and stopped dead in her tracks.

"We don't need an escort anymore." She said in a dismissive tone.

"I'm not escorting, I'm following. I heard what you talked about in there. I'm not getting stuck in here while y'all are going to Las Vegas. I want to fight, all of us do. Miller's got us penned up in here because he's afraid." The guard was nothing more than a private, but he had passion. *I can use passion,* Nida thought to herself. Without a word, Nida turned back around and continued down the hall. The guard followed.

Chapter 34: Threads Unraveling

The Rose Garden's fragrance permeated the air, the pungent scent demarcated a rare dedication to natural beauty of the political aristocracy. The scars on the earth left by humanity plagued this city, the evil seeping out from the coagulated contempt for humanity contained within these vaunted halls spoke to Harold. *How can I be evil in the face of what built this place?* He thought to himself.

He poured a glass of whiskey for himself and took a swig. Standing out in the muggy July air, Harold stood with Rick and James. They had not spoken in a few minutes, lost in a wistful air of longing for days gone by.

"We've come a long way, gentlemen, haven't we?" Harold croaked out and sipped the whiskey once more.

"Yessir, we have," James replied.

Rick didn't say anything but puffed his cigar. The industrial wasteland, the roses, and the cigar smoke swirled together in Rick's head. Nothing could overpower the dread in his soul. Rick sat down on one of the brick steps leading down to the garden itself. He looked at the Secret Service agents around the garden, standing in constant vigil around their master. *Gorillas guarding a snake,* Rick thought to himself.

"We're cascading towards a cliff, now, Harold. It doesn't matter how far we've come together. You've doomed us."

Harold burst into a fit of laughter, James looked at Rick quizzically. Harold walked down to sit beside Rick and bent down, slapping his hand on his shoulder as he lowered down to sit. Putting his arm around Rick, Harold breathed out a heavy sigh.

"I know you're skeptical my friend, but have I led you wrong before?" Harold smiled that intoxicating smile.

"So many times, Harold. So many times." A tear ran down Rick's face. "My entire life has been sacrificed for yours. I've lived every day in a cage created by your ambition." He took another drink.

Harold withdrew his arm from Rick's shoulders and the smile ran away from his face. The smoke from the cigar flowed into Harold's eyes and made them water. He wiped the wetness away from his eyes and coughed.

"Rick, how can you say that? We're going to be okay. This is temporary, rage can only last so long." Harold had been through protest cycles before, but at least now he could lock them up. It was much easier to suppress a rebellion when suppression was legal. The Supreme Court had been packed with Caliphate members long ago, so there was no challenge to Harold's authority. *It's a strange flaw in the system to make sure that the Supreme Court only comes from a small group of universities,* Harold thought. *Much easier to corrupt when the target is smaller.*

"It's not about us being okay, Harold! What we've done can never be reversed! Do you understand that? We've crossed a line here, and we won't survive this. I can't believe how blinded you are, have you convinced yourself that you've done the right thing again?! Honestly, Harold, I can't understand how you continue to rationalize this madness." Rick threw the glass at the doors leading back into the White House. It broke through one of the glass planes and the drinking glass shattered down while whiskey splattered everywhere on the door and the blood ran down in streaks to feed the roses.

The Secret Service agents alerted and walked forward to get control of the situation, but Rick continued, "You convinced me to go on that mission trip. I was only there because of your sexual desires. My entire life was given up because you wanted to fuck Cheryl! I never got a choice because of you! Yet you ignore my advice and my counsel again, and again." The Secret Service had drawn their weapons and were pointing them at the ground.

He continued, "We had everything that we wanted. We had years to make gradual change that would have kept everything on the rails, and you chose time after time to reach towards unnecessary aggression and violence. This isn't leadership, this is amateurism that succeeded on the pure inadequacy of the opponent. I will not give another fucking day to your enterprise of evil, I quit. I quit as Chief of Staff and I'm done with the Caliphate. Leave me alone."

Rick walked into the White House and went to his office. Harold stood in the Rose Garden with James, both of whom remained in a state of stunned silence. James moved closer to Harold, getting shoulder to shoulder with him on his left side, both looking down the hall that Rick had just walked down.

"We should stop him, sir. He knows too much to be outside of our organization." James heavily emphasized the word "stop," heavily implying that he wanted to permanently stop him. This wasn't the first time someone had grown a conscience. James was unsentimental about such things. Harold didn't respond either way but walked back into the Oval Office entrance away from where Rick had gone. James followed.

Rick got into his car and began to drive. He didn't know where he was going, he didn't know where to go. He had been staying at the White House residence for so long, he didn't even have an apartment to return to anymore. Exiting onto I-95, Rick raced south towards Richmond. It had been years since he'd been home. Going to college in Alabama, and then spending most of his life following Harold, he had not had the time to go home.

Tonight, Rick would drive to Richmond and start a new life. *I'll reach out to my mom, I think she's still alive,* Rick thought to himself. He felt light, like a new day was dawning in his life. No more politics, no more struggling, just a quiet retirement away from anything meaningful. He had given so much to the world during his years on Earth that he felt he had earned the right to quit.

He continued to drive down the interstate, music blaring through his radio. It was some rock song, but he didn't recognize it. *I don't know the last time I listened to the radio,* Rick thought to himself. A horrifying feeling washed over him. *Oh god, do I know anything about this country?* The magnitude of the time that Rick had lost began to dawn on him. Fifty-six years old, Rick had spent the entirety of his adult life serving the Caliphate and working in politics.

Rick saw that a bridge was coming up in the road. An idea crossed through Rick's head. *We all have a choice.* A cold resolve set into his heart, he shifted the wheel hard to the right as he crossed over the bridge. Colliding with the guard rail, the force of the car plunged headlong through.

The car landed in the river, and Rick was knocked delirious. He was hanging onto consciousness by a thread. Water was beginning to pour into the car, and Rick passed out.

James approached Harold, not sure how to begin. Harold noticed his approach as the door opened. Shuffling some papers around, Harold pulled out an intelligence report and handed it to James as he walked up. James took the report, but didn't read it right away.

"Sir, Rick is dead." James figured it was best to be direct in this kind of situation.

"I didn't give the order for that, James. Why did you act on your own?" Harold immediately assumed James had Rick killed.

"I did nothing, sir. It appears his car ran off a bridge. Several motorists that witnessed the event said it looked intentional. Here's the police report." James handed Harold the police report.

Harold read through the report, it seemed that James was telling the truth. *Oh shit, what am I going to do without Rick?* Harold began to panic. *Oh shit oh shit oh shit,* Harold had not been without Rick since he had seized control of the Caliphate. *Everything I've accomplished was with Rick by my side, he was my last friend, I am alone now.* A stunned sadness took over Harold. James did not take note, but began to read the intelligence report that Harold had handed him.

"Sir, what are we doing about this? A prison camp uprising? Are we reacting?" An inside source within a

National Guard armory in the area reported some seriously concerning news about an uprising in Las Vegas.

Harold shook his head to clear it. "I feel that in my quest to institute a new order, I've only brought chaos." James detected a sense of doubt in Harold that he had not seen before.

"We don't have time for self reflection sir, we have to respond."

Harold froze. "I-I-.... We're just spread so thin. We've got men locking down the cities, we've got multiple camps throughout the country that are staffed with our men. All we've got left are regular military troops, and they can't be trusted to attack their own people. We could probably gather up a response of five thousand men and a few planes, but that's as much as we can spare that far into the West."

"Sir, I would like to take personal command of this mission." James stood with his hands clasped behind his back.

"Very well, James, very well." Harold poured a whiskey for himself, and took a swig.

Chapter 35: Operation Vegas Crusade

Twelve men in military dress uniforms rung the table in the situation room inside the White House. Harold was seated at the head of the table, and James was standing up beside him. The room was dark, and a large screen began to descend from the ceiling. A map of Las Vegas appeared on the screen.

"Gentlemen, we have received a new mission, designation Operation: Vegas Crusade. The situation is that an armed band of insurgents has taken control of several military compounds including a major supply depot and two national guard armories. We believe that they are planning to make a move into the city of Las Vegas, Nevada to gather recruits and supplies they need."

James continued, "Our mission is to move into the city and occupy it before the insurgent band can gain control of Nellis Air Force Base and become a real, credible threat. The execution of this plan will include five thousand soldiers of the Special Corps, a detachment of the 192nd Artillery Company, and ten C-130 gunships flying air support. The ground forces will be split into five detachments of one thousand men each. Designations Alpha, Bravo, Charlie, Delta, Echo, command of each of these detachments has been assigned as listed in your mission briefing report." James paused for a moment while the men read their report.

"Alpha will attempt to march down the main ingress on Interstate 15. Bravo will swing south to the city of Henderson, and then advance up Interstate 11. Charlie will detach and occupy Nellis Air Force Base. Delta and Echo will remain with the artillery detachment in the rear

330

guard as a reserve force. Prior to Alpha and Bravo's advance into the inner part of the city, the 192nd artillery detachment will use rolling suppression fire to bottle the insurgents up. Once they are trapped in the inner part of the city, they will be forced to either flee and expose themselves on the highways or bottle up in a single place."

Arrows appeared on the screen as James talked, showing the strategic outlook of how the advance was being planned. It showed the locations of each of the detachments and where each involved party would be located at the times.

"Gentlemen, it is imperative that the men understand that we will accept retreat as an outcome for this battle. We do not have the manpower to crush this insurgency, if they run out of the city, do not pursue. Controlling Nellis and the city will give us a base of operations in the area to establish control of the region."

The screen changed to a bullet point slide, "This is the command and control. As you will see, I will be in direct field command over the division. General Altman, you will be in command of Alpha and Bravo. Your role is to coordinate the advance into the city. General Del Rio, you will be in control of Charlie and securing Nellis Air Force Base. I will remain in control of the reserves, the artillery, and the air detachment of C-130s. Are there any questions?"

General Altman spoke up first, "This is a good plan, but I think you're being overly cautious, sir. We should send the reserve forces to trap them in the city. These are untrained amateurs, we can crush them here and solve the insurrection and control in one fell swoop."

James bristled, "You're wrong. You're making an assumption that they will commit all their forces. If we let them escape, they will inevitably retreat towards the rest of their forces. From there, we will be able to track their movements."

The group collectively considered the disagreement for a few moments. Many spoke in favor of both, and there was not a clear consensus. After the group debated for another minute or so, Harold finally had enough.

"SILENCE!" He boomed, speaking for the first time in an hour. He continued, "We will surround the city. I will crush this rebellion here and now."

James, and a large portion of Secret Service stationed at the White house began to prepare for their journey to Las Vegas. This was going to be a heavy logistical lift, they had to prepare a convoy to leave in a single day for five thousand soldiers. Even in the best of times, this was a tough ask, but they began to work towards their goal.

"What do you mean you want to kill Harold Drum?" The Dons sat in silence. August was the only one who spoke up.

"I've made up my mind. It's the only way. He's a tyrant, and that's what tyrants get." Luther had years to think about this. Though the thoughts were in the very dark recesses of his mind, sometimes they peeked through his blissful ignorance of the world for those years. An endless cycle of life and death, played out in front of his eyes. The end of life was a hard point in time for all people, now was Harold Drum's time.

"How do you propose we do that?" August said.

"Gather everyone we can, every gun we can, and every vehicle we can. Drive them straight to the White House, take it, and put a bullet in his head."

The table still gave no response. Eventually, Jartavius broke the silence, "We all know that Luther is the President. We should listen to him."

Luther laughed, but everyone looked at him simultaneously, expectantly. Luther responded, "Guys, I'm not the President. I haven't been that guy in a long time."

His declination only made them want to follow him more. It wasn't Luther the man that they were following, it was the last legitimate member of a government that for whatever reason, these men still believed in. Daquan Hightower stood up and looked at Luther.

"LIBERTY OR DEATH!" All of the dons at the table immediately echoed, "LIBERTY OR DEATH, LIBERTY OR DEATH!!"

Survive. Remember who you are.

Nida walked into an audaciously bejeweled hotel. It had been shut down after a federal crackdown on gambling shut everything in Las Vegas down. The people that remained here had become impoverished overnight as their entire way of life was shattered by someone else's moral crusade. A gathering of the city's leadership had agreed to meet her here. Winters had taken a detachment to the other National Guard base to attempt to get them under their banner. She had to trust him to take care of something, so she was going to trust him with eighty men and a couple of vehicles to try and convince a bunch of infantrymen to follow a new cause.

Initially, Winters had objected to the idea, but Nida had convinced him by giving him command of whatever troops he was able to obtain. He would still be a part of her army, but her intent was to have him operate separately to cover more ground. They would work together to move their cause forward. Nida wouldn't make the mistake that others make by keeping power too close, she would share. She could trust Winters, or so she hoped.

The Mayor of Las Vegas, a tall black woman named Constance Sharpe, stared back at Nida. Constance had deep brown eyes and hair that was braided and pulled back into a ponytail. She had on a gray skirt suit, and black circular glasses. She was older than Nida, but Nida couldn't tell by how much. Nida assumed that she was in her mid-forties.

"You're going to get us all killed! You're gathering an army, Drum is not going to tolerate this, you know that." She was scared, they all were.

"I understand that you are afraid," Nida put her head down, looking at the floor. "I was afraid once." She lifted her head up and began to walk forward, placing her hands on her hips as she approached Constance.

"I had a husband and a child once. We lived in a beautiful little house in a charming little neighborhood. It was bliss." Nida paused for a moment, but put her hands out and began pacing in a line before the gathered assembly of city leaders. "It was all taken from me by this

334

new Christian States of America. They killed my husband and child right in front of me, all because I had the audacity to fight off a rapist pig."

Nida got loud now, channeling her fury, "I will not stand by and do nothing while this evil consortium of zealots tears apart everything that remains! I will not allow anyone else to experience what I have been through as long as I draw breath! I *will* liberate every single person from every one of these abominable camps, and I *will* march this army all the way to Washington if I have to."

She slowed and came to a stop back in front of Constance, placing her hand on Constance's shoulder, "I don't need you to join me, brothers and sisters. I just need you to stay out of my way."

The group was awestruck. The gravity of Nida's thirst for vengeance was enticing. The righteous indignation which oozed from her being stoked the fires of their souls and reignited a passion and longing for freedom. A time before fear and paranoia gripped the nation, a time before Harold Drum seized power and pulled the final brick out of the illusion of democracy that everyone deluded themselves into thinking was real. They wanted to believe.

"What would you ask of us?" A short man, no taller than 5' 5" with brown, shaggy hair stepped up to Nida. He had an olive complexion, and wore a bushy mustache. Nida remembered his name from the introduction as Leonardo.

"If you are willing to help, any soldiers you can muster would be the first ask. We currently have 800 soldiers in our group. Most of them are stationed at a supply depot out at the western outskirts of the city, but a group of them are going to recruit more troops from another armory Henderson where another 200 or so additional soldiers are located. We're hopeful that they will join the cause." Nida decided to be open, hoping that honest dialogue would further convince them to involve themselves.

Leonardo turned towards Constance, "I agree with her. I can't live like this anymore. The entire country is imploding."

Constance simply nodded. Nida smiled and turned to leave, but before she could make it to the doorway, Constance called out to her, "Where are you going?"

Nida turned back around, smile still wide, "I'm going to signal my army to move into the city. We will make this our headquarters and train anyone who wishes to fight here."

Constance retorted, "Who said you could bring your army here?"

Nida snapped right back, "Who among you could stop me?" She continued to walk to the door. Power began to feel natural, and more intoxicating.

The Henderson National Guard armory was smaller than the one that they had taken outside of Las Vegas. It was basically just a brick building. No vehicles were stationed here, and most of the men had abandoned it long ago. It was a dead end, there were only twenty men that still remained at the armory. Those twenty men were determined to function as a city militia to keep the order until the country calmed down.

Winters was disappointed. Obviously, this could not be counted as a failure, there was simply nobody to convince. However, it couldn't count as a success, either. He wanted to be successful for Nida, he wanted her to know that she could count on him.

Suddenly, Nida's voice came over the radio from Las Vegas, "Billy, we've made contact with the city leadership and are moving our forces to this hotel to make a new base here. How are things with you?"

"Great news, Nida. Please use 'over' to signify when you're done talking, I feel like it's pretty ludicrous that I have to keep reminding people. Anyway, things did not go well here. Most of the soldiers that were stationed here fled a long time ago, there's only around twenty men left and they are not interested in leaving. Over."

"Sorry, nobody else does it, so it just feels kind of silly saying 'over' when you're the only one who uses it. Sorry to hear there's no troops here, bring your detachment back to the palace." Winters waited for a moment. "Over." Came the call from Nida. He burst into laughter, and replied, "Yes, ma'am. We're on our way."

Winters turned to his captains, "We're heading to Las Vegas. Get the convoy moving, I want us rolling in 45 minutes." The group of men saluted and dispersed. Winters had not had the chance to get to know his men yet, Nida let him command the prior Army troops because she felt it would be more natural for them, but he had not been in command long. Still, they acted more like soldiers than he was used to with the former prisoners, even if he had no idea how to be a General.

"Sir, it looks like the main force is moving in the city and the secondary detachment is remobilizing in that direction, as well. Our drones also reported that the remaining civilian leaders and people have moved to Nellis Air Force base as we agreed before they met with the girl." Lt. Col. Miller reported gleefully to James.

"Excellent. Dispatch our fighters to the column heading up from Henderson. Once the primary force gets into the city, bottle them up with artillery while the main columns move in. I want Alpha to engage and take whatever hardpoint they try to make a stand in." *Everything is going perfectly,* James thought to himself.

About an hour had passed and the vehicles were starting to roll once more. They had raided a few gas stations on their way in, so most of them had enough fuel already to make the trek back into the inner city. *I wonder how long these fuel supplies are going to last us out here,* Winters thought to himself. As a logistics officer, Winters knew that amateurs win with tactics, but professionals win with logistics. *These vehicles won't make any difference if we run out of gas.* Winters lost himself in his thoughts as his truck finally got rolling. It felt like things were coming together finally after years of hardship.

A small wave of thunderous noise apprised itself of Winters' countenance. It was subtle at first, barely perceptible but unmistakable. *Jets.* Winters looked out of the window and saw something on the horizon. He grabbed his radio.

"All units, be advised we have aircraft approaching from the North! Over!" As soon as Winters' call came through, the first of the jets unleashed a barrage of gunfire and a missile. The lead vehicle in the column was struck by the missile and exploded into a fiery cloud of black smoke. Another jet attacked the column, striking three more vehicles with gunfire as it strafed the column.

Winters called over the long range radio, "NIDA, WE'VE BEEN TRAPPED ON THE ROAD, THEY HAVE FIGHTER JETS IN THE AIR, GET OUT OF THERE, IT'S A TR-" Winters' mouth was engulfed by flames.

"BILLY?! BILLY?!" Nida was panicked. No response came. She looked towards Leon and Irene, "I-I…" Irene stepped forward and embraced Nida. Winters had meant something to her, neither of them knew what, but something. He saved her, and she saved him. They had a bond beyond time and life. His loss stabbed into her heart. *This is what I get for trusting,* Nida thought to herself. *I let myself get too close to someone. That won't happen again.*

"Leon, put our forces on high alert, bring everyone inside the palace. Station a few men on top of the neighboring rooftops, we have troops inbound." Leon raised an eyebrow, not knowing if she was serious.

"WINTERS IS DEAD, THEY ARE COMING FOR US, GET MOVING!" Leon eventually left and began to give out instructions to the soldiers. They shuffled to different locations that they were told to, but they looked scared. At the periphery of her hearing, Nida heard a faint whistling sound. It seemed like it was getting closer and closer to them, but she couldn't tell what it was.

Suddenly, the world was steel and chaos. A huge, concussive blast rocked the ground outside of the hotel. Nida fell to her knees due to the force of the blast. There was blood and remains everywhere as several of their people were hit. The whistling noise returned, but this time it sounded like a chorus.

Again, the world exploded around Nida. Explosion after explosion rocked the ground where they stood. Dozens of people were completely destroyed by the blast, leaving nothing in their wake. The shells continued to drop as Nida regained her senses.

"GET TO THE HOTEL!!!" She shouted as she waved for her people who were still out on the street to move into the relative safety of the structure. They ran quickly, but many were cut down by blast after blast as the steel rain continued to shred them apart.

Nida ran back into the hotel and began shouting orders that they needed to move barricades out into the main room and create a defensive wall. Her people were shaken, they had just watched almost fifty of their comrades completely destroyed with no enemy in sight. They had never fought something that they could not see. The people froze.

Fifty-eight vehicles rode in a continuous column up I-95. Inconspicuous to any onlooker, it could have been just a pocket of traffic. Cars, trucks, SUVs of all sizes carried in them a gang of thieves and bandits to liberate the country from tyranny. Armed to the teeth, these vehicles brought with them the iron hand of justice riding on a wind of industrial fury, but nobody would know it.

Luther sat shotgun in a black SUV that Jartavius had brought for the attempt. A pistol sat in Luther's left hand while an AR-15 sat in between his legs. Nobody talked. They had been driving for hours at this point, Luther couldn't remember how long it had been, but he knew they were getting close. He had driven this route to Washington so many times, he knew exactly how close they were to the destination.

They were in the middle of the column. A few especially reckless young men had volunteered to lead the column. The plan was to have the lead cars ram right through the gates and allow the rest of the group to move into the White House on foot. These first cars were absolutely crucial, if they failed the whole plan failed.

The column began its final approach as it turned on to Pennsylvania Avenue. The column began to pick up speed, wailing on their horns to warn any misbegotten souls on the road to clear out of the way - there was to be no slowing. The front of the column approached the gates going as fast as their manufactured cars could muster. They slammed into the gates. The first two cars managed to break apart the locking mechanism and four additional cars collided with the leads to break through the gate entirely. The rest of the column came to a halt and the rest of the gang exited the vehicles and moved towards the gate.

There was a suspicious lack of gunfire, but they proceeded onto the grounds without fear or hesitation. Advancing to the front door, a guy who Luther didn't recognize stepped into the hall and immediately the death wail of a revolver rang through the halls and caught him in his stomach. He clutched over and was riddled with bullets by the Secret Service defending the halls.

One of the other people signaled to a rocket propelled grenade launcher strapped to his back. *God, I love America,* Luther thought to himself. He motioned for the man to fire into the breach. The man pulled the RPG from his back and took aim parallel to the hallway and then quickly centered himself, launched the rocket and moved back out of the opening. Bullets rang out, but he managed to avoid their effect. The RPG round exploded with fatal purchase on the hallway defenders.

Luther motioned in a group of men who advanced and took the initial hallway. Once the men were further inside, they were met with another round of bullets as the depth of the White House defenses was beginning to take a toll. Three additional men took shots, one went straight through the head of a man who Luther knew as Pete. Luther closed his eyes as he approached him while maintaining cover in the preceding hall. A bullet rang out towards Luther's arm, but didn't hit.

A stalemate ensued where neither party could push the other. The hall defenders held firm and there was nothing that Luther and his compatriots could do about it. Luther poked his head around the corner and saw that the hallway that these agents were guarding had a window on the farside. Thinking quickly, he dashed through the hallway and into an adjacent door. The defenders weren't able to react fast enough, so he passed through unscathed. He saw a service exit at the far end of the hall that he was now in, and ran towards it.

Exiting into the central courtyard, Luther then went into the courtyard and found an angle on the defenders. Readying his AR, Luther gunned down the four men that had been holding the hallway. His men advanced. There were no other defenders, the White House was a ghost town. Making his way to the Oval Office, Luther was dejected thinking that they had missed their only opportunity to capture Drum.

As he made his way to the large oaken door, he pressed it open. To his complete surprise, Harold Drum sat behind his desk, drinking whiskey.

The sounds of small arms fire began to ring out in the streets. Calls came over the radio to Nida that the federal forces were advancing into the city, coming straight for them. The defenders were unable to hold them, every time they hit a defended location they just called in artillery fire on that location. It destroyed the entire building, and allowed their troops to advance unimpeded.

Alarmingly, she began to hear reports from the civilian camp back at the supply depot that a column was marching from the west as well. They were pinning the rebels in, and the vise was almost completely locked down. Nida began to hear the gunfire getting closer and closer. The walls began to close in.

"Get ready!" Nida shouted to the defenders still remaining inside the Palace. A group of about 150 of their fighters stayed at this final defensible position. Bullets began to rip into the interior of the casino. The defenders returned fire, holding their position.

Ratatatatatatata, rang out from a 50-caliber machine gun from the federal forces. It ripped a line through ten of Nida's troops. The men surrounding the carnage broke and fled, leaving a large gap in their defensive firing network exposed. The federals began to advance into the casino, but they were mowed down for the most part by the defenders. The stalemate continued for several minutes, with no side gaining a clear advantage.

Then, a volley of RPGs launched out of nowhere from the federal troops. The explosions rocked the defensive positions of the defenders. However, no final push from the soldiers came. In fact, they began to retreat out of the building. A raucous cheer went up from the men remaining, only about fifty from what Nida could discern.

Why would they retreat? Nida thought to herself. Then she heard a strange noise. A buzzing that she couldn't place. Flashbacks to the artillery rang through her head, and she knew what was coming.

"Sir, the C-130s are in place." Lt. Col. Miller reported to James.

"Good, have the ground troops fall back to defensive positions and then order the bombardment." James smiled. His victory was complete.

"Right away, sir." Miller replied and waddled off.

The buzzing became a roar. Nida's heart began to pound. *Not like this,* she thought to herself. On the ground, the American flag that had flown above the hotel lay in tattered ruins in front of her. It was intact enough to recognize what it was. *Funny they never put the new flag up.*

Nida grabbed the flag and the pole it was attached to and held it up.

"FOR FREEDOM!" She yelled as she began to charge out of the doorway. The men followed her out of the hotel and were met by a hellstorm. Shells rang down all around them, blast after blast exploded on the hotel. Nida was pushed over by the blast and fell down. She lifted up her head one more time to see the angels of death circling above. Then, blackness.

Harold looked at Luther. "Well, we meet again, Mr. Washington." Harold cackled.

"So, you finally remembered?" Luther smiled and walked cooly into the room. Harold stood up and moved into the sitting area. Luther sat on the large couch while Harold sat in a single chair that was arrayed parallel, facing towards the couch. There was a fire burning in the fireplace and Harold poured a drink for Luther and handed it to him.

"I don't suppose you came here for a chat about the past, did you?" Harold smiled as he sipped his drink. He was clearly drunk.

"No, I came here to kill you." Luther said, bluntly.

"Well, that's what I figured. I don't know how you knew to attack right now, but you could not have timed it better. Sincerely, bravo." Harold grinned as he continued to drink.

"Don't patronize me, you demon." Luther's bottled rage began to come to the surface. Overwhelming every sense, he began to tolerate this banter less and less.

"See, you never understood Luther, you just never understood." Harold took another drink, "power exists through loyalty. If the people aren't loyal to you, you have no power. That's why we had to put God in control, don't you see?" He was so convinced he was right, Luther almost believed him for a moment. Almost.

"I've learned a different lesson in my life, Harold. Loyalty means nothing in this world." Luther stood up and pulled out his pistol. He racked a bullet in the chamber and looked at Harold, "when you stand before your God, make sure you let him know the truth."

"Oh yeah, what's that?" Harold scoffed as Luther walked behind him.

"As long as men still die, true power is in the sword." Luther put his pistol to the back of Harold's head, but he heard his grandfather's voice in his head, *Never forget who you are!* His father's voice rang out, *Survive!* Luther roared out loud with primal fury, Luther's own voice shouted into the void of his mind, *THIS IS WHO I AM!*

Returning to himself with malice dripping from every word he spoke, "Sic semper tyrannis." Luther pulled the trigger.

Milton Keynes UK
Ingram Content Group UK Ltd.
UKHW010625290424
441924UK00001B/16

9 798988 926306